Caged Souls

by

Gina Leuci

A Well of Lies Novel, Book 1

Caged Souls

Cover Art by *Diana Carlile*

The Wild Rose Press, Inc.
PO Box 708
Adams Basin, NY 14410-0708
Visit us at www.thewildrosepress.com

Publishing History
First Mainstream Thriller Edition, 2018
Print ISBN 978-1-5092-2053-3
Digital ISBN 978-1-5092-2054-0

A Well of Lies Novel, Book 1
Published in the United States of America

"Where are we?"

"Wellington."

I shook my head. "Impossible. According to the website, that's in Kansas. There is no way we drove that far overnight."

"I'm not sure what you looked at, but our town doesn't have a website."

I think every ounce of blood rushed from my head. No longer able to stand, I sank into the seat beside him. "But, I told my parents we were going to Kansas. They'll worry."

"No, they won't."

I turned my head. His voice was calm. Controlled. There wasn't enough light to fully see his expression, but I felt as though his eyes could see through me.

"I need to call them. Tell them where I am."

He shook his head. "You are exactly where you said you'd be. In a town called Wellington, with no access to phones or internet. They aren't expecting to hear from you anytime soon."

Dedication

To the Bunnies:
This book wouldn't exist without you
turning it inside out and upside down.
You are all amazing.

Chapter One

"Yes, Dad, I did my research."

I held the cell phone away from my ear as if doing so would stop my father's lecture on safety. After one shake of my head, I went back to reassuring my over-protective parent.

"We talked about this. We're going to do a summer work program in some small town in Kansas. Wellington or some such place. Anyway, they tout it as a chance to live off the grid and get back to basics, or some such thing. No phones, TVs, or computers. Sounds very Amish."

The drone of a powerful diesel engine signaled a bus pulling in to the parking lot while I sipped on my second extra-large cup of dark roast coffee. I unzipped my sweatshirt as the sun burned off the mid-morning mist and my dad continued his fatherly advice. I wasn't listening because of the distraction. My college roommate, Caroline, jumped around in a childish dance.

"I promise, Dad." I wasn't sure what I'd just promised but I'm sure he'd asked me to do something. "There's nothing to worry about. It's not like I am backpacking in South America or anything. It's the middle of nowheresville in the mid-west USA. Gotta go. Tell Mom and Sarah I love them."

I slipped the phone into the front pocket of my jeans just as my roomie gave out one more excited squeal. "Ooh, Grace, I can't believe we're doing this."

Neither could I.

While I'd assured my father he didn't have to worry, my deciding not to come home during summer break from college wasn't my norm. I simply didn't feel right about letting my friend traipse off alone.

She whipped around to face me and her earlier squeal morphed into an intense whisper. "O.M.G. That's him getting off the bus. Do I look okay?"

What a question. With long blond hair and baby blue eyes, Caroline Parker was striking on her worst day. Today she wore white jeans and a navy blue, three-quarter length sleeved shirt with wide shoulders. With a hint of eye shadow and a touch of lip gloss, my roommate was more than okay. She totally rocked it.

She looked over her shoulder as the man in question spotted her. "Should I go say hi?" The lopsided grin he sent her way had her gushing. I was afraid she'd melt into a hormonal pile of goo.

I pulled my sunglasses down from the top of my head and over my eyes so I could study this man without him knowing I stared.

While I'd assured my parents working on a farm for a summer would be a fabulous growth opportunity, the man walking toward us was the real reason. I could hardly tell my folks my best friend was head over heels in lust with a man she'd met a few short weeks ago and had decided to follow him to some backwoods town. I, in good conscience, couldn't let her go by herself when she was only setting herself up for heartbreak.

However, I couldn't fault her for her taste. The man wasn't bad to look at. He was quite handsome—in a rugged cowboy sort of way. Nice, solid build. Denim jeans fit in all the right places. His hair was a bit too long for my taste.

Cowboy took her hands in his and lifted one to kiss the back of it. If temperatures can rise with a single glance, it happened between those two. She giggled, then took to fiddling with her cross necklace, one of her nervous habits.

Thankful for the shades, I rolled my eyes. My work was cut out for me.

"Who is your friend?" He looked my way as Caroline released her necklace to grab my hand, pulling me forward.

"This is Grace, my roommate." She barely looked at me as she continued the introductions. "And this is Aaron."

Of course, it is. He's all I've heard about for the past three weeks. He took my hand in a friendly shake and gave me a smile filled with charm. "Nice to meet you. What brings you along with us this summer?"

"I'm only here to make sure you don't break my friend's heart and ensure my roommate gets back on the bus at the end of the summer."

That's me, blunt and to the point. Caroline's smile faltered and I'm pretty sure her new boyfriend's face froze for a moment, but he recovered nicely. "Who knows what the summer will bring."

I felt a slight hesitation as he released my hand. "You just might fall in love….with our little town." The hesitation put me on edge but when he spoke again, his eyes were back on my friend. "Why don't we load all your bags and get you both settled."

A sudden tingle along my spine sent the hairs on my arms to attention. I turned to find another man standing at the open door of the bus. Even behind his own dark shades, I knew his eyes were on me and that he'd overheard my conversation. I'm not sure how to describe him except to say he lacked personality. He appeared older than the rest of the group milling outside of the bus. My guess, somewhere around thirty.

Don't get me wrong, I don't consider thirty old. It's just somehow this man exudes an aura of someone much older. While Cowboy Aaron's body is all rugged outdoor active type of fit, the stone wall of a man staring me down has more of an 'I work out because I don't allow weakness' sort of physique.

Caroline tugged at my sleeve. "Let's go. You need to put your suitcase on the bus."

I turned away from the silent observer and realized I'd stopped breathing for a moment. Who knew a man could intimidate a girl with one look. I made a mental note to stay as far away from Mr. Lack of Personality as possible.

Once I stored my luggage, I slung my backpack over my shoulder and went to board the bus. The Stone Wall maintained his watch at his post by the door. To enter, I needed to brush past him. While one part of me told me to lower my head, keep my mouth shut and go inside, I have a side that refuses to behave. I shoved my sunglasses to the top of my head, raised my chin, and stared up at the silent wall of a man.

"Excuse me." I nodded toward the bus door. "Do you mind if I enter?"

My tone implied he was in my space. Maybe he was, a little, but I could have passed without making a scene. He gave a slight nod, stepped a foot to the left and waved a hand toward the door. While his silent capitulation gave me the win, as I stepped into the dark, cool interior of the bus, I had the strangest sensation I'd started a game where there would be no winners.

"Over here." Caroline waved at me from her seat about one third of the way down the aisle. "I gave you the window seat."

I took a moment to sit and settle my nerves while my roommate bounced in the seat beside me. Another girl, maybe around eighteen, had been out in the parking lot with us. I nodded to her as she moved toward the back of the bus. I'd noticed a few others already occupying seats, so we weren't the only ones heading to crazy town.

I looked up as a familiar and welcome figure moved into the seat in front of mine. "Holy shit, Jake. What the hell are you doing here?"

I've known Jake Collings since third grade. We'd both grown up in Bennington, Vermont and ended up at the same university. He kneeled on his seat, facing me. "My father heard from your 'rents what you were doing this summer. He thought it would be, and I quote, 'a valuable life lesson' for me to be shut off from distractions for fourteen weeks."

I don't know whether to laugh or cry along with him. He was used to having everything he wanted at the snap of his fingers. "Oh, Jakey, this is going to kill you."

He put his hands up in surrender. "That's what I told my father, but what Doc Collings wants, Doc Collings gets."

He swung around and sank down as a line of people took their seats and the bus doors closed. A young girl around my age, twenty-ish, stood up in the aisle. She wore shorts, a tank top and a denim shirt tied at the waist. Gorgeous with blond hair, high cheekbones, blue eyes and long, long, tan legs, she was everything a short brunette like myself resents.

"Hi, all. My name is Hope."

I groaned. Not only was she gorgeous, her voice carried in a sing-song, cheerful manner that had Jake sitting upright in his seat. "I want to welcome you here on this fun adventure. As you know, this summer is all about getting away from the distractions of the outside world and focusing on reconnecting with people face to face. That starts now. As I come down the aisle, please put all phone and electronics into this bag."

Mr. Personality, or lack-thereof, motioned to the tall girl. She leaned in while he spoke in a low tone only she could hear. She nodded then directed her attention back to us. "Please put in all watches as well."

While my watch tracked my exercise and sleep, I hardly considered it electronics. "Going a bit overboard, if you ask me," I mumbled but took it off my wrist. I also turned off my phone and waited for the runway model to make her way to us.

She stopped at Jake and gave him a smile that showed off perfect teeth. "The last part was meant for you, handsome. I heard you have a computer watch."

He raised his left arm. "Guilty. Tell me you're not at least a little bit curious."

I didn't have to see my friend to know he was throwing down his rich boy charm. Blondie was not immune. She shifted from one foot to the other, then pushed her hair behind her ear. I bit back a laugh. I'd watched him work his magic for many years.

When she threw a look to the front of the bus,

checking to see if big brother was watching, Jake leaned toward her. "I can pretend to put my watch in the bag and later, you and I can sit close and explore the web together. Come on. Don't tell me you aren't tempted."

She giggled. "You're going to be trouble, aren't you?"

Yep, he was definitely trouble, but when she cast another furtive glance to the front again, I knew the man in charge held a stronger hold than my friend's legendary charm. She held the bag up and I saw the watch disappear inside.

After Hope finished her trip down the aisle, collecting her goodies as she went, Aaron came up behind us and tapped my travel buddy on the shoulder. "Come sit with me."

Of course she went. I had a feeling I wasn't invited to their *tête à tête*.

The passing scenery captured my attention. We'd left I-89 and took Route 91 south. Normally, I'd have my headphones on, but knowing our destination banned the use of electronics, I'd decided to ship them home for the summer along with my other belongings. I dug into my backpack, looking for one of the paperback books I'd brought. Before I found my source for entertainment, a sound from the back of the bus had me whipping my head in that direction.

Dear God. The cowboy had a guitar and was singing. I pinged Jake on the head and leaned forward between the seats. "She's got it bad."

He got up and moved back to take the empty seat beside me. "Let me guess, you're not here to be one with nature."

"Hell no. My fear that she'd do something stupid is front and center. Look at her."

He did. I did, too. Not only was Aaron playing the guitar, several people now joined in to sing along. "She's having fun. Maybe you should stop worrying about her and join in. It's time to start having fun again."

I ignored the barb and slid a look over at him, taking in the pressed khakis and collared shirt. "Is that your plan? Because unless you packed something other than your country club attire, I can't see you joining into the group activities down at the hog farm."

"Hey, I like pigs." He grinned. "Everything is better with bacon."

It was good to have him here. I had a sneaking suspicion having a friend along would be needed. Hope stood again and called for attention. "It's lunch time and we have turkey or ham sandwiches for everyone. But first, let's bow our heads in prayer."

Jake and I made faces at each other but did as told.

"Heavenly Father, please bless this meal as we share it with our new friends. Keep us safe on our journey and keep us on our path. Amen."

A loud chorus of amens echoed in the bus before our newly appointed hostess and a short, pimply-faced boy began handing out sandwiches and chips.

"If they serve Kool-Aid," I whispered, "I'm jumping ship."

We'd been on the bus about three hours when we made our first stop in Worcester, Massachusetts. The bus meandered across the state to Amherst and finally made its way to another stop somewhere in Connecticut. Each location was a college town to pick up more summer interns; in the end I counted eleven of "us", all heading to parts unknown.

After each stop, Hope the Goddess got up to collect phones and watches. Every time she stood, I felt like a passenger on an airplane instead of a bus. If she'd point her fingers toward the emergency exits, my view of her as my flight attendant would be complete.

After collecting the items from the latest to join the group, she rose once again, this time holding a stack of papers. "This is your contract for the work-study program at Wellington. It states that during the duration of your stay, you understand you will have no access to internet or phone. Your jobs will consist of things such as farming the lands, working with animals, or any job deemed necessary with the running and survival of our town. You agree to follow all town rules and policies which includes no drugs or alcohol or acts considered to be immoral. There is also a W-4 to fill out for employment with the understanding your salary reverts back to the town as room and board."

Jake scribbled his signature without reading it. "Maybe my father should sign one of these which says marrying a woman four years older than your son is immoral."

"Ouch. You'd mentioned his new girlfriend, but not her age. No wonder you've disagreed with him lately."

He nodded. "Wife number three. God help us if he procreates with this one."

I knew what he meant. He was the oldest of eight. When his parents were married, they had him and his three sisters who were triplets and five years younger. But then Doc Collings had an affair with another doctor and got her pregnant. Jake's mom retaliated by sleeping with one of the dads she'd met at the girl's gymnastics who'd already had two kids, a boy and girl. Both parents remarried. His dad and wife two had a boy, while his mom and her new husband had a girl, making the magic number eight.

Distracted by my friend's revelation, I signed the contract quickly and handed it in. "Your dad's not a bad guy."

He smirked. "Maybe not. For a doctor, he doesn't know jack shit about using condoms."

"But you have a stock in the company."

"Sure do. They're like one of those credit cards. I don't leave home without them."

"So, what's your girlfriend think of you disappearing for the summer?"

"I broke up with Layla last week. She was getting too clingy. Would you believe she tried to become a patient of my dad's?"

That got my attention. "Your dad is a cardiologist. It's not like looking for a PCP."

He snorted. "She claimed I broke her heart and wanted him to fix it."

"You sure can pick them. Maybe getting away will be good for you."

He shook his head. "You have no idea. I have it on good authority she was about to go all psycho bitch on me."

I'm sure he would have filled me in on the juicy details had we not stopped once again. This time at a rest area where we were informed we would have dinner. With the multiple detours to pick up passengers, we were still only in Connecticut.

I loitered inside the building for a while before returning outside where I found several of 'them' attempting to bond with the newcomers by tossing a Frisbee. A few others set up to grill burgers and dogs.

The sun played peek-a-boo above the trees as the sound of cars whizzed by on the highway. City noises. I wondered what it would be like in Wellington, Kansas. I'd never been outside of New England. Would it have lots of trees? Or would it be flat? I'd told my dad I'd done research. I'd done nothing more than locate the town on a map and discover it would take about twenty-four hours to get there. Of course, that hadn't figured in the nearly seven hours it took between three states to gather the summer help. At this rate, we'd be lucky to get there by August.

I spotted Caroline, glued to Aaron's side, along with a small group sitting on the grass. It looked like the musician had taken one of the young college boys under his wing by showing him how to play the guitar.

Hope kept Jake occupied. Not surprising the blonde goddess would gravitate toward my friend. Women only had to look at his wardrobe to know he came from money, but it wasn't the reason they were drawn to him. His dark black hair, electric blue eyes, and the perfect 'never had braces' smile all helped tie in with his playboy charm.

I sipped on the horrible coffee I'd procured from one of the vending machines inside and made my way to a picnic table. I pretended to read my book, but my attention kept reverting to my friends and their choices for summer flings. Jake could handle himself, but Caroline was too emotionally involved.

Aaron now had control of the guitar again and

began crooning out a song. With my focus on them, I didn't notice Stone Wall until he sat beside me. "Not going to join in?"

While I'm sure his question wasn't meant to be accusatory, my shoulders tightened and I gripped my book like a lifeline. "I don't see you playing games."

"I have other duties." This man didn't seem to talk much but his answers were concise. "So, if you don't plan to participate in the project, why did you choose to come along?"

I shifted in my seat. I was at a picnic table with my legs underneath. He sat with his back to the table, making me twist around to talk to him. Hot damn, the man was big. Linebacker shoulders, massive chest, and arm muscles bulging against his tee shirt. I might as well be an ant next to him, but I refused to let his size intimidate me, even if I had a hard time not focusing on his chest.

"I'm pretty sure you heard me this morning before I got on the bus."

He gave a slight nod. "Maybe you should stop worrying about everyone else and figure out your real reasons for being here."

"Caroline is my reason."

His raised eyebrow and intense stare made me squirm inside. Before I knew it, I was spewing information. "You don't understand. She was home schooled. She is brilliant but a bit naïve. Since she came to college, she tends to go overboard with wanting to experience everything. Following a stranger to a secluded town is just a bit over the top, even for her."

"She seems to be enjoying herself."

I waved a hand in her direction. "Of course she is.

The guy is serenading her with *Sweet Caroline*. I don't see this summer ending well."

His lip tilted just slightly as he glanced toward the group on the grass. Not a full smile, but enough to make him seem almost human. Almost sexy. For a brief second I thought I was making a connection, then he spoke. "Your friend is an excuse, Grace. I would wager there is another reason you didn't want to go home to your family. As for Caroline, she'll be fine. You don't have to worry about her. Trust me when I say we don't believe in sex before marriage."

Stunned, I sat in silence as the man walked away. How did we go from joining in the fun, to talking about sex and marriage?

I tried to make my way toward my friends just to vent, but was waylaid by another one of 'them'. This one was a male version of Hope. Blond, blue eyes, tanned skin and a country-boy accent named Leland. While his attention might have been flattering I'd already noticed his deliberate attempt to mingle and welcome everyone. Despite his current attention to me, my eyes continued to watch Mr. Personality as he took over manning the grill.

Tall and lanky Leland talked non-stop, diverting me from making my way to my friends. Even after getting my burger, he joined me back at the picnic table, continuing his constant litany of questions.

"Who is that guy over there?" I nodded toward the man in shades at the grill, not caring I'd interrupted him mid-sentence.

He followed my gaze, then sighed. "Oh, that's Caleb. Why do you ask?"

I gave what I hoped was a casual shrug and turned

my attention back to him. "No reason, he was talking to me earlier and I didn't catch his name."

Based on the grimace as he looked at the man in question, I gathered there was no love lost between these two. I refocused. "So, did you grow up in Wellington?"

It worked. "Born and raised. It's a great town, but you'll see it soon enough. Tell me about your hometown."

I was never more grateful when we all boarded the bus again so I could focus on my novel and ignore the chatter. By ten o'clock, the overhead lights were off and one by one the reading lights went dark.

I'm not sure what woke me. The rain maybe? The downshift of the bus's gears? Thanks to their 'no electronics' rule, I had no idea of time, but it was still dark and everyone on the bus continued to sleep. Despite that my seat back was reclined, my head rested against the window.

It took a few moments before my brain registered the view was not what I expected.

Chapter Two

We were no longer on the highway. Instead, we were traveling a tree-lined road bordered by a chain-link fence. The downshift of the diesel engine as the bus slowed caught my attention. When a six foot iron gate slid open, my brain jumped into full gear.

No. This isn't right. I turned to scan inside the bus. Caroline had stretched across the two seats to my left. I could hear Jake's gentle snore in front of me. I stood, keeping one knee on my seat. Everyone around continued to sleep.

Except the driver and Caleb.

The bus turned down the road past the gate and my stomach clenched. I moved down the aisle, holding on to the seat backs as I worked my way to the front. My eyes never left the scenery. I heard the rattle as the gate closed behind us. On either side of the road was a thick forest of trees. The swipe of the wipers kept a tempo, mocking my rapid heartbeat.

"What can I do for you, Grace?"

I stopped at the edge of the seat that Caleb occupied behind the driver. "Where are we?"

"Wellington."

I shook my head. "Impossible. According to the website, that's in Kansas. There is no way we drove that far overnight."

"I'm not sure what you looked at, but our town

doesn't have a website."

I think every ounce of blood rushed from my head. No longer able to stand, I sank into the seat beside him. "But, I told my parents we were going to Kansas. They'll worry."

"No, they won't."

I turned my head. His voice was calm. Controlled. There wasn't enough light to fully see his expression, but I felt as though his eyes could see through me.

"I need to call them. Tell them where I am."

He shook his head. "You are exactly where you said you'd be. In a town called Wellington, with no access to phones or internet. They aren't expecting to hear from you anytime soon."

Shit. He spoke the truth, yet every fiber of my being screamed we were walking into something much different than what we'd been led to believe.

My roommate was blind to anything but what her new infatuation had told her. Knowing how gullible she could be, I thought I'd done my research. Obviously, I'd been looking someplace different. Thinking on it now, it made sense a town living off the grid would not have a web presence.

What about Jake? He'd been forced into this survival boot camp by his father who'd got his information from my parents. None of our parents would know where we were. And what about the others on board? Had they been duped too, or had I been the only one to look in the wrong place?

"Don't over think it." Caleb's baritone voice penetrated my thoughts. He didn't seem fazed by my fear. So far, nothing appeared to ruffle this man.

"I don't know that I can do this," I whispered. The

line of trees ended to reveal rows of corn fields. Still no sign of a town ahead, though we'd traveled a few miles, at least, since the gate.

"Just do as you're told and you'll be fine."

Those words didn't reassure me. I couldn't stay near him any longer. The man was too large. To confident. Too calm. Too much a reminder I was heading into the unknown.

Numbly, I moved back to my seat. Our conversation must have disturbed others because I heard a few mumbles near the rear of the bus. I kept my eyes on the horizon, looking for a sign I was wrong.

Maybe Wellington was what it claimed to be: a small town living without distractions of electronics who invited college students to help with their farming operations each summer.

Caleb was right. This is what we signed on for; what we'd told our parents. So, I got the location wrong. Relax.

In the distance I saw the scattering of lights. A few houses among the fields before the outline of the town. Main Street was dark, save for the street lights, still too early for stores to be open. We passed a gas station, a dentist's office, and even a diner. A normal small town.

Our bus driver meandered several blocks further before pulling into a large garage, almost large enough to be an airport hangar. The bay doors closed behind us. There were some kind of lights on in the building, not bright overhead ones, but somewhere lights kept the garage from being completely dark.

Caleb moved down the aisle and stopped by my seat. "Go back to sleep. We have a couple hours before the town wakes up and we can get you settled."

He continued away, giving the same message to those who'd woken. I zipped my sweatshirt, suddenly cold. I put my hood over my head, wanting to hide from my own fear. I didn't think I'd fall back to sleep, but I woke again, this time as several people talked and moved off the bus.

I sat up. Out the window, I saw the overhead lights in the garage had been turned on. Food was being set up at a table against the wall. Another table was set up just outside of the bus door.

Caroline wasn't in her seat, neither was Jake. I made a quick visit to the restroom before grabbing my things and exited the bus. Hope greeted me with a much too perky voice. Without my daily IV infusion of caffeine, she was lucky I didn't ram my fist down her throat.

"Good morning. Breakfast is ready over in the far corner. But first, we ask that you bring all personal items to the table over here where we will inspect them for any contraband."

"Contraband?" I looked to the table in question and noticed two men rummaging through suitcases. "Seriously?"

"They are ensuring no form of electronics, drugs, or alcohol have been smuggled into town."

My brain still hadn't come to grips that we weren't in Kansas, though I still didn't know where we were. Now I had to allow my luggage to be searched? What was this? Some sort of rehab center for cell phone addicts?

I spotted my suitcase and rolled it to wait in line for inspection. I didn't pay attention to what they were doing at the table, instead, my eyes were in search of my two friends. They were at the food table. Good. I needed to speak with them. And I needed coffee. Maybe not in that order.

"Good morning, Grace. Let's start with your backpack."

I sighed at the deep voice. Caleb, again. It was my turn and I handed over my bag. One of the men whom I didn't recognize because he hadn't been on the bus with us dumped the contents onto the table. There wasn't much. I'd expected to be on the road at least two days, so I'd stuffed a couple changes of clothes, a few toiletries, pen and paper so I could write home—you know, old school. Two paperbacks and my wallet, which they thumbed through, making me twitch, but I held my tongue. They took my bottle of ibuprofen and threw it into the trash.

"Hey. What the…?"

"No drugs of any kind," the guy quipped as my birth control pills also went by way of the metal bucket. The kid probably wasn't even out of high school and was enjoying his role of "contraband police" too much as he inspected each item with fierce concentration.

"Oh, for God's sake."

"Please don't use the Lord's name in vain."

My mouth dropped. The prim and proper rebuke from this man-child was more than I could handle without my coffee.

I sent a challenge directly at the man who stood to the side, back to being a stone wall, watching the interaction. "Come on, Caleb, are you not going to do anything? Birth control and ibuprofen? Really? What if I get a headache? Or cramps."

Playing the woman card usually made men

uncomfortable. The kid, suddenly unsure of himself, shifted from one foot to the other. It worked with him. He looked to the older man who responded by raising an eyebrow at me. "Do you get headaches often?"

I didn't, but I wasn't going to tell him that. "This place is already giving me one."

"Any medical issues will be reviewed with our doctor," Caleb stated with cool authority. "Should I set up an appointment?"

Damn. He called my bluff. I wanted to stare him down, but the man was unflappable. "What about my pills? They're a prescription."

"There's no need for them. Sex without marriage is not allowed here."

What was this? 1960? That was the second time he'd brought up sex and marriage. I didn't plan on hooking up with anyone here, but still, it was weird. My suitcase became the next target. I fumed as my clothes, including panties, were man-handled by these strangers. The only other thing they tossed was a box of tampons. I threw my hands up, ready to argue again, but one look at Caleb's stony stare and I knew it was useless.

"Give me your wrist," one of the men at the table ordered.

I immediately put my hands behind my back. "Why?" The man held a black band with a blinking light on it. It was similar to my watch they'd confiscated yesterday but wider and without a screen to show the time. "What is that?"

"It's, um, well…" He couldn't even answer. I guess the rest of the sheep on the bus hadn't questioned him.

Caleb took the bracelet from him. "During your

stay, Wellington takes care of all your needs. This will track your purchases, whether it be food, clothes, or medical, so we can itemize for taxes."

I narrowed my eyes as I took in the explanation. It made sense, in a weird sort of way. He stepped from behind the table to stand in front of me. I had to look up, past his large muscled chest, broad shoulders, and square chin to his steel eyes. I gulped.

"Give me your wrist."

When I didn't move, he took my arm, forcing it up. His eyes never left mine as he secured the band. My arm tingled where he touched me. Part of me wanted to check out my new bracelet, but I couldn't tear my gaze from his.

"I don't like black. Do you have purple?" I swear I saw a spark of amusement flash in his eyes before he went emotionless again. "I thought we weren't allowed any electronics."

"The contract says *you* will have no access to electronics. I don't have the same rules."

The man took up all the air, making it difficult to breathe around him. Maybe it wasn't his size that intimidated me. No, I probably had to do with his 'don't mess with me' attitude. "I see."

He released his hold on my wrist and stepped back. "No, you don't. Not yet."

My knees wobbled as I took my backpack and rolled my suitcase over to where the others from the bus had gathered to eat.

"Morning," Caroline said around a mouthful of bagel. "Aaron said to let you sleep a little longer."

I held up my wristband. "What do you think of our new wardrobe accessory?"

Jake put down his cup of orange juice then held his up. "A bit odd. Supposedly it tracks all our purchases."

"So they say." I twisted my wrist to inspect it. There was no clasp. It was somehow latched electronically. "I don't even see how it unhooks. Can we take it off?"

"Nope. It's even waterproof," he said. "I asked."

"I don't buy it. None of it."

My roommate frowned. "It makes sense. Please don't worry so much. We're here to have fun."

I grimaced. "No, you're here to have a summer romance and I'm here to make sure Mr. Wonderful doesn't break your heart."

"Aw, Gracie, you need to relax. I know what I'm doing."

"Yeah, Gracie," Jake piped in. "Take a chill pill."

I stuck my tongue out at the two of them. "Can't. That would be considered contraband." I rolled my eyes. "Seriously, how can I relax? I haven't even had my first cup of coffee yet."

I put down my backpack on an empty chair and turned to the tables against the wall.

"Oh, um, Grace..." I looked back to see the two exchange glances. "Never mind," she muttered.

I narrowed my eyes at them, letting them know I knew they were keeping a secret. I stocked my plate with a variety of fruit and pastries then headed for my morning caffeine. Instead, I found only an assortment of juice, milk and teas.

I tapped the shoulder of an older woman who stood by the food. "Excuse me, where can I find the coffee?"

The woman turned and gave me a kind smile. "I'm sorry, sweetie, but we don't drink coffee here."

Chapter Three

"You don't… Oh, hell no. No one said I would have to give up coffee."

I put my plate down and stormed across the garage to Caleb, interrupting him as he spoke to an older gentleman." I've changed my mind. When is the next bus out of here?"

He nodded to the other man who turned and walked away. "And what is the problem now, Grace?"

I stared at him, my hands on my hips, only just not tapping my foot. "No coffee? That's obscene."

"Ah, yes. There is always one who has difficulty with that rule."

"It's a stupid rule."

He smirked. Sure, no emotion on anything else, but he thinks this is funny? I was not amused.

"Coffee, along with alcohol and drugs, contain ingredients limiting our abilities to choose or think clearly. Living a healthier lifestyle allows us to have a better connection with each other and with God."

My jaw dropped. He was serious. "I get cranky without my coffee."

"So I see." The hint of sarcasm was my undoing.

"Shut up," I yelled, then I pushed him. Okay, maybe pushed is the wrong word. I attempted to shove him, but he didn't budge an inch. The entire room went quiet and I had a momentary sense of clarity as my eyes connected with his dark steel gaze.

"Okay, I should not have done that. Because you are…" I gulped and instantly became contrite. I slowly moved my hands from his rock-hard chest, "…really big and you could probably snap me like a twig. So don't. Okay?"

"Then go sit down." His voice slipped down my spine like lava, ready to erupt.

"No."

"No?" Caleb crossed his arms and his muscles bulged. I was playing with fire but was no longer at a point where I could control my words.

"No. I mean—You're not hearing me." This time, I did stomp my foot. Childish, I know, but I swear the man was being deliberately obtuse. "Fine. Let me put it this way. I have been coffee-free since ten a.m. yesterday when I got onto your damn bus, which means I have a clearer ability to choose and I choose to leave. Now."

"No."

Well, hell. That backfired.

"You signed a contract. You belong to Wellington now."

Arrogant. Smug. Pompous. I'm sure there were more words to describe this man, but my caffeine-deprived brain was far from clear.

"By the way," he drawled, "your last cup of coffee was not when you got on the bus. It was at the rest area at dinner time." Technically, he was right, if you can call the vending machine sludge coffee. But mentioning it was his way of making a point he'd been watching every move we made.

"Trust me, Grace, when I tell you giving up coffee

will be one of the easiest adjustments for you to make."

"Is that supposed to make me feel better?" I looked around. "Because it does *not* make me feel better. Not even close."

"Join your friends. Have breakfast. There is a lot to do to get you settled today." He put his hands on my shoulders and turned me around. All eyes were on us. No one even pretended to eat. They waited to see my next move, or maybe how this large, unflappable man would handle me.

He released me and I turned my head to find he'd walked away. I have been dismissed without a second thought on his part. Damn him.

I stormed over to Caroline and Jake. "What kind of place is this?"

Before either responded, Aaron joined us, effectively silencing my questions. I wondered where he came from as I hadn't seen him before now. And I wondered if he'd come to us at this moment on Caleb's directive. While my roommate got all giddy and distracted, I think I had Jake thinking. He leaned back in his chair and began to observe the room.

I picked at a croissant, its buttery flavor lost on me as I tried to regroup. For the second time today, I felt I'd made a mistake coming on this trip. Ten minutes. If I could get that much time alone with my friends— maybe a little longer with my Caroline—I'm sure I could convince them we needed to bail.

Caleb returned to the room, gave a high sign, and suddenly there was a flurry of activity. Aaron stood. "Okay, everyone, next stop on today's agenda is to get you settled in with your host families.

Host families?

I hadn't thought about where we were staying, but host families meant we would be separated. I leaned over to Jake. "I have a bad feeling about this place. I think we should leave."

"Okay. Let's…"

"Hi, Jake." Hope, super perky goddess, interrupted. "I get to be your guide today."

He gave me a barely noticeable nod before turning on the charm with the leggy blonde. "Well, aren't I the lucky one. What's the first stop on today's adventure?"

I slung my backpack over a shoulder and reached for the handle of my suitcase only to find Leland had it first. "Ready to see your new home?"

I saw his hesitation. He'd obviously witnessed my tantrum and probably wondered if I planned to take his head off. Tempting, but I restrained myself. I nodded and walked with him toward the exit. "I was wondering," I asked. "Are you and Hope related?"

"We're twins."

Of course they were. The God and Goddess of Enthusiasm. Dual Cheerleaders for the Damned. I stepped outside, expecting to walk to our destination. Instead, there were three shuttle vans.

My heart sank as I boarded my ride. I'd already been separated from my closest friends. I recognized one girl, Leigh, I believe. She'd joined us when we stopped in Connecticut at the final stop. I spotted Marcus. He was the young kid learning the guitar. Caroline had mentioned his name during her evening ramblings about her day with the Amazing Aaron.

Last was a girl who'd already been on the bus when we boarded yesterday. I don't know her name, but she appeared to be painfully shy by the way she continually wrung her hands together whenever anyone spoke with her.

I noticed each of the escorts were of the opposite sex. By design, I'm sure. Although, I think the poor shy child would have preferred a woman by her side.

The van meandered through town, which appeared livelier now that morning had arrived. People walked down the streets, rushing by with their heads down due to the rain, but a few stopped to glance at the vans. Hoping to spot the new arrivals?

"We're coming up on The Square. It's the center of town where most of our activities occur," my new personal tour guide explained. "On Sundays, we all meet for services then we gather in The Hall for a fellowship meal."

By Leland's hesitation, I knew he expected a response. "How many people live here?"

"Almost four hundred."

That got my attention. "And everyone gets together at once?"

He nodded. "Every Sunday. Its family time and we're all one big family."

Oh, joy. "Sounds…overwhelming."

"Nah, you get used to it."

I doubted it, but kept my mouth shut as the shy girl and her companion exited the bus.

"We'll be the next stop," he said. "You're staying with Kurt and Amy. Their kids are all grown and out of the house so they have plenty of room."

The bus drove two blocks down and one to the left before we stopped in front of a white split-level home with blue shutters. The lawn was perfectly manicured and the walkway was lined with flowers. I gathered my bag. A couple, maybe in their sixties, came out onto the porch to greet us.

The man was tall with white hair and a thick mustache. His hand was on the shoulder of a much shorter woman with brown hair streaked with gray. She was so thin, it looked as though a gentle breeze could blow her over. But both had wide smiles and warm hellos.

"Welcome. Welcome," he said in a booming voice. "It's so nice of you to join us."

The woman stepped forward. "I'm Amy and this is my husband, Kurt. What's your name, dear?"

"Grace Adams."

"A beautiful name for a beautiful girl." The tiny woman clasped my hand in hers, patting it with her other. "Come in. We'll show you your room. Leland, be a gentleman and carry her bags in."

"Yes, ma'am."

I followed them down the stairs "We've put you in Lola's old room." It's a bit smaller than the others, but we thought you might enjoy the privacy down here."

The walls were a shockingly bright pink, but the single bed with the handmade quilt looked comfortable. A wooden dresser and nightstand with an alarm clock/radio completed the entire décor of the room. No pictures on the wall. No homey touches. I wondered if they'd recently gutted and painted it for their new summer guest. Which, I'll admit, is sweet.

"The bathroom is upstairs, second door on the left," she explained. "We all take turns making dinner so you'll be expected to do your share. But we'll give you a couple days to get settled."

"Thank you." I smiled at my hosts. "It's all very

kind."

Amy looked anxious to be the perfect host. "Come upstairs, then. I made banana bread."

"Would you mind if I took a shower first?"

"Of course." Kurt motioned for his wife and Leland to follow him upstairs. "Get yourself settled. We will set out a towel in the bathroom for you."

I sat on the bed, thankful for a moment to myself. The day had not started the way I'd expected. Being in another location than I had planned on, well, that was on me. I never asked Caroline about Wellington's location. And perhaps I over-reacted regarding the personal items they'd tossed. I knew going in no drugs of any kind were allowed. Whatever. I don't see coffee as a drug, but obviously, this healthier living philosophy included it on the No Use List.

So perhaps I did need to chill. My hosts seem nice enough. They'd prepared a room for me, and even thought of giving me privacy. I opened my suitcase and found a change of clothes and my toiletries. A shower would do me good.

I turned on the water then stripped down, except for my new bracelet. When the damn thing didn't zap me after the water hit it, I calmed down a bit more, though I still didn't like it.

After the shower and feeling more like myself, I joined everyone in the kitchen. It was homey with light oak cabinetry, and a sunflower décor; it made me smile. I felt myself begin to relax as I had a few bites of the homemade banana bread while the older couple regaled me with stories of their children and grandchildren.

It wasn't long, though, before Leland stood and said the van was outside waiting.

"Where are we going now?"

"You have a meeting with Town Council," he spoke as though this was a normal thing. I didn't even know who my town reps were back in Vermont, never mind needing to sit down with them.

"Let me get my wallet."

He took my hand and lifted my arm. "No, need. You have your wristband. No need for anything else."

"Oh. I forgot."

We were the only two on the van as it headed back into the center of town. My personal tour guide sat across the aisle and I was thankful for the space. "Are we all meeting with the Town Council?"

"Everyone will, but separately."

I could tell he wanted to talk but I felt a bit overwhelmed and lost so I turned away from him to stare at the passing scenery. If Jake and Caroline were with me, they'd know what to say. They were much better at small talk. I had a tendency to say the wrong thing.

Town Hall was a tall building with a steeple tower, enormous windows in the front and wide wooden steps to the entrance. Exactly what I'd expect in any old-fashioned town. Still, having a gate closing the town off from the outside, I'd been surprised to see an actual town and not a few cabins in the woods.

Inside the entrance were a set of stairs and we walked down to the lower level. Instead of a conference room, the basement held a large file room, filled with cabinets along the walls. The inner part of the room was empty except for five men sitting behind an eight-foot table. There were two more folding metal chairs. One at the end of the table. The other was in front, about four feet away facing the inquisition squad,

"That will be all, Leland." The man who spoke sat in the center of the group. Tall, blond, blue-eyes, in his late forties, with a voice which sounded familiar. I looked back and forth between him and the younger man who'd brought me here. Yep, this had to be the twins' father. Not surprising the golden siblings' parent would be some big-wig townie.

"Hello, Grace," the older man spoke to me. "Welcome to Wellington."

I nodded and waited. I pressed my hands together, not sure what to expect from the men staring me down.

"I'm Roger, the Town Administrator. With me today, are Harry, Bill, Scott, and Jay."

The speaker looked to be the youngest of the group. If any of the other council members were under seventy, I'd be shocked. I heard the door close behind me then booted footsteps approached. I turned in my seat to see who would be joining in on the interrogation and was only slightly surprised to see Caleb.

A part of me was thankful for a familiar face, but did it have to be him? He'd showered and changed. He still wore jeans, but it was the blue shirt with the patch on his sleeve which caught my attention.

"You're a cop?" I didn't mean to speak outwardly but his uniform took me by surprise.

The administrator answered, ensuring I knew who was going to be in charge in this room. "Caleb is our chief of police. He oversees your safety and security."

Police chief. That explained a lot.

While I watched the local lawman take a seat, Roger was talking again and I did my best to pay attention. "Our job today is to get to know you better, so we can make your transition to our humble town easier."

Easier? Didn't they realize a six man on one woman interrogation did not equal comfort on any level. I shifted in my seat to refocus on the table of men watching me.

"So, tell us about yourself. Your family. What is your major at college?"

I rubbed sweaty palms over the thighs of my jeans. I could do this. "I assume you know my name is Grace Adams. I'm twenty. Born and raised in Vermont. My parents own a small restaurant in Bennington. I have a younger sister, Sarah. And I'm a Business Management major."

Simple. All answers ticked off.

"Why did you choose to come to Wellington?" This from Bill, who might be nearing the age of ninety, with eyeglasses thicker than an old coke bottle. He tapped a cane against the tile floor and his voice warbled as he yelled his question.

I looked to Caleb who pressed his lips together and I knew he was hiding his amusement. His eyes dared me to answer. I lifted my chin. Challenge accepted.

"Honestly? My roommate met one of your towns folk and has become—uh—interested in him. He sold her on this summer adventure. I chose to follow her to keep her—uh—focused."

The man to Roger's left grunted. Harry. He was a beefy man whose tie looked like it was about to strangle his gargantuan neck. "I take it to mean you are not sold on the idea of working in our town?"

"I didn't say that." Man, I thought I could be blunt. "I have every intention of doing my part here, as agreed. But the reason I came had more to do with worrying about my friend following a stranger to a town where she can't pick up a phone to say she wants to leave."

I slid a pointed look at Caleb. He was back to being the emotionless drone.

Roger leaned forward. "You don't trust us to take care of your friend."

I leaned forward, meeting his stare. "Trust needs to be earned, Roger." His eyes went up with my use of his name. "Besides, I saw the gates we went through to get here. You are either keeping people out. Or in."

The man leaned back, a gleam in his eyes. "The gates are to keep our farm animals in."

My heart beat rapidly in my chest but I was determined to keep my emotions in check in front of the interrogation squad. "I'm from Vermont. We have farms. And I've never seen six-foot gates blocking a main road used to pen in livestock."

Bill tapped his cane louder and stared me down with old, wise eyes, enlarged by his glasses. Scott and Jay remained silent, but both scribbled notes every time I spoke.

Harry pulled at his tie when he spoke next. "You do realize you have signed a contract stating you will follow our rules."

Back to this. "Yes. Caleb has made that clear." The man in question sat in silence at the end of the table. His arms crossed as he observed everyone and everything in the room. My direct responses had the members of council riled up. Not the police chief, though. Nope, I'd been correct in thinking him a stone wall.

Roger tapped his papers on the table and gave a thin smile. I'd bet his offspring's joyful dispositions were not traits from their father. "Well, then. Might I suggest you put aside your preconceived notions and immerse yourself in the program? You might find it beneficial in the long run. Leland will take you to your next stop."

I opened my mouth, ready to ask my own set of questions, but the interview was over. He nodded to Caleb who stood and walked to me.

"Come this way."

The police chief may not be the person in charge while in this room, but my encounter with him this morning had me deciding not to push any buttons. I stood on rubbery legs but I thrust my chin up and my shoulders back as I followed him to the door I'd entered.

The room seemed bigger leaving than it did when I arrived. I felt every eye on me as I tried to keep up with his long strides. I kept my eyes firmly on the blue shirt in front of me.

A freaking police chief? Seriously? In charge of my safety and security? Huh. The bracelet on my arm suddenly felt like a lead weight. There was something off about this place and I made a mental note to stay far, far away from this man and his merry men of council.

When I stepped out into the lobby and the door closed between me and the inquisition squad, I let out a breath I didn't realize I'd been holding, Leland sat on a bench waiting. Maybe my tall, blond tour guide wasn't so bad. He certainly was a lot less intimidating than the man with the badge.

I stuck my hands in the pockets of the college sweatshirt I'd put on after my shower, hiding how shaky they were. I'd held my own in there, careful not to show my nervousness. I gave a smile to my escort as he motioned me out of the building.

The rain had stopped and we walked through town as he tried to engage me in conversation. He pointed out the street leading to the school a few blocks away, and the library located behind the town hall. The town also had a movie theater and bowling alley. Those piqued my interest, at least there would be some form of entertainment.

When we stopped in front of the town's medical clinic I finally stopped thinking about what had happened at the town hall and focused on the here and now. "Why are we here?"

He walked in front of me and I trailed behind, wanting an answer. "You need to meet with Dr. Todd. He'll make sure you don't have any medical issues preventing you from working on the farms."

Okay. That I could buy. I'd fill out a form, answer a few questions, and sign a waiver.

A pretty redhead with the name tag Bridget checked me in and gave me a questionnaire to fill out while I waited. When I was done, I looked at the magazines on the table. They all either had to do with prenatal care, fertility specialists, or equestrian life. Considering the décor on the wall of nothing but horses, the last didn't surprise me. Still, none of the literature interested me, so I twiddled my thumbs while I waited. I missed my smart phone and aimless amounts of apps that would have passed the time.

The nurse called my name and buzzed me through

a set of doors. We walked to the office located at the far end of the corridor. A man in a white lab coat sat behind a large wooden desk with a single lamp perched on the corner. He had a stack of folders on one edge. Behind him was a bookcase, neat and organized, not a thing out of place. He stood as I entered and offered a smile and a handshake. He was younger than I expected. Mid-thirties, at most, which set me more at ease.

Bridget handed him my med forms and left the room. "So, Grace, is it? I'm Dr. Todd."

I nodded. I found it strange everyone used their first names here. Very informal.

"Let's take a look here. No serious medical conditions. No allergies listed. Good." He went down the list. "When was the first day of your last period? You didn't fill that in."

I shifted in my seat. "I, um, it was a couple weeks ago. I don't know the exact date."

"Hmm. You should keep better track of that information." He gave me a stern look and I knew then and there that Dr. Todd and I would not become friends.

"Actually, I keep track just fine on the calendar on my phone, which you people took away from me."

He sighed and made a note on my forms. "After your blood work, we'll have to do an exam to determine if you are pregnant."

"What?" I sputtered. "I can tell you right now I am not pregnant. No need for an exam to tell you anything."

He no longer held that welcoming smile. "I can't just take your word for it. Do you know how many females have come in to this office and lied in order to get a sign off on activities? As a medical professional, I must see the results for myself."

I felt my usual sarcastic self return in full glory. "While I am sorry you have a patient load of liars, I am not one of them. If you need to confirm my pregnancy status, I will pee in a cup, but I do not consent to anything more. I have a doctor at home whom I see for my annual physicals."

He didn't argue, simply jotted more information on my medical forms before pressing a button on a phone.

Wait. He had a phone. There were phones in this town? The button must have been for an intercom. "Grace is ready to go down for her blood work." He looked back at me. "You can go with Bridget now. Give her this lab request. I will see you later."

Good riddance, Dr. Todd. I followed the nurse down another hallway until we reached a door marked 'Labs' where she pointed me to a waiting room and handed my lab orders to another woman behind a desk.

She typed everything into a computer. Gee, more electronics. I thought this town lived off the grid. Maybe it was only the hospital, in order to keep up with technology. That was probably a good thing, but still annoying.

When I was called, I took off my sweatshirt as requested and put out my arm for the blood draw. I still don't understand the need for all this hoopla. As far as I'm concerned, I put all the pertinent information on the medical survey when I came in.

She stuck me in one try and the first vial of blood filled quickly. She plugged in the second. "When you are done here, we'll send you down the hall for your pregnancy exam."

Exasperated, I tried not to jerk my arm. "I hope you mean a urine test," I stated firmly. "Because I only agreed to a urine test."

The nurse scanned my paperwork. "Oh. I see." She finished, took the needle out and had me hold the swab down. "I'll be right back."

She left the room for a couple minutes then when she returned, I assumed she'd forgotten the band aid as I still held the swab in place, she went to my opposite arm and jabbed in a needle.

"What the hell?" I managed before the world went black.

Chapter Four

My stomach rolled. I struggled to keep bile from rising. A repetitive *beep beep beep* sounded in my brain that I couldn't shut off. Then I realized the noise was in the room, not inside my head.

I heard the mumble of voices and smelled the distinct aroma of bleach. I opened my eyes as I felt my arm being pinched. A blood pressure cuff? Heart monitor machines? Why was I in a hospital?

The last thing I remembered was…

Oh, dear God. They didn't. I looked down. I wore a hospital gown and nothing else.

No. No. No. Please. Not again.

As I sat up, the bile nearly had me, but I managed to keep it down. I tore the cuff from my arm and the monitor clip from my finger.

A nurse, concern painting her face, raced in. "Where do you think you are going?"

If looks could kill, the poor woman would be laying in a puddle of nothing but her clothes on the floor. "What…did…you…do…to…me?"

Nausea wasn't my only problem. Whatever drug they'd given me made me dizzy and I put out a shaky hand to grasp the bed rail.

"Now that you're awake, I'll call the doctor to see you. You'll want to lay back down."

I may not be able to stand, but no way in hell was I

about to lay back down. I took slow, deep breaths as I waited for the doctor. While it did help ease my nausea, my temper increased with every breath.

When the doctor appeared, the only thing keeping me from punching him in the nose was my lack of strength to get out of the bed. "Oh, good, you're awake."

How dare he be so happy? "What did you do to me?"

He carried a clipboard and looked down at it. "Just a complete physical including a routine pelvic exam, pap smear, and breast exam."

It took a full minute before I could even speak, another half before I was able to yell. Loudly. "You had no right! I did not consent to an exam. There are laws against this."

Dr. Todd shrugged as he continued to look down at my chart, avoiding all eye contact. "You signed a contract agreeing to follow all rules and one of our rules is a full physical. Since you were uncooperative, we had to put you out for a while."

"No. This is not happening. Where are my clothes? I need to leave. Now."

He finally looked up. "I can't let you leave until you have calmed down and I know the drugs have worn off enough for you to walk safely."

Calm? There was no way I was going to be *calm*. Instead, I grabbed the pitcher of water from the table beside my bed and threw it at him. It smashed into his face before dumping down the entire front of his body.

Chunks of ice plopped on the floor. Doctor Todd yelped while a nurse came running. "Get her back to bed." He turned on his heel and stormed out.

A second nurse came in and the two of them flanked the bed. "You need to lie back down," one said.

"What I need is to leave," I shrieked. "Where are my clothes?"

The nurses each took an arm and forced me back against the mattress. My body vibrated with energy, either from my angst or the drugs, or both, and I could feel a bout of tears welling. While I struggled against the nurses, I didn't notice the straps they grabbed from beneath the bed until my arms were pinned and the straps tightened.

One placed a blanket over my waist and legs while the other picked up the empty pitcher. I couldn't move. The body trembles started first and then the tears came. I was still crying when Caleb came in.

"Why are you here?" I spat the words at him.

"I heard there was a bit of a physical altercation between you and the doctor."

"Is he pressing charges because I threw something at him? Well, he deserved it. He violated me." My voice cracked and I turned my head away, unable to look at the large man in the room. "There are laws against that. You should arrest him."

The tears started again. I knew it had to be the residual effects of the drugs, because I'm not one to be reduced to tears. "And now I'm being treated like a criminal." I pulled at my restraints. "See?"

He walked to the side of the bed, ignoring the puddle of water on the floor, then sat down on the bed at my side. "Why did they have to sedate you? What did you do?"

"What did I do?" I yelled. "All I said was they could not do an internal exam for a pregnancy test."

"You haven't been here one full day. Can't you cooperate?"

"I said I would pee in a cup. That works, you know. I thought that was very cooperative." I sniffed again. I'm sure, by now, both my nose and eyes were a bright red. He reached over and wiped a tear from my cheek and gave me a small smile.

"Yes, Grace, I believe for you that is a big step toward working with us. Why don't we get you dressed and I'll bring you home."

Home? My heart leaped for a moment; until I realized he meant my host home, but I nodded. When he left the room, I heard him talking to someone in the hall.

"What the hell, Todd? Restraints?"

"Watch your language," the doctor admonished. "We had no choice. She was unstable."

"Do you blame her? The girl is scared."

"We don't tell you how to do your job. She was uncooperative. I did what I felt necessary."

The voices faded off as I struggled to keep my eyes open from the fatigue associated with the drugs. I heard the footsteps a moment before the lawman reentered the room with a nurse. She took my clothes out of a cabinet and put them on the bed. "I'll take these straps off if you promise not to throw anything."

Caleb answered for me. "She'll be the perfect patient. You have my word."

In other words, if I did try anything, I'd be answering to him. Message received. I didn't move a muscle until both straps were off.

"Can you leave the room now so I can get dressed?" Without a word he left and I swung my legs off the bed for the second time. Nausea was gone. So was the dizziness. My body still felt weak, but not too bad. I slipped the gown off and began the process of dressing. I had everything but my shoes on when he called out.

"How are you doing? Can I come in?"

"Guess so."

I held one sneaker in my hand. He took it from me and lifted my foot to his thigh. In a few short moves, my sneaker was on and tied and he was working on the other.

"Let's go." He took me by the arm, I think to hold me up. If it was to keep me from escaping, he needn't worry, the reality was I couldn't run even if I wanted to. I felt completely weak and helpless. A position I thought I'd never be in again.

His police cruiser was a new model SUV. Caleb helped me step up into the vehicle and slid the seat belt across my body. For once, I didn't mind his overbearing nature.

It wasn't quite dark yet but getting close, and I wondered how long I'd been unconscious while they did unimaginable things to my body. I shuddered.

"Are you okay?"

"No." I mumbled as I kept my arms wrapped tight around my body. He kept his eyes on the road, making a few turns before pulling up in front of my new summer residence. He shifted into park but didn't shut off the ignition.

"Want to talk?"

To him? Hell no, but I spoke anyway. "They violated me. They had no right to do what they did. And how do I know they didn't do more than what they said they did?"

He sighed. "They're good people. Things will go a lot easier on you if you'd just do as you're told the first time around. Follow the rules."

"How am I supposed to know what those rules are? I thought that meant no phones or Internet." I hugged myself tighter. "Not this." I looked out the window. "Another question. Didn't anyone else have an issue with what they wanted?"

"They're not fighting it. They were all done with their physicals within fifteen minutes and sent back to their new homes to get settled."

"Why aren't they questioning this? Why are they following along like cattle?"

Caleb turned off the ignition. "Maybe because they want to be here. Let's get you inside."

He walked around to my side of the truck and opened the door for me and helped me to the ground. I felt steadier than before as we walked to the house, but I didn't refuse the arm he put out to lend support. He gave a quick knock on the door before opening it and calling out.

"I'm in the kitchen," Amy yelled back.

I thought, now that I was home, he'd leave, but he followed me inside and up the stairs to the kitchen. The older woman stood by the stove, stirring something in a pot. She wore an apron with a large daisy on the front. "Caleb, what a surprise, and Grace, you're home. Come in. Sit down."

I sat while my escort crossed the room to give the cook a kiss on the cheek. "What brings you here?" she asked.

"Grace had a reaction to medication at the hospital

today. I offered to bring her home."

I silently thanked the man for his tact, but there was no way in hell I would say the words out loud.

"Oh, dear, not the most pleasant start to our town." She looked at me. "I was making spaghetti, but if you'd like, I have leftover soup in the freezer I can warm up for you."

I shook my head. "No, don't go to any trouble. Whatever you are making will be fine."

"What about you, dear?" She looked back at the man still standing. "Can you stay?"

"No, ma'am. Heading home now. I'll see you tomorrow." He nodded to me and left.

Day one had not had a good start. I hoped tomorrow would be better.

****

According to the radio when I woke, Sunday's weather predicted to be in the mid-sixties with mostly sunny skies, a nice difference from the rain I'd woken to yesterday.

I hadn't slept well. My mind raced with the previous day's events: Arriving in Wellington sooner than expected; not having a drop of coffee; Dr. Todd and his forced physical; and a certain arrogant police chief who'd shown a hint of kindness at the end of the day.

With a huge yawn, I forced myself to get out of bed. Before heading to my room last night, I'd been informed I'd be expected to attend the church service. I threw on a pair of white capri-style pants with a navy blue blouse and white sandals. At the last moment I grabbed my denim jacket and walked with my hosts to The Square.

All the newcomers and their host families had front row seating. I'd never had much of a religious upbringing so my mind wandered as the man up front droned on about the reading.

The church was pretty, in a simple way, with its stained-glass windows filling the large room with plenty of light. The benches were a dark stain with deep seats. The room was filled to overflowing, but there was no way it fit four hundred, especially with the number of children sitting prim and proper beside their parents.

I picked a non-existent lint from my sleeve and swiped at any wrinkles. I felt a bit under-dressed in the short-legged slacks. Most of the women wore dresses. Children were in their Sunday best. Even the men wore button down shirts and ties, even though most were paired with jeans and dusty boots. I noticed there wasn't a single hat on any head. If they had one, it was clasped in their hands or shoved in back pockets.

Near the conclusion, the priest or pastor, or whatever he was called, said he wanted to introduce the newest residents to Wellington. I thought it strange terminology as we were only here for the summer, but I stood by the altar with the others as he handed each of us the microphone to announce our names to his congregation. Maybe I've been a bit self-centered and too worried about Caroline, but I hadn't taken the time on the bus to make new friends.

Besides me, Caroline, and Jake, the brown-haired girl who'd got on the bus in Vermont near our college was Christy. The super shy girl who'd been on the bus when we boarded was Isabelle, she was from New Hampshire. I already knew Marcus, the guitar player, he'd boarded at the first stop in Massachusetts, while Jessica and Kevin were from the college in Amherst. That left the remaining girls from Connecticut: Leigh, Penny, and Maria.

When the service finished, I followed everyone out a side entrance to a covered courtyard with glass walls. The courtyard was filled with benches and I noticed an oversized screen on the wall. Kurt explained the service was projected live on the screen so those not inside the church could also participate.

I watched a bustle of activity as people took the benches they'd sat on, flipped them up and connected them to another bench creating picnic tables to now use for the meal. The covered patio area connected the church with a second building where lines of people weaved in and out. We made our way through the crowd slowly as more people than I will ever remember stopped to introduce themselves.

Once we entered the second building, I noticed tables of food along with more of the bench-tables. I stared in amazement at the amount of food, and so much of it fruit and vegetables. It was like walking into an indoor farmer's market.

When I had a full plate, I excused myself from my hosts to make my way past a throng of people, and children, and there were a lot of children, to search out my friends.

Jake waved to me from a table near the door inside the cavernous hall and after I put my plate down, I threw myself into his arms. I'd known this man practically my entire life. Everything about him was familiar and I needed familiarity now more than ever.

"Whoa. What's this about?" he asked as he

wrapped his arms around me and put his cheek down on my head. He smelled like home and I clung to him.

"Yesterday was the worst day of my life," I mumbled into his white Oxford shirt. Leave it to him to have the proper clothes for a church service.

"Hey." He pulled away far enough to look down into my face. "What happened? Are you all right?" I wanted to tell him everything, but the noise of people around us made it hard to talk normally, never mind a conversation about breach of trust.

"No, but we'll have to talk later. Not here."

He nodded as Caroline joined us, a huge smile on her face. "Isn't this place wonderful?" She gushed. "Everyone has been so nice."

He released me and I sat down as my roommate went on about how friendly everyone in Wellington is. I wanted to gag. Kurt and Amy had been the epitome of welcome hosts, but my ordeal at the hospital yesterday lingered.

Not knowing our duties after eating, I excused myself from my friends. I meandered around tables and clusters of people until I located my host family at a table in the courtyard.

"Excuse me, Amy." She looked up with a warm smile.

"Hello, dear. How was your meal?"

"Um, it was fine. Very nice, actually." I shifted from one foot to the other. "I wanted to ask what is next for today. I mean, do we need to stay for clean up? Is there something we typically do on Sundays? Or can I take a walk and explore?"

They sat with two other couples about their age. All had finished their meals and sat talking. "Oh, no, dear. This is your first day. Go and explore the town. You can help us *red up* next week."

I wasn't familiar with that expression, but I assumed it meant to clean. A nice breeze kept the courtyard cool, and I noticed the glass doors had all been opened, allowing a flow of people to mingle both toward the front where the street was, and the back where a large park and playground were filled with families.

I spotted Caleb at a table by one of the open doors. He held a toddler in his arms, a girl maybe about three, who slept with her head nestled into his neck. A little boy, slightly older, came by and tugged at his pant leg. He put his hand on the child's head. His face was relaxed and open as he gave the boy his full attention.

"Holy crap. Caleb is married and has kids?" I realized in my shock, I'd said the words out loud.

Kurt looked over to where my gaze was fixated. "He has three kids. You seem surprised."

I tried to be tactful. "Yes, well, I've only seen him as very stern and, and, well, police chief-y."

Amy shook her head as she made a tssking sound. "I've seen that side, too, dear. But he's seen some things, the poor child."

One of the other woman at their table piped up. "Caleb left Wellington when he was eighteen and joined the Marines. Everyone told him not to go; told him he'd regret it. But, he left anyway."

"Got himself married," another woman continued. "They had their children, then while he was away on duty, his wife… oh, it's so tragic."

Kurt patted his wife's hand. "Ladies, we shouldn't gossip. It's not right."

Damn, were they really going to leave me hanging?

"You're right, not our place. Grace, Sunday's are family day. After our fellowship meal here, we are free to mingle and spend time together or, of course, you may take a walk. All stores and the diner are closed, though."

I thanked them and headed back to the hall to hook back up with my friends, but my eyes shifted back to Caleb as he spoke to a group of men. The child he held must have weighed thirty pounds or more, but he held her with one arm as though she weighed no more than a feather.

He spotted me watching him and I spun around to dash into the hall, anxious to escape. Jake remained at the table where we'd sat and I joined him again, but Caroline had moved to the far side of the room where Aaron and a group of people were setting up instruments on the stage.

"Oh, hell, don't tell me he's in a band?"

"Yep." He grinned and rolled his eyes. "And that one is his muse."

"I can't watch this. Let's go for a walk, please." We tossed our trash into the receptacles by the door and exited out the front doors. The mid-day sun counteracted the breeze, making it a perfect day to explore.

Leland had pointed out all the highlights during our van excursion yesterday, but I'd been a bit preoccupied with a looming interrogation to pay close attention at the time.

The brick buildings and window fronts were typical Main Street, USA, circa early 1900s. Everything was well maintained and updated, but I couldn't help feeling I'd stepped back in time as I spotted the post office as nothing more than a narrow entrance within the line of bricks.

We walked, not talking, not touching, for a couple blocks, until he pointed to a black iron park bench along the sidewalk. "Sit and spill, Grace."

I sat, looking up at the blue sky and the billowy cloud cover. "That obvious?"

He nodded. "Usually you don't stop talking. What the hell happened?"

I shifted on the bench, taking in the quiet of the quaint town. Cars and pickups lined the street, but few people were out and about as most still gathered inside for their meal. "First, what did you do yesterday?"

He shook his head. "No stalling."

"I'm not. I just want to know if you and I had the same experiences."

Jake shifted sideways on the bench and glared at me and I surrendered. "Fine, I'll talk. First was the interview with their Town Council."

"Yes." He nodded. "Odd, but not too bad. Did they give you a hard time?"

I lifted a single shoulder. "I mean, they weren't happy when I told them I didn't trust them and my sole reason for coming was because Caroline was following a guy."

I spotted the lift of Jake's lip and knew my response was normal—for me, anyway. "Okay, they didn't like it, but did they flog you for it?"

"No, of course not. But then I was taken to the medical center for a physical."

"Ah huh."

"Don't 'Ah huh' me. Did they make you take a

full-fledged physical?"

"Do you mean, turn and cough?"

"I told them no, in no uncertain terms I would not allow a full physical. I have a doctor at home for that."

"And?"

I took a steadying breath and looked into the distance. Even with Jake, this was difficult to admit. "They drugged me and performed the physical while I was unconscious."

"They did what?" He jumped up off the seat and faced me, eyes huge with fury. "Holy shit." He began to pace. "What the hell? After what you've been through, this must…Damn. Shit. I'm sorry."

I crossed my arms and leaned back, closing my eyes against the glare of sun. "I want to go home, Jakey. Forget this place even exists."

"Okay. Then we go home."

I opened my eyes. He stood in front of me, blocking the sun. His face was in shadow. "That's just it, everyone keeps reminding me I signed a contract. *We* signed a contract. I don't think they're going to be forthcoming about the town's bus schedule out of here."

He continued to pace. He was angry for me, which was great, since today I was past angry and instead felt more shock about what the doctor had done to me. "So we walk out. Let's go pack our bags and meet back here in an hour."

"What about Caroline? She's enamored with this place. I don't know if she'll come?"

My friend continued his path back and forth on the sidewalk. "Let's tell her what they did and she'll change her mind."

I hoped he was right. As much as I wanted to get out of this place, I didn't feel comfortable leaving Caroline behind. Who knew what would happen to her. We needed to stick together.

"Okay, here's the plan." He took my hand and pulled me up to make our way back to the hall. "I will find the little groupie and get her outside where we can talk. In the meantime, if you run into anyone inside, act normal. Don't give any indication you want to leave. We can't have anyone alerted we plan to break our contract."

I nodded. He was right. Act normal. Fit in.

A crowd still remained in The Hall in order to listen to the band. Aaron played his guitar while a young girl who couldn't be more than thirteen, belted out a song I'd never heard before. The crowd erupted into applause as the song finished. I stood at the edge of the crowd as Jake made his way to Caroline and whispered in her ear. I was so intent on watching them, I didn't notice anyone coming up behind me.

"Grace, I've been looking all over for you."

Chapter Five

My heart sank.

"Hi, Leland." I slowly turned toward him. "I went for a walk. I wanted to explore the town a bit."

When he smiled at me, I realized how pretty he was, and I mean pretty. His skin had an even tan and he had long black eyelashes any woman would kill for. His Sunday clothes were pressed and neat, showing off his tall, thin physique. Even his blond hair could have been styled by Hollywood. He may be the male version of his twin, but his features were almost a bit too feminine.

"You should have found me." He took my hand. I wanted nothing to do with him or this town, but I resisted the urge to pull away. "I would have taken you around. I am your guide, after all."

I scanned the room. Where were Jake and Caroline? "I didn't think about it."

He moved closer. "There's a small group of us getting together to hang out. Come with."

I stood on my tip toes and spotted my friend as he tried to pry Caroline from the front row of Aaron's performance. "Thanks anyway, but Jake and I figured we'd take it slow today. You know, ease into things. Get to know our host families better." I tried to pull my hand from his grasp but he squeezed it tighter.

A big, dark-haired guy came up behind Leland and slapped him on the back. "What's up, cuz? Ready to hang?"

"A.J., this is Grace. I'm trying to convince her to join us.

A.J.'s eyes slid lazily down my body then back up. It was bad enough being sized up like a side of beef, but the glare Leland sent back to the newcomer screamed 'back off.' I'd been here one day and already was over the male preening drama.

"Don't worry about me," I said. "I'm waiting for Jake. We are, uh, going to…"

Hope joined the group interrupting my excuse. "So, are we heading out? Oh, hi."

Leland tugged on my hand causing me to step closer. "You have to come. The best way to get used to being here is to get to know us."

I felt Jake step behind me. "No go," he whispered.

I gave a slight nod. After three years being Caroline's roommate, I knew how stubborn she was when she set her mind to something. Right now, she was fully entrenched in being near the new boyfriend and experiencing everything about this town. I could give her a couple hours. We should wait until dark anyway for our big escape.

With the arrival of my male companion, I saw the gorgeous blonde's eyes light up seconds before she latched onto his arm. "You're just in time. We're all heading out to hang for a while."

He gave me a questioning look. Every fiber of my being urged me to go hide out where no one could find me. Instead, I shrugged, rolling my eyes at the same time. We'd agreed to play along. We had to pretend to fit in.

They led us through town until we got to the school

and then the length of the football fields onto a path in the woods. The rough terrain wasn't what I had in mind when I got dressed this morning, but I managed not to ruin my white sandals.

We headed off the path a bit until we reached another group of people. A.J. introduced us to Tim, Byron, Wayne, Theresa, and Barbara.

There was room to sit on the side of a moss-covered, fallen tree. I took off my denim jacket, placing it down first; my feeble attempt to save my white pants from my woodsy adventure.

Tim lifted a gallon jug filled with what looked to be cider, took a sip, and passed it around. When it got to me I took a giant gulp and nearly spit it out. "Shit." My eyes watered, but the Wellington crowd laughed. "What is that?"

"Hard cider." Leland handed the gallon to Jake.

"I thought alcohol is forbidden here," my partner in crime said as he took a long drink.

Hope giggled. "Lots of things are forbidden, doesn't mean we don't find a way around it."

The jug continued its pass around the circle as we answered questions from the group. When I took the drink for the second time, Jake raised a surprised brow. On the third round, he understood that finally I was going to let loose a bit more than was usual for me.

It turned out, he and I were the youngest at twenty. All the others in the woods were between twenty-one and twenty-five. Wayne took a swig then turned his attention to me. "So, Grace, I heard you had it out with our illustrious police chief."

Hope answered on my behalf. "She actually pushed him."

Byron stared at me. "No way?"

"Not only did she push him," the male twin said, all wide-eyed, "but when he told her to sit down, she said no."

Barbara opened a backpack and pulled out a bag of brownies. "Girl, you are my new hero. Messing with Caleb takes balls. Here, have a brownie. You've earned it."

I took a bite into the chocolate fudge dessert bar. "It was only because I'd just found out I have to give up coffee. I drink about a gallon a day of the stuff. No one warned me."

A.J. grinned. "Stick with us. You want it, we can find a way to get it."

That sounded promising. I took another gulp of the potent liquid as the jug was passed to me again. The taste was barely tolerable, but I managed not to spit it out. It was my fifth round with the jug and my eyes no longer watered when drinking.

"I have a question," I said. "Why does everyone use first names around here? I mean, you refer to Caleb by his name and not Chief Whatever and I noticed a dental office with the doctor's first name."

'They' shared a strange look but Theresa elected to speak. "Because we are all Wellingtons. The entire town is one big happy family."

Jake sat forward. "How is that even possible?"

"The farmlands were purchased by five Wellington brothers in the late 1800s," she continued. "Over the years, their descendants have grown the property and eventually incorporated the town."

"Wow. Amazing." I continued to listen as I worked on my second brownie, washing it down with the cider.

"Obviously, not *everyone* is a direct descendant. We're not into that whole, my sister is my aunt or anything like that," Barbara insisted.

"No, of course not." The alcohol had definitely kicked in. I was relaxing. Yesterday's incident still weighed on my mind, but this group had taken the time to welcome us. If everyone continued to be this nice, and if we weren't planning to sneak out tonight, the summer might not be all that bad.

Hope pulled Jake to his feet. "Come with me. I want to show you something."

I watched my friend leave me behind as the afternoon sun sparkled between the tree branches. Barbara and A.J. started arguing after he made a comment about her ass which made her storm off. Wayne followed to calm her down. Tim, Byron, and Theresa began a heated discussion over Marvel versus DC comics. Not being a comics fan, I had nothing to contribute to their conversation, which suited Leland as he appeared to have other plans.

He handed me the cider and moved closer on the tree trunk. His long legs pressing against mine. "I'm glad you came with us today."

"Thanks for inviting us out. I did need a bit of a distraction." I didn't mean to lead him on. There was no way I was getting into any summer romance. But when he took my hand in his I knew he was hitting on me and would probably try to kiss me soon.

I pulled my hand away and reached for the bag of brownies and pulled out another. It was my third. *Gawd*, what a sow, but tight pants were better than this would be suitor kissing me right now. I'd had way too much alcohol, and I rarely drank for exactly this reason.

"Want to go exploring?"

I giggled. Yeah, right. Somehow, I didn't think he was talking about the woods.

I heard a bird call and suddenly everyone scrambled to their feet. "Shit," A.J. swore. "Big brother is coming."

Leland grabbed my hand and pulled me up. "*Run.*"

They all took off in different directions, but I couldn't. I'd stood way too fast and the earth moved beneath my feet. I took a couple steps and pressed my hand against a tree trunk to steady myself.

Damn, the cider was potent. I spotted my jacket and gingerly made my way back to it. Leaning over to grab it might not have been a great idea but I managed to keep my feet on the ground and turn around. I heard a snap of a twig and hoped Leland had come back for me but it wasn't him on the path.

"Oh, look. It's Police Chief Caleb. Now I get why everyone took off." I pouted. "You broke up our party." I put the brownie in my mouth, holding it there so I could shove an arm into the sleeve of my jacket. I managed one but couldn't find the other sleeve.

The unexpected arrival shoved a cell phone in his pocket as he stopped in front of me. I had to look way up to see his disapproving glare. But despite his sigh, he lifted the other side of my jacket so I could put my arm through.

I finished my brownie in two more bites while he gave me an evil eye as he waited. "Oops. Someone is grumpy." I reached up and put the heel of my hands on either side of his face and pressed up. "You need to turn that frown upside down, mister." I couldn't help myself. I rubbed at the scruff on his face. "Hey, this is softer than it looks."

He grabbed me by the wrists and forced my hands down. "You're drunk."

"Yep. I am." I forced one hand away from his grasp, or he let it go, I wasn't too sure which, and gave him a poke in the chest. Storm clouds formed in his murky blue eyes. "I am drunk. Snookered. Pissed."

"What were you drinking?"

I put my finger to my lips. "Shh. I'm not supposed to say." More giggles from me. "Can you keep a secret?"

He gave me one of his stony stares he was so good at. "I won't tell you what we drank, but, if you look right over there…" I waved my hand in the general direction of the jug hidden behind the stump. As I did, I spun around with my arm and lost my balance.

Caleb didn't let me fall. He reached out to steady me and as he did, I placed my hand on his biceps. "Whoa, Nellie. Your arms are tree trunks. Redwood Forest trunks. How much can you bench press?"

He released me in order to pick up the empty jug and took a whiff. "I'm going to kill A.J."

I rocked back on my heels, my hands clamped behind my back. "Nope. Wrong again. It was Wayne. No. Tim." I covered my mouth. "Oops. I wasn't supposed to tell you. It's not nice to rat on friends."

He took my arm again and led me down the path. "You made friends today."

I struggled to keep up with his long stride. Plus, my sandals were flimsy against the stones. "Yep, Leland and Hope brought us to a party in the woods. There was, A.J. and Tim"—I slowed my pace as I put my fingers up with each name—"Wayne, Byron, Theresa, and… and…" What was her name? "Oh yeah, Barbara. Right. Barbara brought brownies."

Caleb stopped and frowned. "How many brownies did you eat?"

I held up my fingers. Did I have two or three up?

"That many."

"See, your problem, Chief Uptight, is that you need to relax. Slow down. Don't be such a worry wort."

"Is that right?"

"Like me. You even said so. Remember?" If he did, he didn't say anything. "I had a few drinks. Big deal. I needed to unwind."

We reached the field and Caleb picked up his pace again. "I bet you know how to relax. I saw you with your kids this morning and you weren't frowning then."

"Do you want me to treat you like one of my children?"

I held back a laugh. "Nope. I'm not a child." He was walking too fast. I pulled back and he slowed. A little. "But, this place freaks me out. If it weren't for Caroline, I'd never even consider staying where I couldn't drink coffee."

I stumbled and my legs crumpled. In a swift move, the large man wrapped an arm around my waist and swung me up into his arms.

"Whoa. Everything is spinning. Look at those clouds go round and round." Instead of curling into him, I threw my arms out wide, straightening my back and causing him to stop in his tracks.

"For goodness sake. You're not making this easy." He made an attempt to shift me in his arms but I put my head back to stare at the clouds. "Put your arms around my neck, Grace."

I finally did as told, laying my head on his shoulder. He moved across the football field with long, even strides as though he carried nothing more than a grocery bag, never mind a girl weighing…well, we won't go there. I'm not fat in any way, but still, it's not something I'll mention.

I closed my eyes and the world stopped rotating. "Oh, this is much better. Wish I'd thought to do it before." I nuzzled into his neck. "I only came with the group to pretend to fit in."

"Pretend?"

"Mmm hmmm. You smell good." Then before I knew what I was doing, I pressed my lips against his neck. Then another one slightly higher, near his ear.

"Grace?" He slowed his pace which gave me a chance to curl into him more.

"You smell of soap mixed with outdoors." A third kiss. Now he stopped walking. I nuzzled his neck with my nose.

"Tell me why you need to pretend?" I liked his voice. It was deep and husky.

I yawned. "And you're really warm."

"Tell me."

I sighed. "As soon as Jake and I tell Caroline what that horrible doctor did to me yesterday, she'll agree to leave with us."

"Uh, huh."

I closed my eyes against the afternoon sun and breathed in the scent of Caleb. I'm not sure how a person can smell of strength, but he did. Strength and the woods and all man.

As he began to walk again, I welcomed the soothing, even stride. I couldn't stop the yawn. "We're supposed to leave tonight, but first, I think I'm going to sleep."

Chapter Six

I rolled to one side before my head exploded. My cheek rested against a cool slab as I curled into a fetal position. Voices screamed inside my skull. I grabbed my ears, begging them to stop.

But they weren't in my head. A scrape of a chair on the floor pierced me and I groaned.

"Caleb," a man yelled as a door slammed shut. Oh, dear God, did everything have to echo?

"Hello, Roger." As usual, that man's tone remained unflappable.

"I understand you have my children here. Under what charges?"

"Public intoxication and contributing to the delinquency of minors."

"It's that girl's fault." The town administrator's voice carried across the room. "She made it clear she didn't want to be here or follow our rules. Release my children. They had nothing to do with this."

The police chief didn't seem surprised at Roger's demands. His tone was direct as he handled the civilian invading his station. "While Leland and Hope may not have directly provided the substances, they brought our newcomers to the school with the direct intention of drinking and getting them high. The use of alcohol or drugs is an offense. They will spend the night in a cell, like everyone else involved."

The older man continued to sputter. "You just admitted they didn't provide anything to anyone. Release them, or I will call the judge."

Caleb sounded almost bored with the over-protective father. "That's your prerogative. My plan is to let them sleep it off, spend the night in jail, and perhaps do a bit of community service. If you want to get a judge to come into town, it means I have to write this up. They are adults, now. It will go onto their permanent record."

"You listen here, Caleb. You abandoned this town and when you discovered we were right about life out there, you crawled back, tail between your legs. We didn't have to give you this job. We did it because—"

"You did it because I am the most qualified for the position. Your kids stay here in a cell. Or do you want to clean up after them when they puke?"

There was a moment of silence before Roger's voice lowered from a roar to a more tolerable tone of resignation. "Fine. I'll be back in the morning."

The slam of the door crashed through my head causing another groan.

"If you're going to hurl, use the bucket I put beside your cot."

I opened my eyes, a very bad decision, to find the chief of police standing on the opposite side of the black bars.

"Worst hangover ever," I mumbled through my cotton mouth. My tongue moved around, searching for saliva.

"Serves you right."

I forced myself to sit up. Nausea rolled in my stomach but I managed to keep it at bay. Someone had placed a wool blanket over me. I pulled it up to my chin as I placed my head on my up-turned knees. I'd heard what he'd said to Leland and Hope's father but wanted to make sure I'd heard correctly. "What are the charges?"

"Underage drinking, public intoxication, illegal drug use."

Hmm, not the same as what he'd stated to Roger. "I don't do drugs."

Caleb's grunt had me opening my eyes again. I turned my head slowly to see why he didn't believe me.

"T.H.C. brownies." At my blank stare he shook his head. "Marijuana."

"Oh." Then what he said made sense. I put my hands to my head, trying to hold it from spinning off my shoulders. "Oh! How long am I in here for?"

"Everyone will be staying the night."

God, my head hurt so bad I couldn't think straight. "You arrested others?"

"Leland, Hope, Jake, A.J., Tim, Theresa, Wayne, Byron, and Barbara. Did I miss anyone?"

Damn. I tried to remember what I said to him when he picked me up. I'm pretty sure I ratted out who I was with. Well, there goes the new friendships. "No. That was everyone."

"Are you hungry?"

I'd more than likely missed dinner, but there was no way I was mixing food with everything else rolling around inside me. "I'll pass. Do you have anything for a headache?"

"Nope. You'll have to suffer. You can have water, though."

Sadist. But I nodded.

He returned a few minutes later and didn't force me to get up. Instead, he opened the door to the cell and came to me, handing me the bottle. "Take small sips," he ordered then walked away, closing me behind the bars again.

I pressed the cold bottle to my forehead for a few minutes before cracking the seal on the cap and taking a few drops. I swished it around a moment, hoping to rid the cotton in my mouth before swallowing.

It stayed down, thankfully, and I attempted another sip. I didn't drink too much more before I secured the cap and lay back down on the built-in cement bench.

When I woke a second time it must have been morning because the noise level had increased. A phone rang, chairs scraped on the floor, and I tried to distinguish the voices as they talked over each other.

I sat, rubbing the sleepies from my eyes and took a look at my cell. Cement walls on three sides kept things semi-private between the prisoners. Bars on the outside wall, with a door with a slot for a food tray. I sat on the cement bench and across from me was a toilet. No walls around it. No privacy from anyone.

I gulped as I pulled my knees up and stared at the porcelain bowl. While everything was spotless, there was no way I would expose myself by sitting on that thing. Anyone could walk by. I wrapped my arms around my knees and prayed my bladder would hold out until my release. I played with the black bracelet. It wasn't round. It had angles on it, preventing me from spinning it on my wrist. Just seeing it there made me itchy. It wasn't mine so I wanted it gone.

An officer walked by and spotted me. "Good. You're awake. I'll be back for you."

Fabulous. I heard the clang of metal as a cell door swung open and a second later I saw the officer return with Jake, who flashed me a look filled with chagrin.

I must have been in the first cell because I clearly heard the activity in the main office. When Caleb addressed Jake, I moved to stand at the bars. "How are you feeling this morning?"

"About what is expected," he grumbled.

I rolled my eyes. This was not my friend's first foray behind bars due to drinking. He'd been picked up more than once at home due to his love of partying. Not me, though. This is all virgin territory on my part.

"Looks like you have a previous record, although no convictions."

He didn't respond, at least not out loud.

"Problem here, Jake, is your father isn't around to bail you out of trouble and I have a strong suspicion that's what you are accustomed to. Am I right?"

Again, I couldn't hear a response.

"What about Grace? Is she also in the habit of getting into trouble?"

"No. she keeps me on the straight and narrow most times. She's not big on partying, not since… Well, she doesn't drink."

"I see. So whose idea was it to party yesterday?"

Silence.

"Let me help you out." Caleb's tone was more conversational then interrogatory. "I already know who provided the alcohol and who supplied the drugged brownies. Did you go with Leland and Hope, knowing those would be available?"

"Of course not. As far as we knew alcohol was forbidden here. How were we to know someone would have their own private stash?"

"Yet, knowing it is against the law, once the alcohol was provided, you all willingly participated?"

While he didn't answer outright, I assume Jake nodded.

"Were you aware the brownies were laced with T.H.C.?"

I heard Jake hesitate before he answered. "I suspected as much. I didn't have any."

"The urinalysis will confirm that," the chief said. "Did Grace know?"

He snorted. "I seriously doubt it."

"And yet you didn't warn her?"

Ouch. That was a total slap on the wrist, but the law enforcer had a point. "She was already eating a brownie before I even knew they were there. I didn't say anything, though. We'd been drinking for a while already and it was the first time since getting on the bus Grace started to relax. This place stresses her out."

I gripped the bars and pressed my face against them, hoping to hear more. "Do you know what they did to her yesterday?"

"Jake," I yelled. "You can shut up now."

He yelled back, "You should press charges against that jerk-off who calls himself a doctor."

"Shut up." I mumbled, knowing he didn't hear me. Tears stung my eyes as I pressed against the bars. Here I go again, crying. This place is not good for me.

"Is it true you had a plan to leave Wellington last night?" While he posed it as a question, Caleb's tone was much too casual for my liking. He already knew the answer.

Shit. What had I said last night? I remember him

coming into the woods, but everything after was hazy.

There was no response.

"I'll take your silence as confirmation."

"You can take my silence any way you want," Jake retorted. "I didn't confirm anything."

"Today is a warning." The chief was no longer casual, but more of a force to be reckoned with. "Before you leave here, you will provide a urine sample. You and Grace have already missed this morning's tour of the town; however, you'll be expected to join the rest at lunch in order to receive your work assignments. Officer Brent will return you to your cell and a breakfast sandwich will be brought to you soon."

A moment later my friend walked by again and this time he mouthed sorry before he entered his cell. Then the officer was back and opened the door to my cell, motioning me to follow.

There were four desks in the room and I noticed an office against a side wall with a glass door with the words Police Chief stenciled in. But Caleb sat at one of the desks in the bullpen. He motioned for me to sit in the wooden chair at the side of the desk.

"Can I go to the bathroom first?"

He opened his mouth, I assume to mention the toilet in my cell, but I think he read my mind, because his eyes glistened. I prayed he wouldn't make me beg, but he nodded to the officer. "She needs to pee in a cup."

I returned to my seat a few minutes later, nervous, but with my urine sample secured and in a plastic bag. Caleb is intimidating in the best of circumstances, but this is his domain. He was reading a file on the desk and kept me waiting for at least a full two minutes before he looked at me.

Of course this tactic was to throw me off, I know that mentally, but it works. This was my first time in jail. My first time with a record. My first police interrogation. I fidgeted and showed my weakness. I attempted to sit still by pressing my hands together in my lap.

"I know you overhead my conversation with Jake, do you have anything to add about your trek in the woods yesterday?"

Crap. I expected the same direct questions he'd asked Jake, not this open-ended stuff. "Um, no."

He wrote something in the file and I waited, my palms growing sweatier by the second. "Jake mentioned you aren't much of a partier." He threw a look at me and waited. Was I supposed to answer? He didn't exactly ask a question. I gulped and shook my head.

"Per our earlier conversation, you are now aware in addition to the alcohol, you also imbibed in brownies laced with marijuana. When I located you in the woods, you were high and drunk. Do you remember much of what you told me last night?"

I worried my lip. "Not much."

"You told me you had intentions of leaving Wellington."

Oh. That. I pressed my lips and strangled my fingers together. I don't think the rest of this conversation was going to go well.

"Let me remind you, you signed a contract stating that during your stay you agree to follow town rules and policies which include no drugs or alcohol or acts considered to be immoral. You also signed a work contract."

"You do like to remind me of said contract," I mumbled, which garnered me yet another stern glare. Partnered with his matter-of-fact rehashing of my indiscretions, I'm lucky I didn't start crying like a baby. I pressed my nails into my palms and forced myself to handle this like an adult.

"On your second day in town you have already breached your contract by partaking in a party which included both drugs and alcohol and voiced clear intentions of breaking your work contract."

Yes, those were the facts. What were the consequences? "You're right. I broke the rules. Shouldn't I get sent home?"

"On the contrary, Grace." Caleb leaned back in his seat, one hand on the arm of the chair and the other nonchalantly tapping a finger on the desk. "This means I need to consider you a flight risk."

As he continued to study me, he knew he had the upper hand by keeping me hanging. I knew my chances of leaving this town were slim.

He leaned forward again to write in the folder on the desk. I wondered what he wrote. And why pen and paper instead of logging it into the computer on the desk.

Yep, computer and phone. Both items I am forbidden to use in this god-forsaken town. Both items I thought wouldn't even exist here, never mind be flaunted as a temptation.

"Looking to break another rule?"

"What?" I look up to Caleb's raised eyebrow and realized I had reached out to tangle the cord of the phone around my finger.

Ah, shit. "I guess I'm surprised how many

computers and phones I've already seen here when I expected the town to be, you know, antiquated?"

He looked away, but not before I caught the tiny lift on one corner of his mouth. I amuse him. When I'm not pissing him off.

"You, Jake, and Caroline will be assigned duties located on opposite sides of town. You will be assigned something within town so I can keep a personal watch on your comings and goings."

Freaking wonderful. The last person I wanted in my space was this man. I opened my mouth but I had no words. No sarcastic response. Nothing that would disentangle me from the mess I'd put myself into.

"Officer Brent will return you to your cell. You will be served breakfast there. Once I have my paperwork in order, I will escort both you and Jake to your respective homes to change and meet up with the others for job assignments."

I nodded meekly and followed the officer back to my cell. I sat on the bench and stared at the bars. Seventy-two hours or less since I'd boarded a bus in Vermont and already I'd pissed off the Town Council, garnished a drug charge, and put myself into the cross-hairs of the local police chief. Thankfully, Wellington's work-study was not a college-sponsored program, as I don't think this would look good on my college transcripts.

I ate my breakfast in my cell, still in shock I'd been arrested for the first time in my life. When I told my folks this would be a learning experience, this wasn't quite what I had in mind. On the other hand, Sarah would consider this hilarious.

When I got bored sitting, I moved to the doors,

pressing my face against the bars wondering which cell Jake was in. I could call out to him, but somehow, I didn't think Caleb would encourage the conversation.

I spotted the chief pouring a cup of—

Oh, dear God in heaven, is that coffee? I sniffed, hoping at least to get a whiff. He put a tea bag in to steep and my heart sank. He reached into his pocket to grab his phone. "Hi, Mom. No, just finishing up some paperwork. Fever? No, I'll pick her up from school. I was going to head home to shower and change anyway. Thanks."

He hung up and headed back toward the desks where I couldn't see him any longer, but his voice carried. "Brent. Thomas. Release the prisoners and take them home. They need to be brought to the diner at noon to meet up with the rest of the newcomers."

"Sure thing, Chief."

I was released first so I didn't see Jake again before I left. I was escorted out and got to have my first ride in the back of a police car. I suppose I'd had one yesterday, but I don't remember it. And the ride home from the hospital on Saturday didn't count as I was in the front seat.

It wasn't a bad experience. The inside was meticulously clean, which somehow, I think is Caleb's directive, but sitting in the back, I felt everyone on the street could see me and all were judging me. At least I was on the way home and not to the jail. And no handcuffs were involved. I rested my head against the back of the seat and closed my eyes against the much too bright sun.

Officer Brent pulled up outside of the pristine looking house and walked around to open my door but a thought occurred to me. "Do you think they're home? I don't have a key."

The officer gave me a flat stare—he must be taking lessons from his chief—and motioned me out of the car. "I doubt they are home, they both work. And the door is unlocked. No one locks doors here. There's no need."

"Oh." What do you say to that? Even in Vermont, which is generally a safe place to live, we still lock our doors. I mean, if you watch the news, no place is completely safe.

Unless you live in a town surrounded by fencing and you can't get in without a secret code.

"I'll be back for you at eleven forty-five. Be ready."

I nodded and headed inside. It would be easier to be ready if I had a damn watch, but they took it from me three days ago. At least there were a couple clocks in the house. I made sure I was ready to go with ten minutes to sparc.

Chapter Seven

I grabbed my shades before I headed out to wait for the officer to return and provide yet another ride in a police car. He dropped me off at the diner but didn't escort me in. With the glass windows of the restaurant, I know there were plenty of witnesses to my personal taxi.

I spotted Caroline and made my way to her table just as I spotted Jake being dropped off by his police escort. Finally, the three of us would have a chance to talk.

The diner had the typical fifties theme, except, by the looks of the place, it had actually been built in the fifties. Sure, the seats had been refurbished, as had the appliances I could see through the open window behind the counter, but the stools and counters and even the décor were authentic to the period.

The eleven newcomers had all found seats close to each other. I spotted the Town Council members in a corner where they'd pulled a couple tables together. Caleb was with them as they held a quiet discussion over whatever was written on the pages in front of them. Dr. Todd was also part of the group and my stomach sank at the mere sight of him. I didn't even want to look at that man, never mind wonder about his input regarding me.

After Jake sat down, I punched him in the arm. He

pulled back, feigning a pout. "Ow. What was that for?"

"For letting me eat those brownies, and for taking off and leaving me hanging. Some friend you are."

He gave me one of his hundred watt smiles. "I had you in my sights the entire time, up until super cop came and twinnie number two grabbed you to run. As for the dessert, you were too far wasted with the alcohol to appreciate it. I have to admit it was nice to see you let go for once."

"Don't give me your devil-may-care look you're so good at. I know you too well."

Caroline watched our conversation like a tennis match while sipping on her drink. Lemonade from the looks of it. God, I could use an extra-large dark roast right now. "So it's true. You were both arrested yesterday?"

"Yep. Your college roommate is now a felon." My partner in crime's tone was one of pride instead of remorse. I pinched his arm.

"Careful, I may have to press charges for assault."

He was far too chipper while I slunk down in my seat, shades on, picking at a turkey club sandwich and fries. "Wow, Grace, you haven't been wasted since—"

I cut my college roommate off. "We tried to get you to come outside to talk with us yesterday, but you were too busy with Aaron."

She bit into a tomato from her garden salad. "Talk about what?"

A nod from Jake gave confirmation he was still on board so I continued. "On Sunday, did you go to the hospital and did they do a full physical exam on you?"

"Yeah."

"So you're telling me you allowed them to do a

pap smear and breast exam?"

She shrugged. "Sure. Why wouldn't I? They said they needed it."

The dull ache in my head amped to an insistent throb. Why did she have to be so damn passive?

"I told them no, that a pelvic exam wasn't necessary to determine if I'm pregnant. So they sedated me and did the exam while I was unconscious."

She gave me a questioning look. "They're doctors, I'm sure it's all okay, isn't it?"

I knew she was naïve, but seriously? "No, Caroline. It's *not* okay."

Under the table, Jake covered my hand and gave it a squeeze. "What Grace is saying is they stepped way over the line and we think the best thing we should do is—"

Suddenly he shut up and sat back just as Scott approached our table. "Good afternoon. I wanted to discuss your job assignments." A quick glance around and I saw the other councilmen were meeting up with the other newbies.

I put down my fry. It was hard enough to eat anyway without knowing what crap job they might give me after yesterday's escapade.

Caroline received her work papers first from Scott. "You will be working with Amelia at the herbal farm. I understand you have some experience with gardening from home?"

She nodded and gave an excited squeal. "My family had an extensive garden so this is perfect. I love working outdoors."

"Excellent. This paperwork gives you information as to which shuttle to take in the morning and at what time."

The older man then turned to Jake. "You will work at our furniture factory where we make hand-carved rocking chairs. This factory has been around for over eighty years and we receive orders from all over the country. Ask for Glenn."

Orders from all over? Wouldn't they need a website? Did Caleb lie about that? I wish I had my phone to find this damn town online.

"Grace."

I pushed my shades onto my head and reluctantly accepted the page. Before I could read it through, Scott filled in the details. "I understand your family owns a restaurant. We can use your expertise in the school cafeteria."

Are they shitting me? My entire life I've worked in the food industry and when I take a summer to go play with horses, I get stuck in a cafeteria? Could this trip suck more?

No, it wasn't going to suck, because I still planned on getting out of here. Tonight.

He moved on to the next table, still too close to continue our discussion, not that Caroline minded, she was on to new topics. "Ooh, this is going to be so much fun. We planted a few things at home, but we didn't have a whole farm's worth of herbs."

Roger stood in the center of the restaurant and put up his hand as he called for everyone's attention. "From here, the shuttle is going to take you to the store where you can pick up any items you may need to go to work tomorrow. The papers you received give specific instructions for appropriate clothing, if you should pack a lunch, or if there is food available where you are working. We'll be leaving in ten minutes, so finish up."

I leaned across the table to whisper. "We need to finish our conversation."

Before I could say anything further, Caleb slipped onto the bench beside Caroline and gave me and Jake a knowing grin. I sucked on my straw with frustration at his untimely arrival. Or was it perfectly timed?

"How was lunch?" he asked.

"It was great," Caroline gushed. "This diner is the coolest. I've never been to a place so authentic."

He gave the tiny blonde a warm smile. He liked her. Then again, most people did. She was genuinely sweet, taking in every slice of life and eating it up like candy.

"I'm glad to hear you're enjoying yourself. I bet you'll like the bowling alley," he said. "It was built in the fifties and it comes with an arcade. Great place to hang out on Friday nights."

I groaned. Please don't encourage her. I'll never get her to leave. Or was that his intent?

"Grace, you didn't touch your food." The chief frowned at my still full plate. "Was the meal not to your satisfaction?"

I wished my shades were still down, but, no, I couldn't hide my eyes from this man's all-knowing looks. "Just feeling a bit under the weather today, *Chief.*"

"Drink lots of water. It will help flush out the toxins. How about you, Jake? How are you doing?"

"Right as rain. Not much knocks me to the ground." He slid a fry in ketchup and popped it in his mouth. He bumped my leg under the table with his and I felt his solidarity with me. Us against The Man.

Two shuttle buses pulled up outside. Roger motioned for everyone to leave. My sigh of relief to get rid of our unwanted table-mate was short-lived as he boarded the bus with us and again sat with my tiny friend, keeping her talking and ensuring I would be unable to continue my earlier start of conversation.

His choice of seats, directly behind me on the aisle, also meant Jake and I couldn't have a candid chat, either, for we knew big brother not only watched, but listened.

The store was a few blocks away, off the main street. We could have walked, but the shuttles were more for after, so we didn't have to carry our bags too far. It reminded me of one of those club stores, a large warehouse type building with groceries on one side, clothing and household items on the other. I grabbed a cart and pulled out my list.

I had packed my suitcase expecting to spend my summer outdoors. Now I would need clothes for working in a kitchen. Basically, I needed a wardrobe matching the one I already had at home.

Jake pushed his cart beside me and leaned in close. "We'll go tonight and send someone back for Caroline. I've got your back."

I looked around and saw the councilmen standing by the exits. "Ten-ish?"

He nodded before disappearing down an aisle and I turned to head away. I didn't know if Chief Interloper still walked around with my roommate, but as long as he stayed away from me, I could handle the rest of the day.

I didn't know how much time we had for shopping so I walked fast, scanning the aisles for contents and filling my cart. When I had everything on my list, I had neared the grocery section.

Cooking dinner for my hosts would be a nice gesture. They'd been kind enough to welcome me into their home and the first night I barely ate due to being drugged at the hospital and the second I spent in jail. I hadn't made the best impression. The least I could do was to say thanks by feeding them before I sneaked out of their home to escape from Wellington.

Not knowing what they had in their home made shopping a bit more difficult, but I came up with a quick menu. With a full cart, I headed toward the registers and stopped short. How would I pay for this?

"Did you find everything you need?"

I jumped out of my skin as I whipped around. "Jesus, Caleb." The man was barely a foot away. I hadn't heard him come up behind me. "Sneak around much?"

I felt tiny next to him. He had a good six inches on me but it wasn't just his height. Even his shoulders were massive. I wondered if he ever played football. Would he have been a linebacker, pushing his way through? No. Quarterback. Making the decisions.

"You look lost. Is there anything I can help you find?"

No apologies for scaring the hell out of me. Figures. "I forgot my wallet at the house."

He took my left hand, held it up and nodded toward the black arm band. "You pay with this. It's like your own personal credit card."

His hand was huge. He held my wrist between his thumb and one finger. His touch, though, had me paralyzed. It was like lightening searing my skin. I gulped, hoping he couldn't feel my rapid pulse.

"It seems wrong. Like I'm not actually paying."

"Ah, a conscience. She has one."

That snapped me back. I wanted to tell him where to shove it, but I bit my sarcastic tongue and pulled my hand away.

"Think of it this way, Grace." He still stood too close. I had to stare up at him, at his firm jaw, covered in scruff, at his blue eyes the color of denim. "You now work here and earn a paycheck which goes back into Wellington's accounts to pay for these purchases. Since you don't start until tomorrow, this is more of an advance on your salary."

Great. So when I sneak out of town tonight, I will owe this town at least a day's salary if not more. "Just how much will I be making an hour? I wouldn't want to go over budget."

He motioned me toward the register. "Don't worry, I'm sure your first week's check will pay for it."

A week? Screw it. Once I'm home, I'll hit my savings account and send the town my debt. The cashier rang my items then asked me to show my bracelet, which she then scanned, like my own personal bar code. I carried my bagged items out to a waiting shuttle where I was ushered inside. It was nearly full but neither of my friends were on board. Before I could say I would wait for the next bus, the doors closed and each of us were brought to our new homes.

I left all the new clothes in the bags—easier for someone to return them tomorrow—and brought the food items upstairs. When the homeowners arrived home, I had dinner waiting.

Growing up with parents who owned a restaurant, I

was bound to learn a few things, like how to cook a pork loin to juicy perfection, and season roasted potatoes, carrots, onions, and fennel, and add asparagus for a touch of green.

They were very appreciative of my efforts and talked about having their children and grandchildren over later in the week to meet me. I almost felt guilty about my evening plans. Almost.

I helped Amy with the dishes. She loved to talk and I learned all about her family. Lola had four kids: three boys and one girl. Kurt Jr's wife was expecting their second; they were hoping for a girl, as they already had a boy. Their youngest, Shelby, had decided she never wanted to marry or have kids, unless she found a man who loved horses as much as she did, then she might consider it.

I smiled and nodded a lot as I stacked the dishes in the cabinet. Since they didn't own a dishwasher, I got the impression the only dishwashers in this town might be in the hospitals and restaurants.

As I put the knives away, I spotted the butcher knife and a wayward thought hit me. Should I bring something along with me tonight as a weapon? I shoved the drawer closed and pushed the thought away. Too dangerous.

As soon as I could, I escaped to my room and shoved items into my backpack. I couldn't run away dragging my suitcase, so I took only what I might need. I sat on the bed, a book in my hand, but I couldn't read. I kept staring at the clock beside the bed. 9:02. 9:03.

I waited until I didn't hear footsteps above me then waited a while longer. 9:43. 9:45. 9:46. We had agreed on ten, but I couldn't wait any longer. I went upstairs, leaving my backpack by the front door as I went up to the kitchen. The best way to figure out if anyone was still awake was to pretend I had a reason to be up. I filled a glass of water, stood at the sink, taking a few sips and listened. No one stirred down the hall.

I dumped the water, washed the glass, and put it away. At the last moment I opened a drawer and took out the butcher knife. After wrapping it with a dish towel, I slid it down the back pocket of my jeans. I pulled my sweatshirt down to cover the weapon. Feeling more confident, I snatched my bag and walked out the front door.

Chapter Eight

Jake stepped out from the shadows and I nearly screamed before I recognized him. "Ready?" He took my hand and we walked down the street.

"What's the plan?" I whispered.

"Head east?"

I heard the question and laughed. "It's as good a plan as any."

We weaved up and over on different streets, keeping to the residential areas as long as possible but soon we came to Main Street. We could continue to weave or we could head out of town on the road we'd come in from. We were well past the police station and center of town at this point so we decided to continue on the main road.

"Why did tonight have to be so bright?" I stared up at the sky. "Almost full moon. No clouds in sight. A million stars. We're sitting ducks out here."

Yet there was no traffic. The town disappeared behind us as we walked along beside the vast length of open fields. The moon rose higher and still it didn't feel like we'd gone very far. Flat fields continued on either side of us. The occasional shadow of a farmhouse changed the scenery but no sign of activity anywhere. I stopped walking long enough to move my backpack from the one shoulder I'd slung it on, to put the straps on properly. Positioning the weight better made the pack lighter. Jake hadn't bothered with any pack at all. He probably had his credit cards in his wallet and that was all he'd need.

"Other than the fact this road never ends, do you think this is too easy?" I asked as we moved along.

He stopped and did a slow circle, taking in our surroundings. "I've thought that more than once tonight. I see corn fields up ahead. They should provide better coverage should anyone come along."

"I haven't seen anyone yet." I zipped my sweatshirt up higher as the chill of night crept in. "I think our biggest problem is going to be the gate blocking the road out of here."

"Will you be able to climb it?"

I moved closer and bumped shoulders with him. "Nothing will stop me."

When we reached the cornfields, I became more thankful for the moonlight. The stalks were large and ominous and seemed to reach out to us. I slowed down then moved around Jake to walk on his other side, the side by the street, away from the corn.

"What are you doing?" He looked back and forth between me and the large tentacles. "Are you afraid of produce?"

"No. Maybe." I pointed to the crop. "Look at it. It looks like it could swallow us up."

He gave me a stare. "You're really scared, aren't you? Like the time I forced you to come with us on the haunted hay ride."

"Yeah, and the guy with the chainsaw came running out of the corn stalks, wearing a Freddy mask. I don't think I slept for a week." I grabbed his arm, pulling him forward. "Let's get past these. There are woods before we reach the gate."

We were still passing the cornstalks when we heard the motor. Jake pushed me to the side of the road. "Car. Hide, now."

We ran. I managed to keep hold of him as we moved through the stalks, the leaves crashing around us as loud as my own heartbeat as I tried to keep my fear at bay.

They were sure to find us. Our movement must be obvious with the moon high and bright. Now I wished for clouds. For rain. For any sort of darkness. Even for the large growths of corn stalks to gobble us up in the night.

I crashed into Jake as he stopped short, then turned to shush me. The engine moved closer. No. More than one vehicle. Then they stopped and multiple slams of car doors echoed through the night.

I stepped back and a leaf brushed my cheek. I tried to be quiet but I couldn't help the squeak I emitted.

"You can come out now. I know you are there. You can't hide from me." Caleb's voice carried in the clear night, talking as though holding a casual conversation. "Do you know how I found you yesterday behind the school? It's because your bracelets not only track your purchases, they also have a tracking device in them. All I need to do is look at my phone and I can see exactly where you are."

"What the hell?' Jake whispered. "What do you plan to do with that?"

At first I thought he was responding to the man speaking on the road but then I realized he was looking at me and the knife in my hand. I don't remember reaching for it, but it was there and I wasn't about to let it go.

"I don't know." My voice shook as much as my hands as I whispered. "I don't want to go back. I want to go home. I know we just got here but there's something off about this. Why can't they just let us go?"

"Not coming out?" Caleb called out. "Then we'll come to you."

He must have directed the men with him to move because I heard lots of rustling. They were moving toward us. Should we run? Would it matter?

Jake put his hands on mine. "He'll have it out of your hands before you could even blink. Put it away before you get hurt."

The noises were getting closer. The men were coming toward us, from different directions from the sound of it. "Give it to me, Grace. If these things on us do have GPS tracking, then we aren't getting out of here tonight."

He was right. It was useless. I'd brought a knife to a gun fight. He pried the knife from my fingers at the same moment the officers parted the cornstalks and multiple flashlights blinded us.

Jake lifted his hand to cover his eyes but it happened to be the one holding the knife.

Several hands came up, weapons drawn. "Freeze," one of them barked.

"Don't shoot." I barely had the words out before a man grabbed me at my waist while another stepped between me and my lifeline home. "Don't hurt him," I screamed. "It was my fault. Please. It was my fault."

I spotted a red dot on my friend a second before I heard the buzz. He yelped as the stunner probes hit him.

He went down like a stone.

I heard the echo of my screams as Jake stayed quiet. I had to get to him. I had to be sure he was okay. I struggled against the arm around my waist, not registering that it looked like I was resisting arrest.

"Please don't hurt him."

My pleas turned to sobs. He was no longer visible as the officers pulled me through the thick leaves back to the street. I stopped resisting and went limp as they pushed me against the car. I didn't care when my face slapped down on the hood, or when my backpack was ripped down my arms, or even when my arms were twisted behind me as the cuffs squeezed shut.

I'd just watched the police shock my best friend all because I'd brought a knife.

They opened the back of the cruiser and forced me inside. I twisted around, wanting to see Jake. Wanted to make sure he was okay, but the two officers blocked my view.

The entire force must have been pulled out of bed. In a town of nearly four hundred, four officers and the chief seemed a lot. I heard doors slam. They'd put Jake in a different vehicle.

The officers handed Caleb my backpack and I watched as he dumped the contents on the hood of the cruiser. I don't know what he looked for—maybe to see if I had any other weapons?—but he must have been satisfied because he stuffed the contents back and zipped it up. I expected him to drive, being the police chief and all, but instead he motioned for the two officers to get in while he opened the rear door and sat next to me.

I turned to look out the window as the cruiser made

a U-turn to head back into town. "Please don't punish him." I still couldn't look at him. "It was my idea. He didn't know I had the knife."

"I believe you."

The cornfields disappeared and all I could see was the miles of flat, open fields. I finally looked to the man beside me. "Can I ask a question?"

He nodded.

"If we have tracking devices in our bracelets, why did it take so long for you to come get us? We had to have walked for a couple hours, at least."

"It's twelve miles to the town line where you have to get past the fence. Then, you have twice that until you reach another town." He shrugged. "I knew you wouldn't get far."

My fingers rubbed at the black band on my wrist. "When did you know we'd left?"

"Within minutes of you leaving Kurt and Amy's." His tone was low and direct. "When it comes to the eleven of you who arrived this past weekend, it is my responsibility to ensure your safety and security. I know where you all are at any given time."

I felt a single tear slide down my cheek. "Is Jake—?" I was almost afraid of the answer.

Caleb's tone changed from stern authority to almost something a bit softer, almost reassuring. "He's fine. He'll be checked out at the hospital then released."

The town appeared, too quickly. We'd walked for hours and within minutes we were back where we'd started. I couldn't get comfortable with my arms behind my back but I refused to move even an inch. No way would this man see my discomfort.

They brought me back to my host home. Caleb

stepped out first then took me by the arm to help me out of the cruiser. All the lights were off inside.

"Turn around." In a quick motion, he had the handcuffs off and I rubbed at my wrists. "Go inside. Set your alarm. You have a new job to go to tomorrow."

After he handed me the backpack, I let it hang from one hand. "Ah, Chief?" I looked down at the sidewalk, shuffling from foot to foot. "About the knife."

He waited. He was good at that. Not saying anything which made me want to jump out of my skin.

I forced myself to glance up. "Can I have it back?" He wasn't expecting that and it earned me a raised eyebrow. "I mean, Amy will wonder where it is. I just want to return it."

His hesitation was slight but at the moment it seemed an eternity before he answered. "Come see me tomorrow at the station."

Fabulous. Another visit with the police chief.

I walked inside. Didn't have to bother with wondering if I'd be locked out, because, hey, they don't need locks in this town.

The clock said it was 12:58. I'd been gone three hours and had learned, in no uncertain terms, Caleb basically had me, and the others who'd come to this town voluntarily, under house arrest.

Chapter Nine

When my alarm went off, I grabbed my clothes and stumbled up to the shower. I turned the heat up high, hoping to battle my exhaustion and the beginning of a headache forming behind my right eye. My designated family sat at the table eating breakfast when I came out.

"Morning, Grace." Kurt tucked into his eggs and bacon. His cheerful demeanor could only mean they had no idea of my evening adventure.

Amy jumped up from the table "Can I get you something to eat? I never did ask what you prefer for breakfast or I would have had it ready."

I held my hand, motioning for her to stay seated. "That's okay. I don't eat much this early. Usually I just drink coffee. Lots and lots of coffee." I sunk down in the chair. I was tired, depressed and had been without caffeine for four days. Death had to be imminent.

"Oh, my. That's not healthy at all." She stood again. "What you need is protein and orange juice."

I didn't want to argue, or maybe I was too tired to argue, so I let the older woman bustle around the kitchen. "Please, in future, you don't have to wait on me. I am perfectly capable of getting my own breakfast. Plus, it looks like you are both getting ready for work."

I looked over at Kurt who was dressed in navy work pants and a light blue Polo with Wellington embroidered on the pocket. "What do you do for work?"

"Truck driver. I deliver our fresh produce to neighboring towns. Tuesday's my late day. Usually I'm out of here at five."

Really? People actually leave the gates of Wellington?

Stop. I couldn't seriously be thinking of escape this soon after last night's debacle. With this damn thing on my wrist, I wouldn't get far, anyway.

Amy handed me a plate and I noticed her bracelet. Why hadn't I realized it before? Did everyone in town wear the tracking devices? Or was I wrong? Were the bracelets the townsfolk wore only to track purchases while us newcomers had a GPS?

"What about you? Where do you work?"

She smiled as she sat back down at the table. "I used to be a teacher, but I retired a few years ago. Now, I work a few days a week at the daycare. It's fun to watch the younger kids."

Kurt nodded toward the clock. "The shuttle comes down our street in about fifteen minutes. The next one isn't for another half hour, but if you wait for that one you'll be late for work."

I made quick work of cleaning up my dishes before brushing my teeth. Knowing I'd be working around food, I twisted my hair up into a bun, grabbed my sunglasses from my nightstand and headed out the door.

We boarded a bus going to a shuttle station a block away from the center of what they called The Square. I was told to stay on, as this shuttle headed to the school, but the couple got off, going their separate ways for the day.

I could have walked to the school. It was only a

few blocks and I'd been there before. Or at least behind it. Ironic my source of punishment would be on the very grounds of where I'd gotten in trouble in the first place.

The school was located on the west side of town, away from the rising sun, a fact I was grateful for as I closed my eyes during the remainder of the ride. The school was a sprawling two-story building with multiple wings off the center entrance. I made my way inside and went into the office.

"Oh, you're Grace. Welcome to Wellington School." The girl behind the desk was bright-eyed with a huge smile. "I was told to look for you. I'll bring you to the cafeteria."

"Thank you." I hid a yawn as the girl made her way around the counter and motioned me out the door. "I'm Jenni."

"Nice to meet you." I can be courteous when necessary, although some days it is a struggle. Especially in the morning. My parents taught me well.

"We're going to head down to the left." I followed her down the hall with the bright green walls. "The school is divided in half, with the elementary school kids on one side and the older kids on the other. We find it best to keep such age differences apart in some way including the lunch rooms so we have one on either wing." Jenni, my personal tour guide explained. "You'll be working in the elementary side."

I gave what I hoped was a friendly nod. I'd put my sunglasses on top of my head when I'd entered but the overhead lights were extra bright as the throbbing behind my eyes increased.

"For such a small town, it seems odd to have

enough staff to run a school of this size." The kids hadn't arrived yet, so the halls were empty. A couple of the classrooms had their doors open and lights on, and I noticed every room was in pristine condition. I have to give that to this town; they were almost obsessive about cleanliness.

She laughed. "There's not as many as a school this size implies. The classes are combined. One teacher for grades one through three. Another for four through six. On the high school side, though, there are a few more as they separate the classes out by subject. But we manage."

She motioned me toward a doorway. "I'll introduce you to Sheila. She'll watch out for you. Don't pay attention to Jackie. She's a bit fierce at times."

"Oh, okay. Thanks for the heads up."

"Hey, Sheila, I've got your new girl here." She waved me forward as she turned to leave. "Enjoy your first day."

"Um, thanks."

I turned as a woman in her thirties came out of the kitchen. She had red hair, glasses, and a hand rubbing her protruding stomach. "Welcome."

"Hi, I'm Grace."

"Come with me. I am so thankful they assigned you to us here. I'm at the point where I'm almost too tired to stand by the end of the day."

"I'm sure. You look…" I didn't want to be rude. "I mean, when are you due?"

The redhead gave a wide, white-smile grin. "I have another month. I should make it until the end of the school year, but, it's my sixth, so anything goes."

I gulped. "Six?"

She nodded then turned her focus to the kitchen. "This is where you'll be working. Jackie is in charge. There she is."

A tall, thin woman with silver hair scraped back against her head, walked toward me. She wore an apron over her khaki pants and green polo shirt—a match to my own uniform I'd picked up at the store yesterday, per the list I'd been given. "We have a lot to do today. I hope you're not the lazy type."

Blunt. To the point. And not a smile on her face. On a normal day, when my eye wasn't pulsating, I could take on this scarecrow in a heartbeat. Today, not so much. "My parents own a restaurant. I know my way around a kitchen. What's on the menu for today and what would you like me to prepare?"

She gave a harrumph. I don't think I've ever heard anyone harrumph before, but she did. "I do the cooking. You'll be on serving and clean up duty."

Of course I will.

By noon, the pain in my head had migrated to the base of my skull. The noise of children in the room had increased about a thousand decibels. I played the part, though. I smiled. I said hi to the munchkins, noticing each held their bracelets to the scanner at the end of the lunch line to 'pay' for their food. Big Brother missed nothing and no one.

I did every menial task dour Jackie asked of me without complaining. With my head pounding, I was almost thankful I knew my way around a kitchen so well. Almost. Mucking stalls may have been more fun than being stuck inside with a roomful of screaming children.

When my workday finished, I followed my new

co-worker outside as the bell rang indicating the end of the school day. "Thanks for showing me around today."

Sheila moved to stand with a crowd of parents. "My pleasure, dear. It's nice to have good help and pleasant company."

I caught the eye roll and smiled, knowing I was not the only one at the brunt of Jackie's personality flaw. "May I ask a question?" At her nod, I continued. "I want to see my friend, Jake. See how his first day went. He's working at the furniture factory. Can you tell me how to get there?"

"The factory gets out at four so you'd be best to wait at the shuttle station around 4:30 for him. You can catch a shuttle right over there. It'll be leaving in a minute or two."

I thanked her but decided to walk the few blocks, hoping to clear my head. With shades covering my eyes, I turned to head out, but I caught sight of Caleb waiting in front of the school.

He stood with a group of women. One was older with graying hair and another who looked to be around his age. He took a toddler from the older woman's arms and swung her around, causing the child to erupt in laughter. The woman beside him also held a small child, a boy, who held his arms out to be lifted. Caleb switched children with the woman, gave the boy a slight toss in the air, catching him, giving him a kiss, before taking back the little girl, who snuggled into him.

I couldn't help but watch. He was different with his family. A boy ran out from the group of exiting children, yelling 'Daddy' and leaped into Caleb's waiting arms. He lifted the boy up, still holding the younger girl as well. His expression was one of joy and peace. I remember Amy mentioning he had three kids, but with other children joining both him and the other two women, I didn't know which belonged to him.

None of my business. He was the last one I wanted to know anything about. I turned and walked away. The afternoon sun beat down on the pavement, not too hot, as it was May, but warmer than I'd expected. By the time I reached The Square, I regretted my choice to walk. The fresh air had done nothing for my headache and the strength of the beating sun may have actually made it worse.

According to the large clock above Town Hall, it was only three, which meant my wait for Jake would be a while. I figured the shuttle station would be a hub of Wellington's version of rush hour for me to have quiet, so I plopped down on a bench in the park outside of the church.

I suppose it could have been considered peaceful, if in the right frame of mind. Townspeople moved about saying hello as though they didn't see each other daily. Cars and shuttle buses passed by on the streets, stopping at stop signs, or waving the other driver to pass. No one seemed to rush. There was no road rage.

I breathed in the scent of fresh mowed grass and wondered if they had someone who took care of all the downtown area. Not a blade down the entire block was above an inch. Thinking about it, not one yard was neglected in any way. From manicured lawns to trimmed rose bushes and rhododendrons, every blade of grass was meticulously cared for.

Trapped in freaking Pleasantville.

Ugh. Could a town be this stereotypical? This close

to a nineteen fifties wholesome family television show? Was any of it real? I looked around. Everyone seemed normal. They wore modern day clothes. Some in business clothes, but most in jeans and boots. Baseball caps on their heads. The cars and pickups were modern, well the few that there were. Most of the town relied on the shuttle buses to transport them to their destinations.

A woodpecker began to beat on a tree and each peck echoed as a pulse in my brain. I had to move on before my head exploded, or my imagination took another twisted turn. As I stood, I saw a police cruiser pull in front of the station.

Damn. I was supposed to see the chief to get Amy's knife back. The clock hands had moved only twenty minutes so maybe I should get this over with now and then go meet up with the shuttle. I entered the station and stood in the doorway. Not my favorite place. One officer sat at a desk, on the phone. I didn't see the man in charge. I decided to wait and see if the man on the phone would return the knife to me.

I moved to the desk and got a hand signal to wait a moment. I shifted from one foot to the other. *Please hurry. I don't want to see Caleb if I don't need to.*

"Grace."

Shit. Too late.

He'd come up behind me, from God only knows where. For such a large man, he could move without a sound. "Come in." He moved past me into his office, snapping the overhead light on as he moved behind his desk. Not much there. A phone, computer, and a steaming cup of tea. The bookcase to the right held folders and a photo frame of his three children.

I stood behind the large leather chair as he placed a

folder on top of a file cabinet before turning to me. He knew why I was here, did he have to take his sweet fricking time?

"Take your sunglasses off in my office."

I sighed. No use arguing. I pushed the shades to the top of my head and waited as he took in my squinting eyes. "I'm not high," I defended. "I'm tired. I haven't had coffee in four days. I have a headache and your Nazi's took away my Ibuprofen."

"You can go over to the hospital pharmacy and they'll give you something for the pain."

I snorted. "Or knock me out and do God knows what."

Caleb walked around the desk to stand at my side. "That was the nail in the coffin for you, wasn't it?"

I rubbed at my temple. "Shouldn't it be?"

"You should take your hair down from that bun. Might help." Before I could do it myself, he reached behind me and released my hair. Then, using both hands, fluffed the strands forward around my face.

I think I forgot to breathe. The release of the hair tie did help the headache. But that wasn't my issue. It was Caleb. He was so close. So intense. So sexy male. I closed my eyes against the ache in my head, against where my thoughts were taking me. Yes, that's what it must be. The headache was the reason my entire body zinged from the roots of my hair down to my curling toes.

He stepped back and as much as I wanted to not say anything, I couldn't be rude. He'd been trying to help. "Thank you," I managed to mumble, but refused to look at him.

"How was work?"

"Perfect punishment for my crime. If I'd wanted to work in the food industry, I would've stayed home." Okay, maybe I could be rude, but at this point, he had to expect it.

"It wasn't meant to be a punishment. You know your way around a kitchen and Sheila needs a hand."

"Whatever." I shifted from one foot to the other, more anxious than I can explain to leave. "I'm here to get the knife to return it."

He walked back around his desk, opened his bottom drawer, and walked back to hand the knife to me. "Are you going to see Dr. Todd for your headache?"

"I'd rather die."

I took the knife and walked away. I put the sunglasses back in place as I stepped outside, grateful now for the air. There was no way I could wait for Jake any longer, instead, I made my way back to my host home. I heard Amy down the hall in her bedroom and I quickly put the knife back in the drawer then went down to my room. I closed the shades, stripped out of my work clothes, crawled into bed, and prayed for sleep.

Or death.

Chapter Ten

I missed dinner but the headache had eased a bit. I threw on a t-shirt and a pair of shorts and headed upstairs where I heard people talking. I stopped short when I spotted the guest sitting at the kitchen table. Amy stopped mid-sentence. "Oh, hello, Grace. How are you feeling? Caleb mentioned you weren't well."

"Okay, I guess." Lights still hurt my eyes, but I wasn't about to admit it in front of our visitor.

"Have a seat." She motioned to a chair as she stood. "I kept a plate warm for you and Caleb brought you tea."

"He brought—" I sat down and slumped in my chair as she poured the tea into a mug and placed it in front of me. I sniffed it. "What's in it?"

"It's not arsenic," he whispered.

"I didn't mean…" I took a sip of the warm liquid, giving myself a moment to collect my words and to be gracious. "I'm curious, that's all."

"Ginger for the headache," he acquiesced. "And lemongrass. Plus a few other things."

I took another sip. Not bad. "Cinnamon? It's sweet."

"Yes, and brown sugar to counteract the bitterness."

Amy bustled around the kitchen, taking a plate from the fridge, and warming it in the microwave.

"Everyone loves Caleb's tea. He brought the recipe back from—was it Colombia?"

"Haiti."

Wow. The man was a world-traveler. Who knew?

"You've been to Haiti?" I asked as I held the steaming brew.

"No. I made friends with a Haitian and we exchanged recipes."

"You made this for me? For my headache?" He gave me a slight nod as he sipped from his glass of what looked to be iced tea. As much as I hated to, I forced the niceties out. "Thank you."

The microwave dinged and my host mom moved away giving the man beside me a chance to lean closer and speak in a low tone. "We're not monsters here. Given the chance, you might discover we're pretty decent people."

Before I could respond, Amy placed a plate of meatloaf, mashed potatoes, and carrots in front of me. She was content to have someone to fuss over. Caleb might be right. Other than my experience at the hospital, the people I'd met had been welcoming.

Well, except maybe Jackie, but she looked to be a descendent from a Salem Witch line.

That whole police stunning Jake issue, I suppose they were just doing their job. He did have a weapon, although maybe they'd gone a bit overboard.

And spending a night in jail, again, we'd been drunk. Our fault. If I put Dr. Todd aside, and found a reason not to have to go back there over the summer, then maybe I could conform a bit and enjoy my stay here.

"The meatloaf is delicious. I forgot to have lunch,

so I needed this tonight."

"How do you forget to have lunch when you work around food?" she asked.

I finished a forkful of creamy mashed potatoes before answering. "Oh, you know, first day on the job, not feeling great, just wanted to make a good first impression."

Caleb stood. "I need to head home. Have a great night, ladies." He gave the tiny woman a kiss on the cheek. "Tell Uncle Kurt I said hello."

Uncle? Made sense. Theresa had said everyone was a Wellington in this town.

"Thank you for the tea." I looked up and up some more. He seemed to fill the entire kitchen.

"Have another cup in the morning. It should help. Eat lunch. Skipping meals won't do you any good."

I couldn't help myself. "Neither is skipping coffee." There was that upswing to his lips again. Not quite a smile, but it was there.

"Give it a week or two and you won't miss it at all." He nodded and left.

I stabbed my fork into a carrot and took a bite. "So where is Kurt tonight?"

"Tuesday is bowling night."

I don't think I knew anyone who bowled. I may have gone once in my entire life. I finished my plate and went to wash it. "I feel bad about missing dinner tonight. Would you like me to make dinner tomorrow?"

She dried the plate and put it away. "No, no, dear. I'll cook. All the kids are coming over tomorrow night to meet you."

Well, at least they'd waited a few days before descending on the summer house guest. I suppose it was to be expected, as everyone touted this place to be family-oriented.

"You had a couple visitors. Both Jake and Leland stopped by for you earlier."

"Really? I'm not surprised about Jake but Leland?" Yikes, was he wanting an apology for ratting him out on Sunday? "Did he say what he wanted?"

Amy shook her head. "You're a pretty girl. It's not hard to guess."

No. Not with the way he was hitting on me in the woods. I should let him know now I have no intention of getting involved with anyone this summer. Fourteen weeks and I am heading home.

****

Wednesday looked to be a better day. I had another cup of the Haitian tea with my breakfast of toast and jam. I even borrowed a thermos so I could continue my ginger headache treatment throughout the day.

I faced Jackie with a better attitude and barely cringed at the slop that she called macaroni and cheese and I was forced to feed the poor school children. How could the parents allow this crap to be served?

Sheila regaled me with tales of her children, a few of which I met as they went through the lunch line. After work, I decided to make a second go of waiting for Jake at the shuttle station and instead saw Caroline exiting one of the buses.

"Ooh, Grace, I'm so glad to see you." She gave me a quick hug. "I haven't seen you in days."

"I don't even know where you are staying," I admitted. She pointed to the opposite side of town from my summer home, which didn't surprise me.

"I am having such fun already," she gushed. "My

host family is super sweet and Aaron is just the best."

Great. Here we go again with the super boyfriend.

"Last night, we went down to the diner. Do you know they have an actual old-fashioned jukebox?"

I'd hoped to hear about something or someone other than her current fascination. "How's the job?"

"Fabulous. I am learning all about different spices and how to grow them and Aaron works on the neighboring farm so we're able to have lunch together."

Figures. They have me separated from my friends during the day, but they kept Caroline in direct contact with the all-mighty cowboy.

"Aaron and I are going bowling tonight. Want to come?"

I shook my head. "Can't. Kurt and Amy's kids are coming to dinner to meet me."

"Sounds fun."

That would depend on your definition of fun. Not mine.

"I have to scoot." She gave me another hug. I missed her peppiness. "I want time to change and eat before Aaron comes over."

She might as well have skipped down the street when she left and I shook my head at her enthusiasm. I located a bench to wait for my other friend, wondering if he'd even want to see me.

When he did get off the bus, I stood, ready to run to him. But he already had company.

Hope got off the bus with him, her hands a possessive attachment to his arm as she laughed at whatever he said. Jake had eyes only for the perky blonde so I sat back down.

He didn't appear to have any residual effects from

our failed escape. In fact, he seemed healthy and fine as he continued flirting with his new friend. After a few minutes, he tapped her on the nose and watched as she sashayed her ass when she walked away. And Jake, incorrigible as ever, tilted his head and watched her until she disappeared around a corner. When he finished his ogling, he turned and spotted me and immediately jogged over, with a grin a mile wide.

"Hey, there."

"Hey, back. Enjoying the view?"

He plopped down beside me. "What man wouldn't? That girl is a living Viagra."

I punched him

"What?" He rubbed his arm. "You didn't let me finish."

"Ugh, do I have to hear this?"

He grinned. "She may have the looks, but have you heard her talk? She's a walking, talking Barbie doll, all beauty, no brains. She's got nothing on my best friend. How are you doing?"

I rolled my eyes. "I've been worried about you."

"Because of a little stun gun?"

I nodded.

"Not the first time I've experienced that." He laughed. "How could I not have told you about the time I ordered a stun gun off the internet and Cooper, Seth and I tried it out on each other?"

"Why does this not surprise me?"

"Cooper cried like a baby. Dad got home early and freaked out."

"It's amazing your father has hair left on his head. So you're really all right?"

"I'm fine. I stopped by last night but your house

mother said you came home and went right to bed."

I nodded. "Headache. I miss my coffee."

With energy that reminded me more of my peppy roommate, he jumped up and pulled me to my feet. "Want to find something to do tonight?"

"Can't. Dinner plans."

"Then I'll walk you home."

"I saw Caroline earlier." I swung my hand back and forth within his larger one, noting how comfortable and at ease I felt with him around. He was my tie home. "She's one hundred percent enamored with everything about this place. She eats, sleeps, and breathes Aaron."

"Maybe you should get to know him better. He might be a good guy."

I stepped ahead of him and walked backward to stare him down. "Jake Collings, are you going soft on me?"

He laughed. "No, Grace Adams, I am not. All I'm saying is if Caroline is happy, let her be. What if this guy is the one for her?"

I shuddered and turned back around to walk side by side. "If one of your sisters ran off with a man she'd known a month, would you say the same thing?"

"Depends on the sister."

I poked him in the side. We'd reached my summer residence so we stopped on the sidewalk. From my view of the front window, guests had already arrived. "I guess I've got to go in and meet the family."

He nodded and his hand slid from mine. I already missed him. "Oh, Jake?" He turned back. "Where do you live? You've been here twice but I have no idea where to find you."

He waved back to the way we had come. "Three

blocks behind the diner, then two blocks to the right."

"On the other side of town? Why did you walk me home?"

"That's what friends do."

Yes, it was. I could always count on him.

The house was packed with both adults and children. Lola and her husband, Bobby, and their four children ranging in age from six down to six months. Kurt, Jr. with his wife, Abigail, had two-year-old Simon and were expecting a girl in a couple months. Then there was Shelby, who was the same age as me.

The house was barely large enough to fit the crowd. Fortunately, the weather was nice and we spent the time on the back deck with the kids running around in the yard.

Everyone was warm and welcoming. My headache had broken by mid-day, which was great, otherwise I'm not sure I could have handled the social responsibility of being the gracious guest of honor. I was on my best behavior. Not one rude or sarcastic remark passed my lips. My parents would be proud.

Once darkness settled, we all moved inside for tea. Somehow, Lola managed to corral the children into the dining room area where they played together, all but her youngest which slept in Bobby's arms.

I hadn't spent any time in the living room before now. All my time had been in either the kitchen or my room—or the jail, but I try to forget that night. I sat drinking the tea—some peppermint flavored concoction—and taking in the décor of the room. This room showed off Amy's love of family. Photos of her children in various stages of life adorned the walls, while more frames showing off the grandchildren filled every open flat surface. In one corner table I caught sight of an object which caused me to catch my breath.

A phone. There was a freaking phone in the house. What the hell? How can I be told I can't make phone calls when there is an actual phone within my reach on a daily basis? I could call home tomorrow. Talk to Sarah. It had been a week since I'd had any contact with her when I was used to getting at least four texts a day. She didn't like change, and even though I'd explained why I wouldn't be able to talk to her, I'm sure my sister was having a difficult time.

I missed her. Watching this family interact; the laughing, joking, sharing of memories, it reminded me of what home meant. Of course, in my house we had a lot of discussion about the restaurant, and staffing, and menu changes, almost nauseating at times. Our entire lives revolved around the restaurant. I'd hoped for a clean break from all aspects of food prep this summer, but look what I got.

Watching Kurt and Amy with their kids, I realized my family had become a business partnership and had forgotten what it was like to be a family. Maybe that's why I needed a break this summer. When I called them tomorrow, maybe I would remind them.

Chapter Eleven

My work day dragged. I watched the clock, wondering what time my hosts got home from their employment. Wondering if I would make it home before them and have the privacy of an empty house to make my call.

When did I become such a rules breaker? There were some things I know irritated my parents, such as the need to speak my mind, but they never complained about my work ethic. They always said I was responsible for my age and they didn't worry about me.

I wasn't one to get into trouble. I stayed away from Jake's when he had one of his parties. Way too much activity and drama at those events. I'd been to a few frat parties, but that's normal college fun. When I did go, very rarely did I drink as I tended to be the one getting my friends home safe.

Was that what this was about? Here in Wellington I didn't have control? Shit. I'm a control freak. Why didn't anyone tell me before?

I ran home after work, not wanting to wait for the shuttle stops. I took a deep breath to calm my nerves before changing my stride to walk into the house. I couldn't appear to be anxious or suspicious in any way. "Hello? Anyone home?"

No answer. I walked down the hallway toward the master bedroom. Door open, lights off, all quiet. My heart pitter-pattered in my chest as I moved to the living room and sneaked a peek outside. A few people walked by, but I didn't see my hosts.

I walked to the phone and positioned myself with my back to the wall so I could see out the window and notice if the door downstairs opened. I lifted the handle off the cradle.

"Wellington switchboard. How may I direct your call?"

Are you shitting me? How archaic is this place?

"Amy, is that you? It's Connie." Oh, dear heaven they knew which house had called.

"Uh, no. It's Grace."

"Of course. Grace," the sweet as sugar voice replied. "One of our new girls. How can I help you today?"

Now what do I do? I couldn't exactly demand to call my home number. I lied. "I wanted to find my friend, Caroline, but didn't know how to reach her. Do you know who her host family is and can I call them?"

"Of course, dear. I know where everyone lives." Connie seemed nice enough. Helpful, even. "Any time you need to reach someone here in town, you pick up the phone. We'll connect you directly."

I'd bet a weeks' worth of coffee Connie the Operator loved to talk, which might be to my advantage. "If I wanted to make a call outside of Wellington, how would I do that?"

"Oh, easy."

Yes!

"All outside calls get rerouted to Police Dispatch. They have the switchboard for external phone calls."

Hope deflated like a popped balloon. "Thank you.

You've been very helpful. Would you mind connecting me?"

"My pleasure, dear. Call anytime."

I heard the familiar ring of a telephone. One week. It had only been seven days since I had used a phone, but when being told you can't, the forbidden seems so much sweeter. I never knew myself to be a rebel before now.

"Hello?"

"MaryJane, It's Connie. I have Grace on the line to speak with Caroline."

"One moment, I'll get her."

I twisted the cord, leaning toward the window to check for my hosts.

"Hello?"

My college roommate. Yes. Her voice meant her host family was off the line, but what about the operator? I didn't hear any click of another line hanging up. Was she listening in? Was the line recorded?

"Hi. It's me."

"Grace. I didn't know there were phones here we could use."

"Me, neither." And if we were being monitored, I wanted to keep this quick. "I owe you an apology. I haven't given your friendship with Aaron a chance. Maybe we can all do something together this weekend."

She squealed. "Yes, yes, yes. Oh, Grace, I know you will love him. Tomorrow night. Straight and True is playing. Ooh, we'll have so much fun."

"I assume that's the band he plays in?" I spotted Amy walking toward the front door. Even though my call was more than likely already recorded as being made, I didn't want anyone getting in trouble if even this simple phone call was off limits. "Sounds great. I need to go. Later."

I hung up and rubbed my sweaty palms on my pants. Time to be a good resident and help with dinner.

****

On Friday, my new boss allowed me to prepare pizza for the lunches. One thing about this crazy town: they do not do frozen food. Being farmers, there is always plenty of fresh meat and produce at hand. The pizza sauce is homemade. I chopped tomatoes, parsley, and oregano. I shredded cheese. But Jackie cooked the pizzas.

It is the first lunch she'd made that I could stomach. I'd skipped lunch every day this week because the sour-faced woman's cooking was too bland. No spices. The mac and cheese was runny. Her Sloppy Joes had no flavor. The broccoli was overcooked and tasteless.

The pizza, on the other hand, came close to perfection.

Having lunch put me in a great mood, so being asked to do extra tasks before leaving didn't bother me.

"Grace, I need this box of food to go over to the high school cafeteria. They have a bigger storage area. Ask for Julie. She'll show you the shelves we use."

"Sure thing." I hefted the box. While it wasn't too heavy, it was large and bulky and walking from one end of the school to the other would be a hike.

Sheila spotted me as I crossed the empty cafeteria. "Wait." She bustled over to whisper, "The taskmaster likes to see who will complain, which is why she gave you this task."

Ah. Okay. No complaining.

"The quickest route is out the back and cut across the lawn."

"Thanks. I owe you."

I made the trip to the other lunchroom in great time. My arms still felt the weight, but the shortcut was a hell of a lot better than maneuvering through the hallways at the same time all the kids were exiting for the day.

To avoid the crowded hallways, I headed back the way I'd come, behind the school, and spotted a small group of teenage boys at one of the corners. I smiled. It wasn't so long ago I'd been in high school, meeting up with my friends, making plans for the weekend.

"Hold your hand steady, Jimmy. It won't hurt," one of them told another.

It won't hurt? That didn't sound good.

I stopped to take in the crowd. Four boys, all from the high school side. One had a grip on another's hand, holding it in place while a third flicked a lighter under his palm.

Aw, shit.

"You can do it, Jimmy."

I looked at the one called Jimmy. Large. Overweight. Messy hair. Shirt not tucked in. And an expression of trust on a face that screamed mental disability.

I ran to them, pushing aside the one brandishing the lighter. "Stop."

I turned to the big, teddy bear of a boy they'd called Jimmy and took his hand, looking at his palm, which was slightly red, but not yet blistered. "Are you hurt?"

He looked at me with big, wide, brown eyes. "I'm

okay."

"Beat it," Lighter Boy sneered. "We're having some harmless fun with our friend. No big deal."

"Harmless?" I said. "Playing with fire is not harmless. It's mean and cruel."

"*Fi-yah. Fi-yah.*" The big teddy bear of a boy repeated me, pronouncing the way I'd said fire. "You talk funny."

"Yes, I suppose I do."

He reached out and patted my head. "And you're pretty."

Lighter Boy turned to his buddies. "Looks like someone has a new girlfriend." The boys laughed. "Ever have a girlfriend before?"

With a nod to his friends, the leader of the three moved closer while his two buddies flanked me. I felt small among the teenage giants.

"Jimmy, it's time we taught you how to become a true Wellington man. It's all about making babies."

Uh, oh. I did not like where this was going. My stomach did a flip and I stepped back only to realize my retreat had landed me with my back to the brick wall with the three teens blocking my path.

"First you need a girlfriend, which you now have. Then you need to kiss her. Ever kiss a girl, Jimmy?"

I raised my hand, palm out. "Stop. Now."

No one took me seriously. Maybe it was because they were all bigger than me, maybe they just didn't care. The one directly in front of me just smirked. "Or what? Look around. We're at school, helping our friend with his education. And he won't talk, will you?"

He threw the larger boy a warning glance. "Promise you won't talk, Jimmy."

"I promise I won't talk."

My knees started to shake but I couldn't let anyone see my sudden fear. "Enough. You're being an ass-wipe. Step back or you'll regret it."

But the teen who'd taken charge continued to move forward until he was toe to toe with me. This had gone too far. I clenched my fist and rammed it into his nose.

Blood spurted; he howled like a wounded coyote. "You bitch. You'll pay for that."

I had his attention, but not just his. The two other teens each grabbed one of my arms and held me back as the now furious boy grabbed my face with a bloody hand and squeezed my jaw. I couldn't talk, much less scream.

Three on one, with only a man-child looking on and he wouldn't be of help.

A male voice called out from the far corner of the building. "What's going on out here?" It was the distraction I needed to pull free.

The kid released me but not before he gave me a warning. "This isn't over." Then the three teens ran toward the opposite side of the building.

Jimmy looked back and forth between the bullies and me, while the man who'd interrupted ran toward us. I leaned over and put my hands on my knees. That had been close. Adrenalin pulsed through my veins as fear and relief battled. My knees knocked so hard for a second I wasn't sure I could stand on my own.

The older man reached us. "What happened? You're bleeding."

I stood straight. "I'm okay."

And I was. Mostly. I rubbed my wrist and flexed my fingers. They were sore, but it'd been worth it. I'd landed a solid punch.

"Let's get you both inside."

We went to the center of the building which housed all the offices. "Principal Dani?" He called out as we entered the outer office area. A short, model-thin woman in her forties came to the door.

"What can I do for you, Mark? Oh, my. What happened?"

"This girl was attacked out back. I believe one was Oscar. I didn't see who the other two were. Jimmy knows."

"Okay, I'll take it from here. Make the call, please."

The woman turned to me. "Why don't you tell me what transpired?"

"I brought some items from one cafeteria to the other for storage. On my way back, I noticed three boys harassing this one by holding his hand over a lighter. I told them to stop and they weren't happy with me getting involved."

"Is all this true, Jimmy?" Dani turned to the boy. He pressed his lips together. Not talking.

She took his hands and looked at his palms. "Does this hurt?"

"No, ma'am," he responded.

"Who were the boys who did this to you?"

The man-child pulled his hands away and crossed his arms over his ample chest. Back to not talking. She turned to me.

I shook my head. "I'm new here. I don't know anyone and they didn't use their names at any time."

"Okay. The two of you have a seat, please."

It was a nice looking office with a high counter

separating the students from the office staff. Three desks behind. An office on either side of the room. Principal. Conference room. Large, glass windows giving off plenty of natural light. The walls were painted a subtle yellow.

I stared at a bulletin board with a list of upcoming school activities. Quite a few, despite there being only four weeks left to the school year. The upcoming school concert featuring both band and chorus. Spirit Week. Movie Night.

Normalcy. I'd been here one week and knowing this town lives behind a locked gate, I keep expecting to discover some deep, dark secret they are hiding.

A few minutes later, Kurt Jr. and his EMT partner came in. I repeated my story as I'd told Dani. Again, I left out several details. I'm not sure why I wanted to keep it to myself, but I did.

Embarrassment? Maybe. Fear?

"You've been rubbing your wrist," Kurt, Jr. stated. "May I take a look?"

I nodded and held it out. I must have made a face during his exam because the EMT raised his eyebrows and gave a knowing look. "How did you hurt it?"

"She punched him." Jimmy spoke out.

Was he breaking his code of silence? I looked at him but he'd turned his attention to the other medic who was examining his burned palm.

"Who did she punch?" This from a voice at the doorway.

Shit. Who called Caleb?

Even though he'd been nice by bringing me tea the other day, I still found him intimidating. And if I felt defensive about sharing what happened outside with

Kurt, I felt double about telling the police chief. I didn't need any more issues with him.

The boy beside me fidgeted in his seat as the chief moved into the now very crowded office. Principal Dani, and the teacher, Mark, stood at her office door, two EMTs attending to our injuries, and now him. Good thing I'm not claustrophobic.

"Who did she punch?" Caleb's voice was gentle as he spoke with Jimmy.

"I can't tell."

"Why not?" He crouched in front of the boy, meeting his gaze directly. It was a good move. Less intimidating. But the kid just shook his head.

My wrist was now wrapped in an ace bandage. It had started to throb, but, knowing the policy of drugs in this town, I figure I'd have to live with it, so I kept silent about the pain.

"He's scared," I said, causing the man I wanted to avoid to now turn his focus to me. "The kid made it quite clear not to talk."

"And you don't know who it was?"

I rolled my eyes. "New, remember?"

Kurt finished with my wrist and stepped back, making room for the chief to now stand in front of me. He didn't kneel to my level. Nope, he stood over me from his dizzying height. He had a small notebook and pen in hand. "Let's hear what happened from the beginning."

I sighed. For the third time. "I was returning from the high school cafeteria to the elementary side when I saw three boys bullying Jimmy by holding a lighter under his palm. I stopped them. They didn't like it. End of story."

"So when you saw them, you ran over and threw a punch?"

"Uh, yeah. Basically. I got between them. Told them to stop. We exchanged a few choice words. Then I punched him in the nose."

"And he reacted by grabbing you by the face?"

I gulped. I'd forgotten about that part of it. There must still be blood on my face. I nodded but Caleb remained silent. Old Eagle-eyes probably had it all figured out.

When I didn't provide any more information, he turned back to Jimmy. "Come with me."

He brought the boy over to one of the desks, positioning him so the young boy's back was to me, but Caleb could see both of us at the same time while he interrogated the child. The maneuvering didn't go unnoticed. "Can you tell me what was said just before Grace punched the other boy?"

Jimmy rocked back and forth. I leaned my head against the wall and waited. "I promised I wouldn't tell on them and I always keep my promise, Chief."

"I do know," he reassured the young boy. "It's a good quality to have. But can you tell me what they said without telling me who said it?"

"I said she was pretty." He looked over at me and I gave him an encouraging smile. "Then, *he*," Jimmy stressed the pronoun before nodding to me, "said *she* was my girlfriend and wanted to know if I'd ever kissed a girl."

The chief nodded and I had a feeling he guessed where this was going.

"Then he said he would show me how to kiss her and make her have babies."

Amazing how much can be said in a single glance. Caleb's was a book. I saw anger in the tightness of his jaw; rebuke for me not telling him the full story. A warning that, despite my silence, he always learns the truth.

I also saw the murderous rage toward the boys who'd attacked me. Their only reprieve was I didn't know them and their younger victim wasn't telling. In the one week I'd been here, I'd already figured out this man took his position as police chief, and his oath to protect and serve, seriously.

Though temper fumed in his eyes, the touch and smile he gave Jimmy was gentle. "You did good, telling me everything. You kept your promise."

Then he looked at me. Not so gentle now. I hadn't told him everything. His gaze never left mine as he reached for the mike at his shoulder. "Randy, pull up security at approximately 1425 hours behind the school and find out who was outside with Jimmy and Grace. Have a unit pick them up and bring them to the station."

And the win goes to the police chief. As usual. Fucking tracking bracelets. Why didn't he just make the damn call in the first place?

"Chief, if you are done," Kurt, Jr. said, "we'll take the two to the clinic to be checked out."

I snapped up in my chair. "I'm fine. I don't need to be seen."

The medic looked up from the paperwork he was filling out. "It's standard procedure. All medical issues are referred to the doctors."

"I'm not going." I jumped up, my heart racing. "Caleb, tell him I don't have to go." Like he'd do me any favors after I deliberately withheld information.

"This isn't my call," he stated. "Kurt's right. You need to have your hand checked."

Kurt looked between me and the chief. "Fear of doctors?" I couldn't respond; but I would not go back to that place, either.

"Grace had a bit of an issue with Dr. Todd when she arrived," Caleb explained.

"No problem," the EMT stated. "Todd works in the city on Fridays. Dr. Logan is on call today."

While a part of me was relieved I wouldn't have to see Doctor Doom, I didn't know if this Logan was any better or even if he'd been a part of my unapproved examination.

The chief nodded at me and I knew I didn't have a choice. I had to go.

I was in a foul mood by the time we arrived at the hospital and Kurt chalked it up to fear of hospitals or doctors or whatever as he gave my hand a reassuring pat. First person I saw on arrival was Nurse Bridget, accomplice extraordinaire. She received the brunt of my 'do not mess with me' stare.

I fumed while I waited in the exam room until an older gentleman with gray hair and glasses entered. This man was short, fat, and bald, and had a kind smile, but I'd been fooled once before by his medical partner. "Hello, Grace, I'm Dr. Logan. I understand you have a bit of pain in your wrist?"

"Yes, sir."

He unwrapped the wrist as he spoke. He reminded me of my grandfather and I began to relax, slightly, but my last visit here was too recent and fresh in my mind and I kept my eyes peeled for any unexpected needles. "What happened?"

I shrugged. "Just a slight mishap with my fist coming in contact with a well-deserving nose."

The gentleman chuckled. "That happens. Flex for me."

I moved my wrist as directed as the elderly doctor finished his exam. "No need for the ace. We'll give you a brace to wear for a few days for support, but it should be fine in a week, just don't overdo it."

It was easier than expected. I felt the tension ease from my shoulders. "Thank you."

"The nurse will be in with the brace. Have a good weekend and try to keep the boxing to a minimum."

I nodded. At least he had a sense of humor. The doctor left the door open when he exited and I had a clear view of the corridor. About three doors down was a sign which said x-ray and a counter with a nurse behind it. She spoke to a male patient.

"George, you're next. Please give me your arm so we can remove your tags."

I watched as the nurse ran a scanner over George's bracelet and a second later it was removed and placed in a basket.

Well, halleluiah on a stick, x-rays can't be taken as long as the patient was wearing electronics. If I had known about that a half hour ago, I would have played up my injury. Any frickin' excuse to get this tracker off me. Too late now, but I stored the information away for future use.

Nurse Bridget brought my elastic brace and pain killers. Two to take now, two more to take before bed. If pain persisted, I would have to return to the hospital for another dose.

A bit too Big-Brotherly for my taste. I'll manage

the pain, *sans* medication, thank you very much. But I took the ones for home with the intent to hide them in case I had need for them at a later date and avoid the trip to this place.

I walked out of the hospital and knew I would be late for dinner. Again. My summer parents were going to hate me. While I could walk to their home, really it would take no more than twenty minutes, I decided to take the shuttle. Within five minutes I was exiting the first bus at the shuttle station and looking for my transfer bus to my quadrant of town when I spotted A.J. making a beeline toward me.

"You!" He pointed at me then to the side of the bus station. My stomach flipped. A.J. looked pissed and wanted a quiet location. Not a good idea, but what the hell, doesn't look like I've been making any good ones of late.

Chapter Twelve

I followed him around the corner of the building before A.J. attacked. He immediately pushed me against the wall. "You've been nothing but trouble since you arrived. First I end up in jail, now my kid brother is in the slammer. What the fuck is your problem?"

Not one to back down, I lifted my chin and pushed him in the chest with my good hand. "First of all, I remember spending a night in jail, too, so we're all to blame. Second, who the hell is your brother?"

He nearly spit in my face. "The kid you gave a bloody nose to." Being this close, I did see the family resemblance, then again, this town was practically inbred.

"Maybe you should be down at the station asking him why I punched him instead of harassing me. Big creep is lucky his nose is the only damage."

He squinted and I saw the rage. This was heading downhill fast and I really didn't want another run in that would cause me to see Chief-I-Know-Everything again today.

Before this encounter became a repeat of earlier in the day, there was a welcome interruption. "Grace. Hey, what's going on?"

Jake. Relief hit me but my anger didn't dissipate as my best friend came to stand beside me. He planted his feet in a stance which screamed 'ready to fight on my behalf.' My latest attacker stepped back and from the corner of my eye, I noticed the Bobbsey Twins—Hope and Leland, making their way toward us.

"Your girlfriend," A.J. sneered to Jake, "is nothing but trouble."

"Take a look in the mirror," I retorted. My hands curled into a fist, not because I was ready for round two in the boxing matches, but more to keep myself from shoving the self-righteous, donkey's spawn onto his ass. "I believe it was you and your friends who provided the alcohol and it was your brother and his friends torturing an innocent child. Seems to me, you and everyone in this place are the problem."

He lunged toward me and all hell broke loose. I moved forward, ready to defend myself but Jake stepped between us.

Leland pulled at the shorter, but physically stronger man "Austin James, you're making a scene. Keep this up and we'll all be back down to the station."

A.J. shrugged Leland off him and stepped away. He pointed a finger at me. "Stay away from my family," he warned before storming off.

"Kinda hard to do, dumb ass, when you're all one big, convoluted family," I mumbled. The adrenaline dissipated and the shakes set in. I felt all the emotions of the day rising to the surface. I slid down the wall and hid my face at my knees.

"What the hell was that about?" My long-time friend crouched beside me while the siblings stood close. "And what did you do to your hand?"

"Coming here was the worst decision of my life," I wailed, ignoring the question. No way could I tell the story again.

"What you need," Leland declared, "is a night out having fun."

I groaned. "I promised Caroline I'd go out with her and get to know Aaron better, but all I want to do is go back to my room and disappear.

"Nonsense." The tall blond took my good hand and pulled me up. "We'll all go out together. It'll be a party."

"Yes," his sister gushed. "Let's. We'll take your mind off your day and show you the fun side of Wellington."

****

Despite my reluctance, I managed to keep my promise. The band, Straight and True, was good. Really good. Plus, my roommate's child-like exuberance lifted my spirits a bit.

I spotted Isabelle, one of the girls from the bus, across the room with two young men vying for her attention. She threw me a shy smile and I nodded back. There was no doubt she was enjoying herself. Like my best friend and all the other girls in the Hall, Isabelle wore a dress. I, on the other hand wore jeans and stuck out like a sore thumb. No, I fit in with the guys. All in their jeans and boots.

Except for Jake in his usual country club attire, but on him, it worked. He could walk around this backwoods town in a tux and instead of standing out, he'd set a new trend.

Was I the problem? If I stopped seeing red at every turn, would I relax and settle in? It wasn't like any of us were being ignored. No. Hope clung to Jake, staking her claim, while her twin focused his attention on me.

He didn't seem to care I hadn't dressed for the occasion.

The pitcher of diet birch beer on the table went fast. Wine or beer would have been better, but not in the cards in this Podunk town, but I wasn't going to turn down the carbonation. Up to this point, I didn't even know they'd allowed soda here even if it was only caffeine free. If I can't drink coffee, then I think I've found my new drink of choice.

When the band took a break, Aaron headed to our table and placed a gentle kiss on top of my best friend's head, sending a beaming, loving glow across her cheeks. My roommate is beyond smitten. At least the singing cowboy seems like a decent guy, being friendly to everyone he talked to and most important, he is definitely into my best friend.

I had a quiet moment with her in the restroom a while later. "I like him, Caroline. He's sweet on you."

She beamed at me into the mirror as she applied lip gloss. "It's different here. At this place." She explained. "Things move slower. I mean, at college, after knowing someone a month, we'd be hot and heavy in the sack."

I nodded. "True."

"But here?" She turned to face me. "We've barely done more than kiss. And it's sweet. He makes me happy."

"Slow is good."

I said it, but inside my brain had a thousand questions. Slow sounds good, but what if it isn't? Sometimes fast means the passion peters out quickly and I want my roommate on the bus home with me come August.

"I've never felt this way before." She wrapped her

arms around herself. "When I'm with Aaron, everything falls into place."

"Are we talking the moon and stars aligning?" I joked but was only half kidding.

She beamed at me. "Maybe." Her expression softened. "All I know is he balances me out. He's the calm to my storm."

The rest room door swung open and Isabelle came in. She gave us another shy smile but I noticed a gleam in her eyes.

"Are you having fun?" I asked politely.

"Oh, yes," she gushed, not with Caroline's exuberance, but there was no hand-wringing anxiety, either. "This town is wonderful. Everyone makes me feel so welcome. I am having the time of my life."

"I feel the same way," my love-smitten friend exclaimed. I groaned and waited as the two talked.

What was I doing wrong? I'd done nothing but make numerous enemies and spend a lot of time with the local law since my arrival while everyone around me was having the summer of a lifetime.

Back at the table, I looked around. Caroline kept an entranced eye on her boyfriend up on stage. Hope clung to Jake, making it clear she wanted to have him as boyfriend status, and he didn't mind at all having a tall, blonde, model wanna-be decorating his arm.

That left me with Leland who was trying hard to get me to acquiesce to his charms. I suppose it isn't a bad thing. Tonight, I discovered pretty boy is a story teller and funny, as well. He kept us all entertained. He had his arm on the back of my chair but all I could think was that with his metro-sexual looks, is he would be considered the eye-candy in the relationship.

Shrugging off my own insecurities, I will admit to enjoying the evening. As everything wrapped up for the night, Aaron turned to us, his arm once again slung over his girlfriend's shoulders. "Not sure if you're interested, but tomorrow afternoon, a group of us will be playing a game of baseball.

I stopped in my tracks. "Oh?"

Jake laughed. "You said the magic word: Baseball. Now Grace's whole world will stop."

Aaron looked interested. "Do you play?"

"A little."

My buddy punched my arm. "Yes, she plays, and she's good."

The singing cowboy, now baseball player seemed impressed. "You can be on my team."

I held up my wrist in its brace. "Can't, but I'd love to watch. When and where?"

Leland rolled his eyes as I took in all the details. "Two, at the field beside the school. Tomorrow's our first game of the season. We'll play again next weekend. I'll save a place for you on my team if you're interested."

I couldn't help my grin. Finally, something in this crazy town I could look forward to.

****

Kurt Jr. came by the next morning to help his dad hang the American flag on the house in preparation for Memorial Day while I helped Amy change all her indoor décor to a patriotic display.

When he asked about my wrist, I promised I'd take it easy, but it wasn't long before I began helping to bake cupcakes for the Sunday fellowship. I may have over-done it slightly so I did take one of the pain pills

I'd received at the hospital, but I hid the bottle, determined to keep the last one stashed so I wouldn't have to report every instance of headaches or whatever ailed me.

Despite his obvious lack of enthusiasm for the game, Leland came by at one to go with me. He looked like an eighties preppie in his perfectly creased and ironed shorts and short-sleeved knit shirt. He even wore boat shoes. Not me. I had on shorts I'd cut from a ripped pair of jeans, a tee shirt sporting a local band from my hometown, and my hair was pulled back into a pony tail and tucked into my favorite hat from my high school softball team.

If it weren't for the bum wrist keeping me benched, I'd be out on the field, but I refused to let it sour my mood.

Surprisingly, the field was packed with people. I looked for Caroline in the bleachers but instead spotted her over by the visitor's dugout distracting a certain player. Before I yelled to get her attention, Aaron pulled her in and gave her a long, heated kiss and I flushed from my viewpoint with its intensity.

I finally realized why I'd been so resistant of their relationship. Jealousy. My best friend had found love and it was real and genuine and I wished I could have what she had.

Instead, I had a very nice looking, tall, blond man taking my hand to lead me to the middle section of the bleachers. I silently groaned. While he was nice enough, what I wanted would not be with this man. Leland Wellington was not my type, despite his insistent attempt to make 'him' and 'me' a 'we.'

Hope, Jake, Wayne, Barbara, and Caroline joined

us as the bleachers filled with warm bodies. I watched and listened as the Wellingtons talked about games from years past. Baseball really was a 'thing' here. Maybe the only thing I could get on board with.

I love baseball. I have been a fan since the age of six when my grandfather brought me to a major league game between Boston and New York and related the long history of rivalry between the two teams. Over hot dogs and ice cream, he explained the game and a fan was born.

I won't tell you which team I pledged allegiance to—being from Vermont, it could go either way—but I chose a team and by the age of seven I was in little league and loving every moment.

Aaron pitched for the red team and Caleb played first base for the blue team. It was easy for me to choose which side I rooted for. It wouldn't be for the chief, that's for certain.

The crowd was raucous and loud, cheering the players on and I had my roommate's approval as I cheered for her man. About halfway through the game, though, I realized no one around me actually picked a side to support. I heard plenty of 'nice hit' or 'good catch' or 'you can do it' but it didn't matter which team was up. I suppose being related to everyone in some way, they must not want to offend.

Not me. I like competition and loyalty to a team. So the blue team, and one man in particular, became my target. "Strike him out, Aaron," I screamed as I stood to be heard.

Leland tugged on my arm. "Grace, people are staring."

I looked down at pretty-boy, who obviously has

never played ball in his life—might get dirty, was my guess—and shrugged his hand off. "Good. It means they can hear me."

I continued my cheers and jeers as the blue team batted. Then Caleb came to bat. I sat forward, watching intently as he firmly planted his feet at the base. His thigh muscles filled out the denim and, as he pivoted from one foot to another, I found myself staring at his ass. My mouth went dry.

He swung at the first pitch and the ball connected with a loud thwack and fouled.

My first thought was a resounding 'yes!' because I could watch his tantalizing ass again. But I had to stop drooling.

The game, Grace. Focus on the game.

With the current bane of my existence at bat, this was not the time for me to go silent. "Let's go, Aaron," I screamed to the pitcher to get my mojo back.

It worked. I stood again and moved my eyes up past the batter's fine behind and now noticed the amazing bulge of arm muscle as he swung at the ball.

Strike.

At the next pitch, which went outside, Caleb checked his swing. The ump called it correctly, but I needed something to distract me. "Are you blind? That was a strike. Get your head out of your ass and into the game."

The umpire took his mask off and turned to give me a glare through thick-rimmed glasses.

"Or maybe it's time for new glasses. Go see an eye doctor."

Those around me erupted, some in snickers, others in gasps. Leland tugged my arm again. "Ah, Grace, the umpire is our eye doctor."

Oops.

Caleb took two steps back from the plate and also sent me a look—but his was all amusement. As our eyes met, I saw his silent message: Game On!

He stepped back to the plate and I intently watched every move of his amazingly muscular body as he swung the bat, sending the ball over the fence for a two-run home run.

I may be rooting for the opposite team, but watching him run the bases was a total win. And when he crossed home plate and looked my way, I held both hands up with a shrug. He responded with an answering nod.

Red team lost five to three, but my mood was the best it'd been since I'd arrived. We met Aaron by the dugout and he put a sweaty arm around Caroline's shoulder but pointed a finger at me. "You."

Uh, oh. I cringed and waited for the rebuke.

"I like you. I haven't enjoyed a game like that since Trudy and Mike went at it and both benches emptied. Baseball was canceled for the rest of the summer."

I breathed a sigh of relief. "I aim to please."

Jake put his arm on my shoulder. "Nah, you aim to piss people off, but you do it in an entertaining way."

That earned him elbow to the ribs, which I gladly provided.

"Come back to the house," Aaron invited. "We'll get some steaks on the grill."

I nodded but rolled my eyes as the twins kept close to Jake and me. "Can we bring anything?"

"Nope." He shrugged. "My mom and Rita planned plenty of food as this is the beginning of the season.

Tradition."

I had no idea who Rita was, but I've discovered people here talk as though I know everyone they do. I gave an appropriate nod and followed the crowd. Hope and Leland were on a mission to separate me and Jake as much as possible, which I find more than slightly irritating.

My friend, on the other hand, appeared amused. He rolled his eyes but placed an arm around the blonde enchantress and threw her his engaging smile. If I didn't find her so thoroughly annoying, I'd almost feel bad for her. I know my hometown Romeo enough to know this poor girl is nothing more than a summer fling, and with the way she threw herself at him, he figured her for a sure thing.

Aaron wasn't kidding when he said his mom would have plenty of food. He placed a kiss on top of the head of a woman in her late forties as she placed a bowl of salad onto a long folding table in the back yard.

"I'm Karen." The woman smiled warmly at me." It's a pleasure to meet you. I enjoyed your commentary on the game."

I grinned. "Thank you. I get a bit passionate." I looked at the table already loaded with potato salad, coleslaw, salads, and beans. "Do you need a hand with anything?"

"Not today, dear. Rita and I have all the sides ready. My husband, Joe, and Rita's husband, Conrad, are manning the grill. Feel free to put in your order and how you like your steak cooked."

"I will." I turned to see another woman, a bit older than Karen, exit the house and I stared. I'd seen her before. At the school.

"Hey, Caleb." At the mention of the chief, I spun around as Aaron gave him a man hug with the single slap to the back. "Good game."

The newest arrival had his three children in tow and I watched as the youngest rushed straight to the older woman. "*Grammaw*."

Of course. Now I recognized her. I'd seen her outside of the school. I don't know why I didn't think about him being here, and now I would have to be socially polite. Not my best trait.

Jake didn't mind. He headed straight to the police chief. "Great play out there today. You killed it."

"Thanks." the older man's smile was relaxed and genuine. He stood with a little boy plastered to his leg and he casually stroked the boy's head as he spoke. "I had a bit of incentive."

He looked directly at me with amusement. I shrugged, for once not knowing quite what to say. I was too busy trying to figure out why my stomach experienced a sudden influx of dancing butterflies. It most certainly couldn't be due to his attention directed at me.

The pitcher from the red team nudged my arm. "I've already laid claim to this one for my team next week. Don't even think about stealing her."

Caleb looked down at me. "I take it you play?" I nodded. "What position?"

"Second base."

The two exchanged glances.

"You gonna toss Pete from his position?" the pitcher inquired.

I grunted. "I watched Pete. He's good at bat, but he doesn't have the arm to get the ball to home plate. Put me in. You won't regret it."

And like that, I fit in. Everyone had a good time and I felt no animosity toward the police chief. After dinner, Aaron pulled out his guitar and began to sing. Soon, Caleb joined in with a pretty good baritone.

I sat with a can of 'pop', which I discovered was the term for soda here and relaxed by the fire someone had lit in the fire pit in the center of the yard. I chatted a bit with the group, but mostly I listened to the strum on the acoustic guitar and watched as fireflies flitted through the clothes on the neighbor's line.

Despite the difficult week I'd had, this night was almost magical. This was what I'd hoped for when I'd signed up for the summer program. I soaked it in. From the easy camaraderie of the close-knit family; the strum of the guitar; the simple chatter.

Leland sat close, his leg only inches from mine. I know he wanted me to acknowledge him, give him a chance for something more, like Jake was doing with Hope, who now sat on his lap. I didn't. Couldn't. Not that he wasn't nice enough. He had been plenty kind.

I couldn't because my eyes kept straying across the fire, to a certain older man with a deep voice and an easy-going smile. Caleb intrigued me. Tonight, he wasn't the man in charge. Here he was relaxed and having fun. He appeared to be a doting father, disappearing several times to meet the needs of his children, but never seemed frustrated with them.

Maybe he wasn't so bad. Sure, he had his duties as police chief which he obviously took seriously, but seeing him today at the game, and tonight in this peaceful setting, I kinda liked the guy.

It was after ten when everyone picked up to head to

their respective homes. After thanking our hosts, I followed what was left of the straggling team players to the sidewalk. I rolled my eyes as Jake planted a long kiss on Wonder Twin, but with his cue, Leland thought he could do the same. I put my hand on his chest and pushed him away.

"Sorry. I thought I made it clear. I'm here for the summer only and have no intention of leading anyone on. We can hang out as friends, but nothing more. Got it?"

He gave me a look full of charm, which I am sure would work on other women—if he wasn't trapped in a town surrounded by cousins. He attempted to wrap his arms around me a second time. "Aww, come on. Lighten up and have a little fun."

"The lady said no, Lee." The stern voice startled me. I'd thought Caleb had left already.

My would-be suiter threw his hands up. "No harm in asking." I couldn't see what the older, more mature man did, but it caused the boy beside me to shrug. "Okay. I'm going. Have a great night, Grace. Stick with me, though. We'll have fun this summer."

I turned around and spotted the open car door of the cruiser, with the three kids in the back seat, each buckled in right and tight. The two youngest were asleep while the oldest watched Caleb and me intently.

The chief stood by, his stance one of authority. Gone was the man I'd watched all day. I gulped. "I had it under control."

He nodded. I didn't like it when he stayed silent like this. I also didn't like that somewhere deep inside I wanted to see the happy Caleb again. The smiling man of earlier.

I had to break the silence. "Go. Take your kids home."

"You all right to get home?"

I looked around. "It's not like it's a big city full of gangs. I've got it."

He nodded again and took a step back but while I told him to go home, I didn't want to lose this small connection with him.

"Have a good night. I had fun tonight. You know, you aren't so bad when you take off the badge."

I saw a slight lift to his lips. A tiny trace of amusement was back in his eyes. The wayward butterflies were back. "You like to always have the last word, don't you?"

Instead of answering and proving him right, I pursed my lips and pretended to lock my mouth shut with my fingers then turned and walked away.

Chapter Thirteen

Once again, I sat with Kurt and Amy at Sunday morning service. Instead of listening to the words of the readings, I people-watched. I couldn't get over the number of small children there were. Most sat quietly, fidgeting, but quiet. I didn't feel quite as under-dressed this time because I'd 'purchased' a sundress earlier in the week.

Not being the religious sort, I sat there knowing it was expected of me to do so, but eventually, the preacher's sermon caught my ear.

"I have been paying attention to all the crime happening outside our gates," he said. "People protesting and causing riots in the streets. Police officers shot and killed for no other reason than the uniform they wear. Children beaten for doing nothing more than asking for food. It's a terrible, scary world, which is why we must do everything we can to protect our own here in Wellington."

Ahead of me, heads nodded, and peopled murmured their 'amens.' My head turned as I watched those around me listen in rapt attention. Until the pastor continued his sermon from the raised pulpit. "Providing alcohol and drugs to those new to our community does not set a good example of the love and family atmosphere we have to offer those entering into our fold.

I froze in my seat as he regaled the entire town about the transgressions which put several of us in a cell the week before. I could no longer turn my head to watch others, fearing the entire population of four hundred stared at me.

He moved from one end of the alter to the other as he spoke passionately. The headset microphone he wore allowed his words to be heard clearly, not just for those sitting inside the church, but also for all those in the seats in the covered courtyard. "We must seek forgiveness, not only to the Lord above, but to those we have harmed. We must also pray, as we do every week, for our family members who exit our gates daily as they head for jobs in the city or to attend colleges. While their salaries and educations are valuable to the ongoing success of our community, we encourage them to always travel in pairs when they are outside the safety we provide here in Wellington."

I noticed Amy squeeze Kurt's hand which he patted gently. Was she afraid for her husband when he left home each day? The gesture indicated it, but I thought she was the one who came from outside. Why was she so scared?

The litany of fear of the evil beyond the town continued from up front, but now that the focus was no longer on me, I looked around and saw the congregation's total acceptance of the sermon.

Dear God Almighty—hmm, being in church has me thinking of a higher power, not a usual occurrence—- is there more to the tracking bracelets than I was led to believe? Do they think having Big Brother watching over them will keep them safe?

I continued to fidget even when the tone turned

more conversational. "Before we conclude, I want to announce the engagement of Annalise to a young man she met at the university. Kyle has visited several times over the last few months and has accepted a job on Daniel's farm. They have decided on a September wedding.

"Also, Sissy and Joe got the news they are expecting their first child mid-January. Luke and Maryjane are pregnant with baby number four, due in early February. Children are the future of our success as a community and we look forward to welcoming a new generation. Now, let's bow our head in prayer before joining together for our fellowship meal."

I bee-lined my way to Jake after the service as everyone moved to the other building. "Your family goes to church. Was that whole sermon thingy strange?"

He pursed his lips. "A bit. I mean, there are usually announcements about things happening in church but I guess since this is such a small town, everything and everyone is connected."

I had to take long strides to keep up with him. "Sure, but didn't you find it, you know, a little preachy about evil outside the walls of this town?"

"He's not exactly wrong, Gracie. Everything he mentioned is happening."

We had reached the other building and filed in, following the lines to the buffet tables. It amazed me how each week, people made a huge meal to share with the whole community. Didn't they get tired of it all? I continued my interrogation of Jake. "But, he made it sound like there is only danger outside of this place. It's not like that."

When the person to my right responded to my statement, instead of Jake, I groaned. "It *is* full of evil. I will never leave these gates."

I turned to see my boss, Jackie, and saw fear and determination. "Why do you think that?"

"My son died out there." The sour-faced woman took her plate, exited the line, and walked away, leaving me standing with my mouth open. Well, it possibly explained a lot about the crotchety old lady I worked for. Still, she dropped a bomb and just walked away, leaving me with more questions.

I spotted Sheila as I walked to a table and I stopped short. "Oh, my, you look bigger and bigger every day. Are you sure you're going to make it until the end of the school year?"

She laughed as she rubbed her belly. "Maybe not. This one is getting ready to join his or her siblings." I looked over at the table where she stood and shook my head at the brood. Five children, ages two up to nine, lined up like soldiers, eating their meal.

I looked between Sheila and her husband who had the youngest on his lap feeding him while taking bites from his own plate. "They're all so quiet. How do you do it?"

"Teamwork. Cole and I work together. It's what makes us great."

I wanted to ask about our boss's revelation about her son but decided now wasn't the time. Maybe at work we'd have a quiet moment and Sheila could fill me in.

Jake had found a seat next to Hope. Her twin was nowhere to be found, thankfully, and I took the seat on the other side of them. As I settled in, I spotted Caleb across the room with his three children, his mom and stepfather.

I was seeing a different side of him. Yesterday he'd been carefree when playing baseball, grinning at me when I'd urged the pitcher to strike him out. Again when he joined in with Aaron, singing and laughing into the night. It was all so different from the stern, don't-mess-with-me police chief persona.

Currently, he balanced his youngest, Shawna, on his lap, while cutting up food for his son, Justin, whom I learned was five. Eliza, his eight-year-old, came to the table carrying drinks. I had met Eliza through the hot lunch line at the school. A very quiet girl with wide, sad eyes. I still didn't know anything about their mother other than she had died.

I kicked Jake under the table, interrupting his conversation with his summer girlfriend. "Seeing all these families, don't you miss yours?"

He gave his attention to me, causing Hope to huff. "Maybe a little, but it also reminds me how dysfunctional they are, too."

I rolled my eyes. "Your family isn't dysfunctional. It's normal to have divorced parents and blended families."

He pointed with his fork. "Look around. This is what family should be, not the shouting and arguing my parents did every time they exchanged us for visits."

Repeating his gesture with my own fork, I made a sweeping gesture to encompass the entire room. "*This* is not normal, Jake. *This* is a nineteen sixties television show with people pretending to be normal. Your family is real life. Don't you miss your sisters and brothers?"

He shoveled food into his mouth, talking around it.

"Sure. I wish they were here with me."

"Well, I miss Sarah," I mumbled as I went back to my plate. "And my parents."

"Of course you do." He didn't sound open to my point. "Your parents are still married and get along."

"They fight, too, you know," I argued. "They run a business together, their youngest daughter has Down Syndrome. It's stressful. It's not all rainbows and unicorns, but its family."

I pushed my plate away. Watching everyone around me be one big happy family only made me miss mine more. I needed to escape. Without a word, I stood, discarded my plate of food, and headed toward the exit.

Was it homesickness, or something else? The good citizens here were afraid to leave the confines of the gates. From what was said though, several folks, like Kurt, actually went beyond the town to work, but most stayed in Wellington, surrounded by those they loved. I looked down at the black band at my wrist. I couldn't even talk to my family until my work contract was over.

My eyes connected with the police chief's across the room. Damn, he saw everything. Of course he would see me leaving. Whatever. It's not like I could go far.

I welcomed the warmth of the sun as I walked down Main Street. With it being Sunday, the holy day, everything was closed. I'd learned a few things over the past week and one was that Sundays were reserved for family. Only a skeleton crew worked at necessary jobs. One operator on the phone switchboard. A few hospital staff. A limited amount of bus drivers to shuttle families to and from church. Police and medics were always on call, but they weren't required to sit around the station.

I walked the nearly empty streets, roaming aimlessly. Shuttle buses lined the street along with a few pickup trucks and family cars. I didn't want to be around people today. At least not these people. As I passed a store window, I spotted a notebook and made a decision to write to my sister this week. I wouldn't be allowed to mail it, I'm sure, but at least I would feel more connected to Sarah.

I headed back the way I came and of course, there was Caleb coming my way. He had his kids with him, the youngest in a stroller. While it looked innocent enough, I knew better and I was feeling enough out of sorts to not keep my mouth shut. "Spying on me?" I knew my tone was nasty, but I didn't care.

"Out for a walk with my children," he drawled.

"And you just happened to come the same way I walked?"

He looked down at Eliza. "Why don't you take your brother and sister over to the playground? I'll be there in a moment."

He waited until his daughter crossed the street toward the park which was about a half block away before he turned my way again, his voice deep and determined. "I don't have to follow you to know where you are, I've got that covered."

That was for damn sure. I wanted to lash out and tell him to go to hell. Then in one breath his demeanor changed. His shoulders relaxed and his voice lightened as he gave me an inquisitive look. "What's got you bothered today? You seem agitated."

I couldn't keep up with the mood swings. I wanted to fight. To argue. To keep my feelings locked away behind a fierce exterior. Instead, his question had me turning my back to him before he noticed the instant swell of tears.

"Grace?"

No, I would not break down in front of this man. I needed to be strong. I swiped at my cheek and turned around with a determined smile. "Actually, to put it simply, I'm missing my family right now."

He nodded. "Understandable. Tell me about them."

Tell him? "Don't you—I mean, I saw the file on your desk at work. Didn't you do a background check on me?"

There was an almost imperceptible hesitation. I wasn't wrong, but he was back to being nice. I shouldn't throw it back at him.

"Sure. Who your parents are. What they do for a living, your GPA at college, your high school transcripts, medical history. It's cold information. Tell me about them. Who they are."

Maybe it was because I missed them, or perhaps because he'd asked and seemed genuine, but as I walked to the park beside him, I spilled my guts. "My sister, Sarah, is my best friend. She's younger but special. She has this way about her which makes everyone smile and want to be around her. Sometimes it pisses me off, but mostly I find it endearing.

"She usually texts me every day, so not having contact with home is not just difficult on me, but on her, too."

"Because she has Down Syndrome?"

The fact he knew about Sarah almost surprised me, but then again, I'd already figured out he'd done a full background check on me and all the others who'd come to his town.

"Maybe. I guess. She likes routine. Anyway, we're as different as…" I gave a half-hearted smile. "My dad explained it best. Sarah is the sun. She is bright and happy all the time, from the moment she wakes in the morning. There is nothing about her that anyone who met her wouldn't love."

We had reached his children. Eliza pushed Justin on a swing while Shawna slept in the stroller. Caleb took over for his daughter so she could swing as well. I automatically took position behind the oldest and we continued talking as we pushed the kids on the swing set. This park was empty, as most of the other families utilized the park outside of The Hall in the center of town.

"I see. And what does your father say about you?

I gave what I hoped was a nonchalant shrug. "What's opposite the sun? He says my moods wax and wane like the moon. I can be a bit moody, if you haven't noticed."

I squirmed under his assessing look as he used one hand to push his son. "You make it sound like an insult. I wouldn't. The moon is a powerful entity. Come to think of it, poets and songwriters write more about the moon than they do about the sun."

I cocked my head at the comment. Had he just complimented me? Before I could comment, he changed the subject. "Besides Caroline's impulsive behavior, why did you decide not to go home for the summer, knowing your sister expected you?"

"I guess I wanted something different," I said with a shrug. "I grew up in my parents' restaurant. It's their entire life and every day at home I'm helping there.

Actually, even from my dorm room, I've been helping."

"Really?" The kids were bored with the swings and both headed off to other areas of the playground. The meal must have been completed because I spotted a few other families with small children heading our way. "In what way?"

"I'm taking Business Management because while my parents are fabulous in the kitchen, I took over the business aspect of the operation when I was fourteen. I've been tracking the supplies, making the orders, scheduling the employees, tracking their vacation time, basically whatever is needed in the office."

"Quite a big responsibility to take on at a young age."

I grimaced. "Yeah, well, even back then I had a tendency to be outspoken and my parents had to separate me from the diners when I'd tell them to shove it if I thought they were rude. They gave me a task in the office and it turned out I had a knack for it so I've been maintaining it all from school."

The youngest child woke and I watched Caleb gently lift his daughter from the stroller. She was obviously wet so he headed to a picnic table and laid out a blanket and easily changed the pull-up diaper. When finished, he pulled her into a quick hug.

"When are you going to start using the potty, Jellybean?"

"Not today," was her firm answer. He sighed and set her down so she could run and play.

He took being a single dad in stride. I knew he relied a lot on his mother to help. Plus, he couldn't do the job of Chief, needing to leave home at a moment's notice to deal with issues in town, without a support system at home.

"Can I ask a question?"

He gave me a nod.

"The sermon today." I spoke slowly as I tried to word the question in a way that wasn't insensitive. "Is the priest—or pastor, or whatever he is—I mean, does he always preach about the evil ways of those outside Wellington?"

Caleb raised one eyebrow, a look that had me rushing to explain. "It seemed so preachy to me, like 'You need to fear everything and everyone outside the gates.' He didn't really mean it like that, did he?"

"Yes. He did."

Chapter Fourteen

Wow, a three word answer. Not exactly helpful. Nor reassuring.

"But why? You left here. You know what it is like outside those gates. I mean, I know your wife died—"

Shit, there goes my tact. As usual. By the way Caleb stiffened, I knew I'd crossed a line. Since my foot was already in my mouth, might as well eat it. "And I don't know anything more about it, but surely not everyone had something tragic happen to cause such a firm belief to stay behind these gates."

He wasn't looking at me. Instead he had a pensive, faraway look on his sculpted features. I needed to fill the silence. "Although, Jackie said her son died out there, so maybe she has a reason to hide here."

"We're not hiding, Grace. We've provided a safe environment to raise our families. A place where our children can run through town and we don't have to worry if they will be snatched. We don't lock our doors at night because we don't have strangers who might break in and steal from us—or kill us in our sleep."

I went to interrupt but he held up a hand in a sign he wasn't finished. "We've created a self-sufficient town where no money has to be exchanged for food or clothing. We keep in compliance with government laws by tracking our actual expenses, hence the band on your wrist. The truth is, we do everything we can to take care of our own."

"If Wellington is so safe, why does it need a police chief?"

The smile he gave was almost indulgent. "We still deal with human nature. Most of the calls I get are easy. Fights between brothers. Residents who consider it fun to grow marijuana or brew their own hard cider." I grimaced at the reminder while he continued.

"I don't have a difficult job. My officers who work in the cities and towns outside of Wellington full-time see the down and dirty crap of human nature. Gangs. Domestic violence. Rape. It happens every day out there. For them, covering shifts here is a welcome relief."

"You have a town of nearly four hundred, are you telling me you are completely safe from any of that here?"

Caleb shook his head. "No, of course not, but let's look at your situation at the school with Philip, Oscar, and Mike."

I finally had names to attach to my attackers, other than A.J's younger brother.

"What they did was unacceptable. What they threatened was even worse. You, being new here, didn't know who they were, but because of this"—he lifted my arm to show my wrist band—"because of the system we have in place here, I knew in seconds who the culprits were and they were arrested. Out there, the likelihood of anyone being arrested is slim, and if it wasn't you being harmed, it would be someone else. And someone else again until or if they are caught."

Caleb's passion showed through like a beacon. He truly believed in the pastor's fear-based preaching. I walked beside him while he kept one eye on his children in the pristine park. While he believed in what he said, I wasn't ready to give in.

"I spent twenty years outside these gates," I said. "The only time I've been arrested was after I arrived in Wellington, where I was introduced to marijuana-laced brownies for the first time."

He acquiesced. "*Touché*. Although, I do find it amazing, considering your best friend is a well-known partier with the financial means to get into some serious drug related situations."

"Don't drag Jake into this." I immediately jumped to my friend's defense. "He's a good guy. Yes, he has friends he gets into trouble with, but he also knows it's not my scene and he's always protected me from that side of his life."

"Don't be naïve, Grace. Once you go down the path which includes drugs, no matter how innocent it seems at the start, there is no separating from it. Those worlds will collide eventually. If Jake keeps looking at life as one big party his daddy will save him from, he's going to have to face the music at some point. While it'll be a huge slap in the face for him, you could get caught in the crossfire."

He nodded at something behind me. "Speak of the devil, here comes your friends now."

I turned and spotted our topic of conversation with several of our new-found friends in tow, all heading our way. My heart sank. I'd been enjoying my time with this enigmatic man. Our conversation had been lively but easy going. I didn't want it to end.

"Thanks for letting me talk."

His blue eyes glinted in the sun. Despite my run-ins with Caleb the police chief, Caleb the regular guy wasn't too bad.

I left with the group and we meandered behind the school—must be a favorite hang-out spot for this crew—but this time we stayed out of the woods and avoided any contraband that would get us arrested. As usual, Hope clung to Jake's arm like an appendage. I stayed close with Wayne and Theresa, keeping them talking to avoid Leland, though I saw his frustration with not getting the same results as his sister.

Later, as we headed back toward the Square, Jake got in step with me. "So, what was the conversation between you and Mr. Serious about?

"Caleb? Actually, he was very nice."

He scoffed. "Are you going soft on me? I thought you hated the guy?"

I wasn't about to tell him how the police chief had warned me to keep my distance from him, "I had a moment of homesickness. He saw me leave The Hall earlier and came out to check on me."

"Huh. Probably wanted to make sure you weren't making another break for it."

"No. He was very nice. We had a good conversation."

He stopped in his tracks. "A good conversation? With our parole officer?" He snorted. "Whatever."

"Believe what you want. Hey, want to skip out on this crew and head back to my host home and bake cookies?" I knew him long enough to know the topic of food was a great way to change the topic.

"Yum. I'm in. Must be that time of the month for you, huh?"

I punched him in the arm and instantly regretted it

as pain shot through my wrist. "Why the hell would you say that?"

He laughed as I gripped my sore hand. "Ha, serves you right for hitting me."

"You have sisters, you should know better than to talk like that."

I got a grin in return. "I have sisters, therefore I'm not afraid to make comments like that. You only want to bake when you are royally pissed or it's that time of the month. Right now, you aren't pissed."

I pouted, but it got me thinking and doing the mental math. Okay, so I was due for my monthly visit. Maybe that explained my melancholy mood.

"Are you making maple walnut cookies?"

I rolled my eyes. The man was a glutton. "Without real Vermont maple? Not a chance. Let's see what's in Amy's cabinets."

****

Monday arrived with another interesting day at work. After my brief encounter with Jackie yesterday and the bombshell about her son, I wondered what kind of mood she would be in. Besides, I was curious about how her son died and wondered if I could find a way to get her to talk about it.

Instead, Sheila greeted me with the news that half the town was down with food poisoning and our boss was one of them. Knowing how she cooked, I wondered which dish she'd brought to the fellowship meal and thanked my lucky stars I'd skipped out early.

With the head chef being out sick, it meant I had to cook, and I was up for the challenge. I looked at the menu: steak and cheese on a whole grain roll, garden salad, and carrots. Easy.

I turned on the radio, the only electronics I am allowed to have, and hummed along to the music. I sipped on an endless supply of zero caffeine pop; it was a poor substitute for my usual addiction, but I suffered through. As I cooked the shaved steak, I added a little garlic powder, salt, and pepper. I also decided to add caramelized onions as a finishing touch.

Sheila sliced carrots, then boiled them. Deciding to add more flavor, I put them in a skillet with butter, brown sugar, and a touch of cinnamon, nutmeg, and honey. Not too much, as I didn't want to be accused of sugaring up the kids before their next class.

My sous chef almost swooned after doing a taste test. "Sweetie, this is delicious. The kids are going to love it."

She must have mentioned I cooked the meal to the teachers because for the first time since I'd been here, the adults grabbed trays and ate from the hot lunch menu.

I reveled in the accolades. With the town being so small, I'd met a lot of people already, especially those working at the school. Having them see something I was good at felt great, especially as I am sure all the escapades that earned me time in front of the police chief were also public knowledge. I'd rather be known for being a great cook then a trouble maker. Of course, I'm not sure how my perpetually unhappy boss will react when she returns to work but at least the kids enjoyed one meal.

With it being just the two of us, there was more work to do for clean up, but I could see Sheila was getting tired so I sent her home and finished the clean up by myself, working later than usual. I did use the kitchen phone, asking my new friend, Connie the switchboard operator, to patch me through to Caroline and we made plans to meet at the transfer terminal to hit the store after work.

I'd discovered Amy's birthday was this week and last night I'd offered to bake the cake. While my parents had ensured I was more than efficient in cooking meals, I preferred baking. I decided on a chocolate cake with raspberry filling covered in chocolate ganache. Once I had all the ingredients, I walked the aisles while my college roomie talked incessantly about her job.

"So after we combine the herbs, we package them and they are shipped into the surrounding towns for sale. You should try some of the blends. Amelia has me try each one and I know you would find something amazing to use them with your cooking."

"Sure. I'll check them out," I mumbled. I was listening but I was searching the aisles as well and was a bit distracted. Of course, it wasn't long before Caroline's topic turned to her favorite subject. "Straight and True is playing Friday night and on Saturday Aaron wants to know if you want to go horseback riding."

"Sounds fun. Sure, I'll go."

"What are you looking for? I thought you had everything you needed for the birthday."

I pushed the carriage down another aisle, looking at the shelves. "I'm due for my period so I need to get tampons."

"Oh, those are at the clinic pharmacy."

I stopped and stared at her. "Why?"

She shrugged. "I don't know. Guess they consider it a medical thing."

I groaned. "This place is so archaic. Let's buy, I mean swipe, our arm bands and head over there."

I still felt uneasy whenever I needed to go to the clinic, even if this time was only to the pharmacy side. I'd seen Dr. Todd around town a few times and managed to avoid him, but going into his territory made me nervous. I'm not sure why. It's not like he was going to randomly grab me and knock me out again, but still, my stomach twisted whenever I thought about what he did to me. I expected to walk into an actual store like the ones at home. Instead I found a counter with two pharmacists working and all the product was behind swinging doors. My angst about this place quadrupled and I felt my hackles rise.

I looked at Caroline. "Do we really have to request feminine products and have them get it for us?"

She nodded. "Yep. And they ask questions, too. They take it all very seriously."

"I think I'm going to throw up from all this Big Brother bullshit." I stepped to the counter and asked for the product needed.

After telling me to "Please swipe your band first," a tall, string bean of a man in his forties looked at the computer monitor. "I have your name as Grace, date of birth August 9, 1997."

I figured the wristband had all my information, but this was the first time anyone had me verify it. "Yes."

He continued looking at the computer, his voice drone-like as he read from the script onscreen. "You are requesting product due to your menstrual cycle. We don't have the date of your last period in the system."

My stomach clenched. I took a deep breath. "No, you wouldn't. I'm new here."

He gave me a blank stare. "So what is the date?"

"Why?"

Caroline nudged me. "Just give him the information, Grace."

"No, he's not a doctor and it's none of his business." I whipped back to the man behind the counter, plastering a fake smile. "All I need are tampons or pads. Can you please get those for me?"

The man kept his fingers on the keyboard as he looked back and forth between me and Caroline, his eyes deer-in-the-headlights wide. I don't think he was used to anyone refusing to provide what was expected. "I can't until I have all the data logged in the system."

I tried to be good. I hadn't raised my voice at all and even said please, but now I spoke between clenched teeth. "Why in the world do you need to know information about my menstrual cycle? Seriously, I want to know."

String Bean looked around, as if wishing someone would come rescue him. No longer able to be a drone following the script onscreen, the poor man gave a nervous cough. "Uh, this… uh… this way we know if someone is pregnant or possibly pregnant."

Back to the obstetric police routine?

Nope, being good went out the window. I raised my voice. "Really? Because the hospital staff already performed an invasive exam—*while I was drugged and unconscious, by the way*—to determine I'm not pregnant. If I am requesting tampons then obviously I am expecting my period which would also indicate I. Am. Not. Pregnant."

I leaned across the counter in a gesture intended to menace the shit out of the guy. Looking startled, he took a step back. "How about you go and find the damn tampons, or I will go back there and get them myself."

He looked toward the door behind him, then back to the computer screen. Obviously, no one in the history of his job had anyone refused to provide answers to his online script. "Ah, well, as soon as I have the date in the system, I can get what you need."

"Tell you what, you put whatever the hell date you want in the system. Make one up. Pull up a fucking calendar and count back twenty-seven days and choose one for all I care." By this time we were nose to nose. Close enough that I smell the mints on his breath. "I am *not* telling you jack-shit. Got me?"

Caroline pulled at my arm. "Grace, the man is only trying to do his job. You don't have to make a scene. What's the big deal anyway? It's just a date."

I turned back to my friend and saw four other people waiting in line watching the show. "The big deal," I said loud enough for everyone to hear, "is in the real world, we question authority. Our physical health is a private thing, and if we don't want to disclose it, we don't have to."

I turned back to the counter. "Well? Did you pick a date yet, 'cause I don't see you marching into the back to get my item yet?"

"I… I'll be right back." The frazzled man quickly turned and disappeared behind the doors to the back room.

I tapped my fingers on the counter while I waited. The other pharmacist took care of the remaining customers while I continued to wait and mutter to Caroline who kept twisting the cross on the chain around her neck. "It's not a difficult task. Why the hell is he taking so long? Three other people have been taken care of already."

I spotted Dr. Todd coming out of the swinging doors and my stomach clenched. I immediately went into defense mode at the sight of the man I'd been doing my best to avoid since my arrival.

"Hello, Grace." His condescending tone made the hairs on my arm stand up straight and tall. "I understand you won't provide information for Sean to help process your request."

I gave the doctor a sigh of disgust. "As I explained to String Bean here, the information is private and none of his damn business."

He didn't hesitate to respond. "As your physician, it is my business, so what was the date of your last period?"

I leaned forward and hissed, "You are not *my physician*. My physician is back home in Vermont. And after what you and your staff did to me, what on God's green earth makes you think I am going to provide you with any information?"

"You're in a bit of an agitated state, Grace," he said, putting a touch of smarm in his tone. "Do you require something to help you relax?"

Just what I needed to push me over the edge. This vile, loathsome quack pretended to be a professional, but he was nothing more than a control freak who pushed drugs on people in order to have his way with them. My hands curled into fists and I lunged.

A brick wall of a man stepped between me and the doctor, blocking me from my objective.

"They called you?" I nearly spat at the police chief. "Of course they did, freaking cowards. No wonder they took their time coming back out here. Did you hear what he said to me?"

"Calm down, Grace." Caleb's voice was low and firm. He took my arms in a light grip, forcing me to take a step back from the counter.

My entire body hummed with rage. "You heard him, though, right? I told you what he did to me when I arrived and he practically said he'd do it again."

"Doc," he said to Todd the Twerp, "I've got it from here. Why don't you go back to your patients?"

That's it? He was going to ignore the fact the doctor wanted to drug me again? I tried to pull away, tried to see past the stone wall in front of me in order to look at the quack so he could see I wasn't as forgiving.

Ignoring me, Caleb turned to the pharmacist. "Sean, tell me what started this?"

"I'll tell you what—" I started.

His grip tightened. "I didn't ask you, Grace. I asked Sean."

"All, allll I did, Chief, wasss asssk her for the date of her last menstrual cycle and"—his eyes bulged, his cheeks reddened, and he began sweating like a sumo wrestler—"she became belligerent."

The Chief looked at me. "Is this true?"

"Which part?" I knew I was being obnoxious but didn't care. When he remained silent, waiting for an answer, I gave in. "Yes, basically."

"Why won't you give him the information?"

I thrust my chin out. "Because it's none of their business. I'm a private person and I'm tired of everything about me being public knowledge. I'm tired of having Big Brother watching every move I make."

"I know this transition has been difficult on you,

Grace, but when you fight the simple things, you cause yourself more distress. You've made your point here today. Can't you give the date, get what you need, and move on?"

If I did, they'd win. If I didn't, I couldn't get what I needed. Either way I'd lose, but I don't like to back down. I cocked my head and looked up at the stone wall of a man. "Tell you what, if you give me my phone, I can access my calendar of events and look up the date."

He shook his head and actually rolled his eyes. I think I exasperated him. Bonus. Without releasing my arms, he turned back to the stuttering pharmacist. "Can you get me a calendar, please?"

The man rushed to the other side of the counter, looking most thankful for a tangible task. A moment later he laid a single page calendar on the table.

Caleb nodded to me. "If you don't know the exact date, make a reasonable deduction and tell Sean."

"And if I don't?"

He leaned down to speak in my ear. "Then you walk out of here without what you need. Is your desire to make a point greater than what you will endure during the next week without feminine products?"

Seething, petulant, and pissed, I pointed out an almost random date which the pharmacist busily logged into the computer. He looked up from the screen, face now pasty white. "Um, Chief? I'm supposed to ask if she's sexually active."

I may have growled.

I launched myself across the counter, but the police chief maintained a vise grip on my arms, preventing me from reaching my target. But at least he gave a small sigh as he spoke. "Don't press your luck, Sean. Go get what she needs."

Two minutes later, I had a bag of tampons and a police escort out of the pharmacy. Caroline trailed behind us, carrying the bags of food and looking a bit shell-shocked at my outburst.

"Do you need a ride home?"

My friend nodded, but I shook my head. "I'd rather walk over a bed of hot coals barefoot before I spend another minute with you."

"Suit yourself." Caleb motioned for my friend, who handed over all the bags to me and got into the cruiser, leaving me alone with my petty, emotional state of mind.

I hated this place. I hated that man, too. He always had to win.

And I wanted coffee. A really, really strong cup of coffee. Caffeine free soda pop wasn't going to do it today.

Chapter Fifteen

Jackie was back to work by the time Tuesday arrived. Once she heard how good my food was the day before, she turned meaner than a rabid raccoon. Before the day was done, I'd been tasked with cleaning out the soft serve ice cream maker which might not have seen the light of day in ten years.

Fortunately, I'd baked Amy's cake the night before, so when I showed up barely in time for the dinner with all her children and grandchildren in attendance, I was able to almost relax.

I do get cranky when Mother Nature makes her monthly visit, and with my boss on the war path all week, I wasn't in the best of moods come the weekend. By Friday night I joined the usual crowd at The Hall to listen to Straight and True, as had become the norm, Leland sat by my side.

Exhausted from all the extra work I'd been assigned this week, and the lull of the music, my eyes closed, my head rolling back onto my new friend's shoulder. When the tempo of music changed, I opened my eyes and immediately spotted Caleb watching me from across the room

My pulse quickened. When had he arrived? Leland's arm now became a heavy weight on my shoulder. A part of me wanted to push myself away. For Caleb?

Gina Leuci

Huh? The man was a walking, talking rectum. Why should I care if he sees me with someone else?

The blond, breathing, male-mannequin beside me used his arm to pull me closer. "Where are you going, baby? I like having you lay against me."

I attempted a smile for his benefit. "Sorry, I'm a bit tired, but I don't want to be rude and fall asleep."

He nuzzled my neck. "Mmm. It's okay. You can sleep on me any time."

I gulped. I don't know what it is about him, but he puts me on edge. He's beautiful. Funny. Popular. His father is important in the community. He obviously wants to spend time with me, but from the moment he first spoke to me on the trip to Wellington, I felt an undercurrent of a secret agenda and I was ground zero to achieving it. Yet, he's done nothing I can put my finger on to prove I am not once again over reacting to every little nuance in this town. So I continue to let him pursue me.

I watched Hope lean against Jake, fluttering her eyelashes at him as she giggled. I knew her agenda immediately. She planned to put her claws in the rich, attractive, new guy in town in every way imaginable.

Hell, why hadn't I seen it before? This town was starving for outsiders to come in and join the ranks. These young adults didn't have a pool of eligible partners to choose from for future mates.

Unless they ventured outside of the city gates for any length of time—- which the pastor put the fear of God into them not to do—so what chance did they have to find a significant other to spend their lives with? Having a group of college students come in during the summer for a work study program actually brought

168

non-Wellington family members to them. No wonder the twins had immediately attached themselves to us.

The music was fast and upbeat. It seemed the one thing this backwoods town didn't do was censor the music. The band played everything from Jason Aldean to Bon Jovi to Led Zep. Currently, the female vocalist was belting out a song from Pink and I suddenly wanted an excuse to unwrap myself from the hand drawing circles on my bare arm.

I jumped up and pulled Jake to his feet. "Hey, let's dance."

I lost myself in the music, moving to the beat and feeling the stress of the week evaporate. We touched and gyrated in ways that appeared anything but platonic but had the two of us laughing.

It was during one of those moves, one where Jake's front was pressed against my back, his hands moving down my sides, when I felt eyes watching us. I knew without a doubt it was Caleb and I felt the need to kick it up a notch more. I turned to face my life-long friend so our bodies pressed together as one as we moved in a nearly sexual act.

I heard a few gasps and realized we'd probably taken things a bit far for this retro, uptight town, but as his hands grasped my behind as he gyrated forward, I laughed. We were shocking these townspeople and it was just what they needed.

When the song finally ended, my dance partner leaned into me. "Feeling better?"

He knew me too well. I nodded.

"I think we put on a good show." He had my hand as we headed back to the table. "Want to tell me what that was all about?"

"I had a revelation about this place and especially about The Twins. I'll fill you in later."

"Well, that was certainly entertaining." Leland greeted me back at the table. I'd hoped him seeing me get loose on the dance floor would embarrass him—which, from the stares I received, there were definitely those in the room who were—but unfortunately, I think my moves had the opposite effect on my wanna-be boyfriend.

His gaze roamed my body, taking in my flushed skin and focused a bit long on my breasts, still heaving a bit from exertion. Shit. He was definitely turned on. "I'm calling the next dance."

"Oh, um, I need water first."

But he took my hand and pulled me back onto the dance floor. It was a slow number. At first, his hands went into a formal dance position, one hand holding mine, the other casually on my hip, but it wasn't long before he slid my hands to his neck and put both of his on my hips, pulling me closer.

I tried to step back without being too obvious, but his grip tightened. "Don't pretend to be a prude, Grace." He leaned into my ear to talk, his breath warm on my neck. "You are one incredibly sexy dancer."

I moved my hands to his chest and pushed myself back, as much as I could with his hands keeping our lower bodies pressed together. "I barely know you. Jake and I have been friends forever. We know each other's boundaries."

He laughed. "There were boundaries out there? Hardly." But he moved back to his original position, putting a slight distance between us. "Better? See, I am a gentleman."

For a moment, I thought I'd be making an entirely different kind of scene, one in which my knee connected with Leland's family jewels. But this dance wasn't any more comfortable, not with his choice of conversation.

"You say you've known each other a long time. With the way you two danced together, you can't tell me you haven't gotten down and dirty with him."

"What?" I stopped moving; he kept going and his movements nearly had me tripping as I got back into step. "No. we're just friends."

"So you haven't had sex with him?"

This night was going downhill fast. I looked over Leland's shoulder, hoping to catch Jake's eye. Instead, he was wrapped around Hope, swaying to the song the singers on stage sang together about not going home alone.

My dance partner practically whined as the hand on my hip became a vice grip. "So you have had sex with him."

I felt my exasperation grow. "No. We haven't."

His grip lightened slightly. "Are you saying you're a virgin?"

All I wanted to do was escape. Instead I stood still on the dance floor. "I'm not saying anything. This is ridiculous." I bit out the words, keeping the conversation low and between us. "I'm done. I'm going to get a drink."

But he pulled me hard against him, forcing me to continue to sway with the music. "Not until the song ends. It's rude to walk away."

"Then you better change your tone and your topic, otherwise how I walk away won't be pleasant for you."

"You are a see-saw of emotions. I love the crease between your eyes when you get mad. Relax, Grace. I'll be a gentleman. Promise."

And once again he moved a step back and led me around the dance floor. The moment the song ended, I bolted across the room to grab a drink.

But no reprieve for me. Caleb leaned against the wall, sipping on a bottled water. Gawd, the man was intimidating on a normal day, but when he wore that damn uniform shirt with the badge, it put me off my game.

"Having fun?"

I knew sarcasm when I heard it. And I'm an expert. It was just what I needed to get my mind off what had occurred on the dance floor. "Are you?" I popped the top of my soda with the hand not hindered by the brace and sucked down the carbonated liquid.

"It's been a while since this place has had so much entertainment. I had to cool down after watching you and Jake on the dance floor. I felt like a voyeur to a public display of foreplay."

I choked. "It wasn't like that at all."

"No?" He took another sip of water. "I wouldn't be so sure. After your exhibition, I saw several couples head for the door, and it had nothing to do with embarrassment. With the look in their eyes, I'd say there are several married couples who are going to get lucky tonight."

A new flush of heat rushed from my chest up to the top of my head. "There's nothing wrong with what we did," I mumbled. "Everyone at home dances that way."

"You're not at home, Grace," he warned. "And the people here are not exposed to explicit television and movies. Be careful. As it is, I have a feeling the man you are with tonight," he motioned to Leland, "is taking you to bed in his dreams."

With a mock salute, he turned on his heel and walked away. I gulped and frantically scanned the room. I caught a few looks from some of the men full of appreciation, however, I also spotted one glare from a woman, who turned her man away from me.

I needed to get out of here. Fast. I didn't even return to the table to say bye to Caroline, who was in deep conversation with Teresa. Jake was nowhere to be found either. No, I take that back. As I headed to the exit, I spotted him and his summer girlfriend in a dark corner of the room, pressed against the wall playing tongue hockey.

I definitely needed to warn him about my suspicions about our suitors first thing tomorrow, although with the way his hands moved on the girl, my warnings may come too late.

Chapter Sixteen

During my Saturday morning chores, helping Amy and Kurt *red up* the house, as they called cleaning, Caroline called to remind me about horseback riding. "You disappeared last night without saying goodbye."

I wasn't about to explain my reasons. "Yeah, sorry."

"Are you still going on the trail with us today?"

"I guess so. Who's going?" Please don't let it be Leland.

"I don't know. I didn't ask." Which didn't surprise me. My bestie was a go-with-the-flow kind of girl. "Does it matter?"

"Not really." I wanted to spend time with her. I missed seeing my roommate every day. I missed her cheerfulness and love of life. She tended to balance out my intensity.

"We're meeting at one o'clock at The Square and will take the shuttle to the farm. Aaron and Jackson, the owner of the farm, are leading the trail ride."

"Okay, I'll see you there."

"Bring a swimsuit and towel, oh, and a bagged lunch because we won't be back for dinner."

With a stuffed backpack, I arrived at the transit station to see a large group of people. This wasn't going to be a private party, and with Leland looking anxious to get to me, I was more than thankful for the crowd.

There were the people I expected to see: Aaron and Caroline, Hope and Jake, Leland. I assumed I would meet Jackson once we arrived at the farm. More surprising, though was the number of young children. I spotted Sheila's husband, Cole, with their nine-year-old daughter, Louise. Mark, the teacher from the school, and his eight-year-old son, Timmy.

Then there was A.J., who I've been avoiding as much as possible, along with his bully of a brother, Philip. Having those two along could be an issue, except I'm not sure what trouble they would cause with Caleb around. Yep, the police chief was there, and he had his oldest, Eliza, with him.

I had the two bullies who hated me, a tall blond who wanted to be my boyfriend and I wanted to stay clear of, and the police chief whom I had a tendency to piss off. Why had I agreed to come today?

Oh, right, because I'd followed my best friend to this bizarre town with the expectation to be working with horses daily and after two weeks, this was the first time I'd actually be around one. The shuttle bus was full and I was pressed against the window seat with Leland beside me for the fifteen-minute ride to the farm located on the farthest parcel of land from town.

The residents were around horses on a regular basis, so Aaron came to us interns first to see our experience levels. Caroline had no experience riding, so her boyfriend chose a horse for her named Honey, which he insisted was gentle. Jake, a more experienced rider, was given Gringo Killer, a horse they said they'd procured from a farm in Mexico a couple years ago.

After learning I hadn't been on a horse since I was nine, Aaron returned from the barn with Jazzy. I immediately fell in love with the brown horse with the white streak down her nose.

I talked to Jazzy as Jackson walked us through putting on the saddle and checking the strappings. I watched as Caleb made sure Eliza was settled on her horse before he returned with a horrifyingly large black horse with flaring nostrils.

He pulled gently on the reins. "Easy, Galahad."

Ugh. Even the horse knew who was in command. I rolled my eyes and settled into the motion as the group of fifteen eventually headed out into the woods on the far side of the Wellington lands.

Once on the trail, the horses started to show their personalities. Leland's liked to prance and show off, so several times he would disappear toward the front of the line as the horse whinnied and twitched her tail. I tried moving toward Jake a couple times, but Gringo Killer liked to run while my horse, sweet Jazzy, liked to go at her own slow pace. It had been much too long for me to remember how to fully take control so I tended to fall behind every now and then. Although, I was never at the back. Jackson always remained at the end.

At one of the times when I was a good distance from those in front of me, but with the younger kids and their fathers behind, A.J. slowed his horse until he was beside me. "Heard you showed some interesting moves last night in The Hall."

I didn't want to encourage him and hoped he would move along quickly. "Oh?"

"Rumors are you and your bestie were practically doing the nasty out on the dance floor."

I shifted on the saddle, not exactly thrilled with where this conversation was going. "You shouldn't listen to rumors."

He moved his horse closer. "Makes me wonder how much of what you accused my brother of doing to you was true. I'm thinking you came on to him, got caught, and you lied about it."

I gripped my reins tight, ready to tell him where to get off, but I didn't get a chance.

"I'm thinking you should move along," Caleb said from directly behind us. How much had the man overheard?

My new nemesis shot me a frustrated look and sent his horse forward.

"How are you doing, Grace?" the chief asked casually.

"Just peachy, and you?"

He moved beside me. "Relax. Jazzy is a good horse. She'll do all the work for you."

I nodded and tried to do as he said, but I knew all my muscles were tight as I concentrated on moving with the horse so I wouldn't bounce all over the place.

"How is Eliza doing?"

I'd hoped the question would get the large, intimidating man to leave my side, but he gave a quick look behind and continued with the pace. "She's a natural. She loves riding."

"It's been a while for me. I forgot how much work it is."

"You're doing fine."

He nodded his approval then turned around to join his daughter again while Jazzy and I slowly meandered along the trail.

We rode for over almost two hours, crisscrossing through trails in the woods surrounding the town. I had a brief moment of wondering if the entire town was actually surrounded by fencing. Was it possible to escape this locked town by heading out from the opposite side of the wall of trees?

Even if it were possible, there was still the matter of a GPS tracking band on my wrist preventing me from going too far. It didn't really matter, though. I'd made it sixteen days already and most of the time it wasn't too painful. I could make it through the summer, work out my contract and be thankful when I returned to my normal routine in Vermont.

Eventually, we exited the woods into a large field and a gorgeous, sun-kissed lake. The beauty was not lost on me. I stopped Jazzy in order to take in the colors of lush green fields, surrounded by the woods and then the bright blue of the water sparkling as the sun, high in the sky, danced across the still waters.

While this was old-news to the residents of Wellington, and they were all quick to dismount, I stayed in place, until Caleb rode up beside me. "You good, Grace?"

I turned to him, my awe evident in my tone. "It's breath-taking. Please tell me you don't take this view for granted."

"No." He scanned the horizon. "This was one of the things I missed most when I left, and one of the first places I came when I got home." I noticed how his features softened as he spoke. "I come here to rejuvenate."

"I can see why. All I can say is, wow."

"It's quiet now. Come July, it's a popular hangout."

I looked around at the woods surrounding the field

and lake. "How… how do they get here?"

He smiled and I noticed the slight wrinkle around his eyes. "It's actually not far down that path." He pointed off to the right. "We took the long way here to exercise the horses."

He dismounted and motioned to me. "Come, let's take care of the animals so we can enjoy the rest of the day."

I swung my leg over and down, then groaned. I'd forgotten the muscles that are used when riding. If I felt sore now, I can only imagine how my legs would feel tomorrow after taking the ride back.

Once the horses were taken care of, everyone stripped down to their bathing suits and headed into the water. I wasn't far behind. I tossed my backpack on the ground, placed my wrist brace inside the pack then pulled out my towel, and took off my clothes until I wore only my bikini.

I look good in a bikini. I'm not being conceited, but I know I have a decent enough figure to pull it off with confidence. When I saw Leland staring at me with his mouth open, I sashayed my way to the waterfront, strutting my stuff.

Then I saw Jake staring at Hope and I felt a bit inadequate. I mean, my suit was great. It was a black and white striped outfit, with no straps, but the bottom was modest compared to the tall, model-thin blonde.

For a town centered on sheltering their children from the harshness of the outside world, including not even owning televisions, I was nothing short of amazed at the scraps of flesh-toned material which barely covered the girl's ass. There was more sea-shell shaped bling used to hold the scraps together than there were any actual coverage. The top wasn't much better. Again, if it weren't for the sea-shell ties, the color of the material was too close of a match to her skin to know there was anything to cover her.

She swept her long hair to one side as she tiptoed into the water while her prey strangled on his lust. I moved behind my friend and pushed him, sending Jake tumbling into the water where he lost his balance and came up sputtering.

"What was that for?"

I nodded to the goddess, "Thought you needed cooling off."

He looked at the siren and back at me. "Jealous?"

I rolled my eyes. "Hardly." I put my hands on my hips and shifted. "Not when I look this good."

He stood and made his way toward me and I saw the evil grin. I took a step back but he was quick. "You need to be taken down a peg or two. You're much too confident." He grabbed me at the waist, swung me around and tossed me into the cold—no, beyond cold—frigid water.

"Holy Christ on a cracker." I yelped.

Nine-year-old Timmy pointed at me. "She swore."

"S-S-Sorry," I stammered as the adults glared at me. "W-W-Won't happen again." But I had to bite my tongue against the horde of swears echoing in my brain. "How in the world do you manage to swim in this thing?"

Aaron and Caroline came running in behind me, laughing and splashing as they adjusted to the temperatures. I stood, just about thigh deep when Leland came up beside me.

"Grace, I knew you were beautiful, but wow, just

wow."

His heated gaze roamed my body and stopped at my chest. I looked down and saw why. I had full pucker effect and my admirer was in complete guy mode. I could bail and head ashore to wrap myself in a towel or take the plunge and move into deeper water.

I dove under and swam out until I was shoulder deep while Bobbsey twin with the puppy dog expression, followed. Fortunately, Caroline and Aaron were nearby and I joined them.

I did finally adapt to the water and had fun as the group splashed around. We splintered off into groups, with the dads and their kids in one area—which thankfully included Caleb—and the rest of us out a bit farther. Which meant the bully brothers were with us, not so fortunate.

Because I stuck close to Jake as much as I could, and Leland was constantly by my side, things were fine for a little while, but eventually, A.J. started on me.

At first, it was hard to tell. He was splashing and being generally obnoxious with everyone, and when I was splashed in the face the first time, I didn't say anything.

When he swam under the water and butted against the back of my knees, I swatted at him. When he came up, I told him to knock it off.

A few minutes later he grabbed me by the ankles and pulled me under; I came up, pissed and ready to fight. I wasn't the only one.

Jake was quick to jump to my defense. "You touch her again, A.J. and I will throat punch you so hard you'll be struggling to breathe for a month."

He pretended innocence. "What? We're all out

here having some fun. No harm intended."

"Leave Grace alone," my protector warned.

I attempted to intervene, but it was good to know I had my friend by my side. "I can handle myself."

I heard a whistle, and we all turned to see our local lawman lower his fingers from his mouth. He pointed at A.J. and motioned for him to come to him but his response was to raise his middle finger and swim farther away.

"Asshole," Jake muttered.

Philip responded by splashing us in the face, before he dived under and followed his brother out to a large rock in the distance.

I stayed with the group a while longer but eventually, I decided to dry off. Because it was only late May, the sun, while high in the sky, wasn't as warm as I'd wanted, so I sat with my towel wrapped around my shoulders.

I turned my face upward, soaking in the rays and welcoming the joys of warm weather. Eventually, the laughter of those in the water had me watching their antics.

Jake swam under Hope and stood up with her now on his shoulders, she giggled before teetering over with a huge splash. Caroline and Aaron were farther out, floating on their backs and talking quietly. The dads in the group hung together as they took time to play with their kids. Leland had joined A.J. and Philip out on the rocks.

My eyes returned over and over again to Caleb as he lifted his daughter in order to throw her into the water where she would come up laughing and swim back to have him do it again.

He continued to comply, and every time, I found myself staring at his arms as they bulged when he lifted the child. At his firm six-pack glistening in the sunlight. The deep sound of his rumbling laugh had me wishing I was the cause for his happiness.

My cheeks flamed. Where had that come from? No. I wanted nothing to do with Caleb. Maybe I should hit the water again to cool my wandering thoughts. Sure the guy was good looking, but, he was in serious need of a personality adjustment.

Leland walked out of the lake and I watched him behind my sunglasses. He was no slouch to look at either. If he left the gates of Wellington and headed to New York, he'd probably be scouted immediately as a model. I suppose you couldn't work in a farming town without building some firm tones, but the lanky man's muscles were not as defined as…

Shouldn't go back there. At all. But my eyes drifted to the man in the water and I knew the warmth I felt had nothing to do with the sun.

The tall blond arrived, blocking my line of vision. "May I join you?"

I wanted to say no, but I had no real excuse. I nodded and he spread his towel and lay down, leaning on his side toward me. "Are you okay?"

I answered but kept my eyes on the swimmers. "Sure. I'm fine, just wanted to warm up."

"No. I mean, you seem distant. Distracted."

Maybe now, while they were basically alone, would be a good time to lay down the law. "Listen, Lee. I like you. I'm sure you're a good guy, but I need you to know I am not here to have a summer fling. I'm leaving at the end of August and I'm never coming back. I don't want you to think there will be anything between us."

He sat up and turned so his back was to the water as he faced me. "If you're thinking I want what my sister and Jake have going, maybe I do. And I'll admit, the moment I set eyes on you on the bus, I wanted to get to know you better. But, if all you want is for us to be friends, fine. However, if we share a few kisses along the way, I won't say no."

I went to talk but he held his hand up to motion my silence. "I watch you, Grace, and I notice that when you let yourself, you actually have a good time with us, but then you put up a wall and push everyone away."

He wasn't wrong. I do push people away. Especially here where I don't, can't, understand why everyone allows their lives to be ruled by fear. "Your life is different than mine. These bracelets tracking our every move, our every purchase, it's invasive."

He took my hand and traced the outline of the wrist band as he spoke. "See what I mean? You put too much thought into it instead of letting it be what it is. We take care of our own. You don't have to carry cash. You don't have to worry about budgets. You put in an honest day of work and you have food and clothes as you need them. And when the time comes when you can't work because you are old, or sick, or injured, everyone here helps take care of you because we care."

"It's an interesting idea, and I guess it works, but—" But, it sounded rehearsed. Or programmed.

"Shh! No buts. You came here to enjoy yourself. Yes, you have a job, but it's not your whole life. I heard you're playing baseball this weekend."

I nodded.

"Since it's something you enjoy, I will be there to cheer you on. As your friend."

I could deal with that. "Okay."

"However, if I sit in the bleachers and admire how you run the bases, I promise I will try to keep my wayward thoughts to myself."

I couldn't stop the smile his comment caused. Even if I didn't feel the same way about Leland as he did about me, it still felt good to be admired. "Deal."

At some point during our conversation, Jake and Hope exited the water and were currently chasing each other across the grassy field. "Are you okay with those two? I mean, Jake is leaving in August as well, but he can be quite the player."

Lee gave a casual shrug "What my sister wants, she gets. It's always been that way."

I wasn't surprised at his comment. I still haven't spoken with Jake about being careful and I worried as I watched Leland's sister sprint over the field with my best friend in hot pursuit until he tackled her and they splashed back into the water.

I needed time alone to warn him. I sighed and turned back to watch the man beyond them, standing waist deep, with the sun a halo behind him. He talked with Cole as their two daughters splashed and played near them. Two fathers, attentive to their charges. Relaxed.

At this moment, the man in the water was the man who'd approached me on Sunday wanting only to help; to ease my homesickness. Here, he was the man I'd seen last week playing baseball, and later singing along while Aaron played the guitar.

But, I had seen his other side too often. A darker

side I had a tendency to bring out in him. And when Caleb called for his daughter to head to shore, I watched him do a sweep of his head and knew, without a doubt, the man was doing a headcount to ensure everyone who'd arrived was still within his vision.

That man. The man who was completely in control, he was the man I didn't understand. The man who brought out my need to argue and debate.

I decided then and there, the only way I could get through the summer is to be the perfect resident from this point forward. I turned my full attention back to the younger, thinner man sitting beside me, regaling me of another time he'd been here and the antics they'd pulled. I had no idea how long he'd been telling the story, but I nodded and smiled and pretended I had been listening all along.

When dinner time was announced, Leland stood, holding his hand out to me. While I told him we could be friends, I still had my reservations about his intentions, but I dropped the towel and quickly pulled on my shorts before we headed over to join the others.

We stood in a circle, hands joined, in order for Jackson to lead the prayer for our meal together. I should have closed my eyes during the reverent time, but my gaze was drawn to a certain very buff man standing across from me. When the prayer was over, I silently added my own few words: *Please, if there really is a God, then help me not keep staring at a man I could never be with.*

Maybe my prayers were answered, because Caleb grabbed his t-shirt to pull over his perfectly tanned body before grabbing his brown-bag. But maybe I should have added more words, like asking the deity to remind Leland about the friends-only deal, because despite his promise, his eyes rarely moved beyond my bikini-clad chest the entire meal.

Chapter Seventeen

I woke on Monday, Memorial Day, juiced to start playing baseball. Instead, I discovered the day would begin with a prayer service—they did that a lot around here. This time they'd have it at the cemetery before they placed American flags at headstones.

I followed along because I'd just promised God a couple days before I would be a good Wellington citizen. At the earliest opportunity, I sneakered up, put my hair into two braids, added my school baseball cap, and headed to the school grounds.

I spotted Aaron immediately and headed toward his dugout. I heard Jake call my name from the bleachers and I smiled and waved. Leland was beside him. I groaned and waved to him as well. Friends. Right.

Aaron handed me a red mesh pinnie vest which all the players wore to denote their teams. I snapped mine into place over my shirt as the team huddled together. "Okay, we have a new player today. Everyone knows Grace?"

I smiled and nodded to my teammates. From what I'd seen last week, this was a competitive crowd. I'd fit right in, but first they had to see what I could do.

"She plays second base. Pete, are you okay with outfield today?"

Pete put his hands in the air. "Sure. I'll let her have second. Should be a fun game."

I didn't know if he was being sarcastic or not, but I thanked him. Our team was first up, and when it was my turn, I slipped on the helmet and gripped the bat.

Being new, I had a lot to prove, and I swung too early at the first pitch. Not a good start. Second pitch, I fouled. At the third, my bat connected with the ball with an easy out pop-up. Not my best start, but it was still early in the game, I'd get into my groove.

When the time came to cover the bases, I adjusted my sunglasses and pulled my glove on. Like riding a bike, I was soon back in a rhythm.

When A.J., who was on the blue team, made it to second base, he decided to start in on me. "Hope you throw better than you bat," he taunted.

"You'll find out soon enough." I was in too good of a mood to worry about the obnoxious behavior even when he spit, making sure it landed close to where I stood. I looked at the gob near my foot, then glared at him from behind my shades. "It's time to grow up. Move on already."

Fortunately, the next batter sent the ball sailing down the third baseline. I went into play mode while he ran to the next base, only to be tagged out.

Caleb batted next and I felt my mouth go dry as he took his stance. I silently wished for the ball to go anywhere but near me because I knew there was no way I'd be catching the ball unless it landed on my head. He hit a single and I managed to turn my eyes away from him to refocus.

When the chief made it to second base and waited for the next batter, he spoke in a low tone. "Is A.J. bothering you?"

I couldn't look at him directly. Just two days ago,

I'd promised myself I would be good and stay away from this man, yet here I am, trying hard to not notice how the sweat glistened on his brow, or how his biceps bulged under his short-sleeved shirt.

I adjusted my cap to hide my face. "I can handle him."

"I'm sure you can."

The afternoon passed quickly with both teams scoring almost evenly. I did piss A.J. off more when I caught his pop fly in the seventh inning. I wondered if he'd have a comment or two next time he came to second base, but he never made it.

My batting improved after my first attempt. No home runs, but I did hit enough to send runners in.

Blue team was up by one when we got to the bottom of the ninth and my competitive streak was in full play. Aaron struck out the first batter, the next batter was out at first and then Caleb was up again. The bat struck hard sending the ball into center field. Pete grabbed it after a single bounce and threw the ball to me.

Caleb ran like a bat out of hell toward second; I'd be damned before I allowed him to get there. I took a running leap in the air to catch the ball. Unfortunately, the momentum sent me in a direct path of the runner.

We collided and both of us crashed to the ground, with me on the bottom. I hit hard and the wind rushed from my lungs. It took me a full thirty seconds before I could suck air back in, but that was also when I became increasingly aware of the rock solid male and breathing became difficult for an entirely different reason.

He still lay on top of me, although, now more so from the waist down, his legs tangled with mine in a very intimate manner. He leaned up on his elbows staring intently into my eyes.

"Grace? Are you okay?"

Hmm, he had nice blue eyes almost the color of the lake we'd swum in the other day. A part of me wanted to rub my hands along the soft fuzz of his facial hair, but I couldn't get my body to move.

His lips were moving and I vaguely heard his words. "Where are you hurt?" He turned his head away and my heart sank, but only for a second. Now his hands moved across my body. Checking my right arm. Then my ribs.

Ooh, don't stop. But his hands continued their path. "Can you breathe?"

No, No I can't, but not due to our fall.

I heard the pounding of running feet and knew others would join us shortly. It was time to get myself together. Caleb continued to ask questions but I couldn't answer yet.

Was I okay? Yes, I think so. I wiggled my toes in my shoes. Working. My fingers? Right hand moved fine. Left? My arm was above my head, hand still in the glove. When I flexed, I felt the ball still in the grip of my glove.

I blinked. There were now sneakers within my view. The other players had arrived to check on me. I took a breath. Yes. Breathing. In. Out.

"Damn it, Grace, talk to me."

I looked back into the sky blue eyes, full of fear and I felt a need so powerful to reassure him. So I said the only thing I could think of. "You're out."

I heard a burst of laughter from Aaron. "Ha. She's right. Good for you, Grace, good for you."

Caleb's mouth twitched with the suppressed grin he was good at, and his eyes sparkled, first in relief, but as our gaze stayed connected, his deepened and for the briefest of moments, I saw it. I recognized it. I knew it because it mirrored my own.

Attraction. Want.

He knew I saw it. As quick as it happened, he checked his emotions and pushed back onto his knees, holding his hand out to me. "Are you able to sit up?" His voice was back to being controlled and all business.

I nodded. His hand was warm and secure as he helped me sit, but then he stood and stepped away as the other players moved in to check on me.

Leland pushed his way through and knelt by my side. "Hey, sweetheart, are you okay?"

Sweetheart?

"I was so worried," he continued, but I was still stuck on the endearment. Sweetheart? What part of the 'friends only' conversation from Saturday did he not grasp?

"I'm fine." My response wasn't just to my suitor though, but to everyone standing around. I wanted them to move. To leave me alone again with Caleb.

But Caleb was nowhere to be found.

Chapter Eighteen

I figured we'd head to Aaron's place, like we did last week, but the twins had other plans. They brought Jake and me home for dinner with their parents.

I was hot and dirty and didn't want to be there. Especially when I saw Roger and Iris dressed in their Sunday best. Having been raised in the restaurant business, I was not a stranger of Emily Post etiquette of a four course meal. Neither was my companion, which at least put the two of us in a better position with the King and Queen of the town society.

Not that they were actually any better off than any other family. With the town paying for everything, everyone was almost all on an even standing, but this couple presented an air of superiority due to Roger's position on Town Council.

Our host kept the conversation going during the meal. "So, Jake, I understand your father is a surgeon. Quite an impressive job."

"It is, and I am a bit of a disappointment to him as I am three years into college and still haven't declared a major."

Iris did a small cough then covered it with a dab from her cloth napkin. But her husband didn't show any emotion as he continued. "And what do you think of our little town?"

Despite Jake's on-going battle with his cheating

father, he had been raised in the country-club scene and could be the perfect, polite liar whenever necessary. "I am finding it all very interesting. While I have heard of the concept of 'it takes a town', I'd never thought I would actually see one as self-sufficient as Wellington."

The man at the head of the table slid his knife into his steak and cut a piece which he dipped a corner into homemade steak sauce. "I've heard you are catching on quite well with the furniture business. Are you enjoying it?" He bit into his steak as he continued his focus on his guest.

Jake was quick with an answer. "Surprisingly, I am. I didn't think I would enjoy wood-working, but I've been told I'm picking it up quickly."

"Son, if you decide to stay on in our little town, you have a job waiting for you."

I nearly choked on a piece of corn and quickly grabbed my water glass as the man at the head of the table turned his attention to me. "And how about you, Grace? You've had a bit of a rocky start here. Are you feeling any more settled?"

Jake winked at me from across the table, and I bit back the urge to stick my tongue out at him. I could be just as polite as he when I put my mind to it.

"Yes, sir. My job at the school is quite easy. I'm used to helping out in a restaurant so fixing one menu item a day for fifty kids or so makes the day go quick."

Iris piped up. "I've heard wonderful things about your cooking skills. Perhaps you could teach me a thing or two. I am practically hopeless in the kitchen."

"Of course," I muttered then stuffed a mushroom in my mouth before I said something I shouldn't.

I spotted a glance between father and son and knew without a doubt the father was checking out the prospects for his children and had just put his stamp of approval on the two of us.

I wondered why he'd chosen the factory for Jake to work. Originally, I'd assumed it was to keep him on the opposite side of town from me due to our attempted escape. Thinking about it more, he could have been assigned to any number of farms as a young, strong, farmhand while still keeping us apart.

Here, though, at this table, I saw a different reason. Roger's daughter had her eyes set on this particular summer intern. Did she want to be with someone who wouldn't come home at the end of the day with dirt under his fingernails or dust on his boots? Or was that daddy's lofty goal?

And what was the head town councilman's thinking when it came to me and his son? Heaven help me. While Leland was nice enough, I wasn't interested. I found him to be a bit too white-collar for my taste. I preferred a man with a little more muscle; a little more passion about his work; a little more… Well, a little more 'not Leland'.

When the older Wellington stopped grilling me, I found my mind drifting to thoughts completely inappropriate for the dinner table. I did not imagine the look on Caleb's face earlier. No. He seemed as shocked by it as I was. Once I actually caught my breath, there was no denying I'd become completely aware of how intimately his body had pressed into mine. Or how I'd reveled in his touch, even while knowing it had been impersonal at the time.

Sure, I'd admired his body from afar more than

once, but those muscles were more than impressive as we'd landed and rolled. I wonder what it would be like to roll and tangle my legs with Caleb in the give and take of a mattress with no clothes blocking my access to view that span of muscles across his chest. I grabbed at my water glass and averted my eyes from those at the dinner table. Now was not the time or place for these thoughts.

I helped mother and daughter bring out the dessert course. As I put the plate of cheesecake in front of Leland, I wasn't immune to the look of heat and approval he sent my way.

Dear Supreme Being up above, what was happening here? I was meeting the parents of a man who wanted to have a relationship with me, while I was thinking of another man whom I could never be with, but none of it mattered because, in the end, I was counting the weeks until I wouldn't see either one again.

****

I woke in a great mood on Tuesday and I knew it had to do with Caleb. I had to see him. Talk to him. I would get through my work day and pull him aside when he came to pick up his kids at the school.

I had a song Straight and True had played stuck in my head. I didn't know the words, so I hummed as I worked. My upbeat attitude sent Jackie into a sour mood, more than usual, if that is even possible, and she doubled my workload. I wasn't near done when the bell rang at the end of the day and I missed my opportunity to see a certain man pick up his children.

I had no reason to head toward The Square and I wasn't about to waltz into the police station to visit him, so I went back home to help with dinner.

Leland called to see if I wanted to go bowling, which I declined. Instead I went into my room to read. A bit of a letdown to the day I'd planned.

Wednesday was more of the same. While the boss wasn't quite as mean, Sheila got tired early and I stayed late again, to help finish her work. This time I decided to walk down to The Square and hope for an opportunity to run into a certain lawman. I did see him from across the street as I sat on a bench near the diner. He and another officer were escorting two men still arguing loudly with each other even as they were led in handcuffs into the station.

I grinned as I watched. I recognized the brothers as Fred and Dave who had a tendency to argue and occasionally throw a punch or two. I was only on my third week here and already recognized most of the people. Maybe not all by name, yet.

I shook my head and walked away. What was I thinking? Yet? I wasn't planning on staying long enough to get to know everyone. Granted, it was a town with only around four hundred people with a third of them under the age of eighteen and I served a majority of those in the hot lunch line.

I spotted Jimmy in the playground as I walked home and decided to stop and say hello. While his body said he was a teenager, his mind was still a little boy and he made animal noises as he pulled himself across the monkey bars until he spotted me and came running.

"Hi, Grace."

"Having fun?"

He nodded. "Wanna play?"

I looked around at the kids playing and spotted a

couple swings open. "Swing?"

We sat and the oversized teddy bear of a boy immediately started pumping his legs to go higher and faster, while I kept a slow, steady pace. We didn't talk, but I enjoyed watching him, even when he got bored of the swings—- about two minutes into it—before heading to the merry go round to spin.

Thursday was more of the same, except by the time I left work, the students were gone and Leland was waiting outside for me.

"Come out with us tonight, Grace. Don't leave your friends hanging." He gave me a charming smile and I had no good reason to refuse.

We ended up at Barbara's house. Actually, I should say her parents' house. Here in Wellington, it was very rare for someone who was single to move out on their own. There were some exceptions, of course, such as Kurt and Amy's youngest daughter, but she worked with horses and was available to them at all hours, so she had a small apartment on the ranch.

Barbara's parents were in their very early forties and had big smiles and easy going natures. Barbara was the oldest of their kids. Ten in all, the youngest being six, all running around the back yard as chicken cooked on the grill. It seemed big families was the norm in this tiny town.

I thought for sure Friday would be the day I'd finally see my new obsession again. I had my work duties done before the bell rang and I rushed outside, my stomach doing the flip-flop thing in anticipation. Instead, I spotted the police cruiser driving away before the kids even made it outside. I waved to his mom, Rita, and headed to the shuttle with a heavy sigh.

I started to doubt the look we'd shared. If he'd felt the same connection, why wasn't he looking for an opportunity to see me? For the first whole week I didn't go a day where I wasn't in some sort of contact with the police chief. Now, when I wanted to see him, I couldn't seem to find him. Perhaps I would have better luck at The Hall tonight. I took extra care with my wardrobe, put on a touch of lip gloss, and pulled my hair away from my face then headed to meet the crew at our Friday night gathering to listen to the band play.

I participated in the conversations. I found creative ways to avoid Leland's hands when he went to move them from the back of my chair to my shoulders. I even danced, but more modestly than last week. But throughout the night, I kept my eyes scanning the room for the police chief.

I did see Officer Brent standing by the door, though. Obviously on patrol, keeping a watch over the crowd—and by crowd, I am talking a total of thirty people if lucky. Those who came on Friday nights were late teens to late twenties. Mostly single, but it included several young married couples without children yet. Once in a while, I'd spot an older couple or two at a table along the back, but they typically didn't stay for more than an hour.

"Hey, Theresa, is Brent working tonight?"

She looked at the door and back at me. "Yeah, why?"

I gave a non-committed shrug. "Just wondering why. We're not much of a rambunctious crowd."

She leaned in close to be heard over the music. "The chief insists an officer be on duty whenever there is a gathering. Every week, they take turns. I think

Caleb was here last week. Brent this week. Probably Thomas or maybe Greg next week."

I sat back, deflated. So he wouldn't be making an appearance. More than likely he was home putting his children to bed.

Just as well. I'm a fool to even think about pursuing something with him. I need to push him aside. Completely.

Saturday the skies opened and the day was a complete washout. No baseball. No Caleb. I took the time to cook, working side by side with Amy, preparing plenty of food to bring to the fellowship meal on Sunday.

I sat in the pew during the Sunday morning service, trying my hardest to sit still. I still had a hard time with the heavy-duty preaching of evil doings outside Wellington so I let my eyes roam as I tuned out the pastor. I finally had my eyes on the object of my obsession this week. His youngest was fussy so I watched as he carried her out. Without him to keep my interest, I searched out some of the other summer interns. Like me, they sat with their host families during the church service. I spotted Christy, who'd boarded the bus with us in Vermont. She listened intently, taking in every word with wide-eyed wonder.

Penny fidgeted a lot, but then I realized she kept trying to look at someone. Of course, I had to figure out who so I turned around, looking at her, then to where she kept glancing. She'd found a boy she liked. While the skinny red-head barely looked over eighteen, I figured he had to be out of school as I recognized almost all the kids there, if not by name, at least their faces. Even those in the high school, as I made a point to know where the bully Philip, was whenever possible.

When we moved into The Hall for the meal, I caught sight of Maria, another of the girls from the bus, and she, too, seemed to be falling under the spell of one of the Wellington males. As I stood in long line for the food tables. I scanned the room, hoping to spot the one man I'd been trying to find for a week.

Nothing. Nada. Zilch. The man was AWOL.

I barely noticed that the two men in my life, Leland and Jake, sat on either side of me at the table, until they had to lean over in order continue their very boring discussion about cars. For a town with very few vehicles, the Wellington resident was more than knowledgeable on the subject and I was very bored sitting between them. My roommate was nowhere to be found and I had no interest in talking with Hope.

Until A.J. sat directly across from me. I groaned. "What do you want?"

He smirked. "Who says I want anything? Can't a guy come and join his friends?"

I shut my mouth and tried to immerse myself in the world of vintage cars. For a few minutes I thought all would be fine, until I felt a foot sliding up the inside of my calf. I clenched my jaw and moved my legs back. A moment later, the foot was seeking out my legs again. "Knock it off."

He gave a knowing smile. "What? Oh, was that you?"

"Unless you were intending to play footsies with Jake, you know it is."

That got my friend's attention and he sent his own glare across the table. "What's your problem, bro?"

A.J. ignored him and instead turned to Leland. "So,

have you gotten in her pants yet?"

Both men on either side of me instantly reacted. The one on my left stood, ready to pounce, the other gave a terse warning. "Don't start trouble."

But it was obvious he enjoyed stirring things up. "Ah, come on, Lee. You've been hot on her tail for three weeks now. Are you not man enough to get a little something?"

He turned and gave me a cold glare. "Or is she just a hot tease?"

Both now stood. I gulped. The last thing I wanted or needed was these guys fighting my battles. Besides, we were in The Hall, surrounded by the entire town enjoying their fellowship meal. This interaction wasn't going unnoticed.

I put my hand on the arms of the two men beside me and tugged. "Sit down, both of you." I ordered, but neither complied. If it weren't for my grasp, keeping them in place, I am sure one or both would have lunged across the table. I stood, trying to take control.

"Let's get something straight, here and now." I interjected. "You spending a night in jail was your own doing by supplying and drinking alcohol. I spent the night in jail for my participation. We made choices; we paid the consequences. Your brother's choices caused him to land in the slammer. Done. Over. Why you continue to hold onto this is beyond me, but enough already."

The sneer I received told me what I'd said landed on deaf ears. "I don't believe my brother was to blame. His charge was aggravated assault with the attempt to rape which is a crock of bull."

Jake jerked out of my grasp and stared down at me.

"Is that true?"

"We'll talk about it later," I huffed.

The bully across from me continued his tirade. "I've heard how you were out on the dance floor, and I've seen you with Leland. You're a tease. So if anyone was to blame for the incident it wasn't my kid brother. You had to have said something, done something, to lead him on."

My mouth dropped. Before I could respond, Aaron came to the table. "Austin James you've said enough. Move on."

"What? Are you taking her side? No family loyalty?"

"I'm not taking sides, but you're causing a scene."

A hush had settled in the large overcrowded room as nearly the entire town sat and stared at our table. I looked around at the pious group, only this one cowboy had thought to step in to help someone in need. Or maybe it's because I am an outsider, I'm not worthy of their intervention. Perhaps they will pray for me tonight?

I started to laugh. I knew I was about to get myself in serious trouble, but I couldn't help myself.

"Oh, no," Jake muttered. He knew my brain had disengaged from my mouth.

"I understand it all now. You're jealous." A.J.'s eyes darkened as I spoke. "There are all of us newcomers here, eight of which are women, and not one of them chose you. Caroline is with Aaron. You see me with Lee. Penny, Isabelle and Maria have all found boyfriends, and poor A.J. is feeling left out."

"Grace." I heard my name and the tug on my arms as both men beside me tried to make me stop, but I was beyond that now.

"I'm not wrong, am I? I've been watching, paying attention. This town is in serious need of outsiders in order to grow, and here you are at twenty-two with no one to snuggle up with at night."

I turned to Jake, still holding my arm. "Be careful with her." I nodded toward the girl he'd been pursuing for the past weeks. "She doesn't need much encouragement to get her claws into you for good." I looked back at the one who'd started the scene. "This, whatever this is, is over."

I turned and walked away, weaving through the tables of townsfolk, and their twitter of conversations. I heard Caroline call after me, but I kept going. Once outside, I walked with no particular destination in mind. I turned left and kept going, away from the center of the town. I was heading the opposite of the gate we'd entered the first night coming to this town.

Yesterday's heavy rains had stopped, bringing with it heat and humidity. I passed the street leading to the school and kept going. The smell of manure hung heavy in the air, another reminder of the farms near my own home in Vermont. I hadn't ventured much farther down this quadrant of town before and I had no idea where the road would lead. To the cattle farms? I knew they had them, I hadn't seen them, though. Only chickens up on a distant hill.

I wiped the tears from my eyes. I'd cried more since I arrived in this town than any time in recent history. I missed my parents and my silly, always upbeat, sister. I should have gone home for the summer. Should have spent the time, hidden away in the office, doing the paperwork, setting the schedules. Instead, I opted to follow my roommate to keep her from doing something she'd regret.

Who was the one with regrets now?

I heard the engine from behind. Figures. I brushed the tears away, turned and waited. Caleb stopped the cruiser in the middle of the road—not like there was a lot of traffic here—and stepped out. For a week, I'd been looking for an excuse to see him and he'd been nowhere to be found. At the moment, though, he was the last person I wanted around.

"Aren't there any other cops in this God-forsaken town? They had to send you?"

Chapter Nineteen

Caleb leaned back on the hood of the car, putting one booted foot up on the bumper as he crossed his arms. "I heard what happened. Are you okay?"

"I'm fine. You can go."

Not that he would listen. Instead he turned to stare down the road. I hate when he is silent. I have an uncontrollable need to fill it. "I wanted to go for a walk. It's not like I can leave, anyway." Bitterness dripped in my tone.

"Do you want some company? To talk?"

I strangled back a laugh. "What's to talk about? It's the same story every time. I don't belong here. Can't we break the contract and let me go home?"

There was a flash of something in his eyes before he turned back to the horizon.

"What?" I asked. "What was that look? What aren't you telling me?" I moved to stand in front of him, wanting him to look at me and not over my head. "When I asked about the contract you turned away. Why?"

Caleb finally looked at me, but his eyes held no emotion. He was a master at putting up an emotional wall. "I'm not in charge of the contracts, Grace. My job is to make sure everyone follows them."

"Am I to believe I am the only one who is struggling this much? That in all the years this town has had interns, no one else has gone home early?"

Again, he looked over my head, avoiding my eyes. He changed the subject. "A.J. was out of line. I didn't realize he's still been bothering you. Trust me, after today, he won't come near you."

I snorted. "What are you going to do? Talk to his daddy so he'll give him an ass-whooping?" I semi-joked. "'Cause that's what you country boys do, right? Ass-whoopings?"

His half smile caught me off guard for a moment. It's the one he gives when I've amused him. It brightened my mood. Slightly. "We country-boys, ma'am, are taught at a young age to respect a lady. If we don't, then, yes, we suffer the consequences."

"Seriously, though, I don't wish him a beating or anything. I only want him to move on from those stupid incidents."

He gave a nod. "Consider it done."

I turned to face down the road. While the rain had stopped, the sky remained overcast. "Where does it lead? I haven't been out this way before."

"More farmland."

"All surrounded by fences?" I heard the longing in my voice. "Do the roads stop at the fences?"

He shifted his position against the hood of the car. "No, they lead to other towns. Mostly. This side leads to the hills so there's no exit."

I looked forward, then back at the road I'd traveled. "It's strange that a town is equally divided down the middle, don't you think?"

"The story goes, many, many years ago, the Wellington brothers bought a large parcel of land and divided it equally between four of them. Their Mama, being a smart woman, instructed them to each choose a different form of living, two chose livestock, another corn, and the last fruits and vegetables, so if there was a bad year for one, the others could be there to help.

"Then Mama had her home built in the center where the four farms met and demanded they all come to her every Sunday for dinner."

I listened to the deep timbre of his voice as he continued. "There was a fifth son, much younger than his brothers, who took over the homestead when Mama died. His wife was a schoolmarm who taught all of the Wellington children. As the families grew, they built their homes near Mama's original homestead, but choosing their plots along their parents' farm lines."

I cocked my head as he finished. "It's nice, knowing your family history and how the town has developed and grown. I never paid much attention to the history of where I grew up." I waved down the street. "But, when did they, you know, seclude themselves?"

Caleb gazed down at me, his blue eyes no longer distant, but almost warm and inviting. I'd nearly forgotten about my tears and my reason for leaving the fellowship hall.

"The gates went up long before I was born. I believe it was in the late sixties during the height of sex, drugs, and rock and roll."

"Really? No hippies allowed?"

His chuckle was deep. I liked the sound. "I've seen the school photos from back then and the Wellingtons were more pure-bred. No long-hair. No bell-bottoms on the women. And absolutely no smoking allowed."

I giggled. Then I poked him in the chest. "There is

still something about this town that doesn't sit well with me." I looked up at him, at his crossed arms, at his casual seat against his car. But there was nothing casual about him.

I poked him a second time. "No town in this day and age actually lives without televisions, or internet connections, or, coffee." I poked him a third time. "What the hell is it about not drinking coffee? It's madness."

He closed one fist over my hand and kept it pressed against his chest. My hand tingled under his. My breath hitched. I was finding it hard to concentrate on what he said.

"Those aren't bad things. It works for us here. We're happy. Our kids play outdoors and get exercise. They're not attached to their computer games, or their phones. It's healthy living."

I was getting distracted by the beat of his heart beneath our clasped hands. My argument was going to become ridiculous in a moment. That moment on the ball field, I felt it again. And with our hands held together, he had to be feeling it, as well.

Leland had said something similar to me at the lake. Maybe their way of life did work for them. It was too much for me.

"You said it yourself, Caleb, this town is what you know. You've been sipping on the Kool-Aid for all your life and are immune to it. It's all too foreign to me. If I start drinking, it'll be like poison and I'll probably die a long and painful death.

His free hand moved to swipe at the remnants of my earlier tears. His voice was soft but resonated within me, pulling me toward him. "I'm sorry you're so unhappy here."

My mood, my words, hung in the air between us, but my hand remained under his, against the strong wall of his chest. More than anything, I didn't want to lose that connection. "Well, you guys do like baseball, so I guess it hasn't been all bad," I admitted. Like this moment, right now. This was more than not bad.

"I'm glad to hear it." His voice deepened and I lifted my eyes from our hands up to his face. To his eyes as he intently watched me. My gaze lowered to his mouth and I watched as his lips bent down to mine.

And he kissed me.

For nearly a week, I'd thought of the look we'd exchanged on the ball field. I'd wondered if I'd only imagined the attraction between us. Now I knew without a doubt, it was real. All of it.

My heart beat double time as Caleb's lips explored mine and I closed my eyes. For a first kiss, I can't say I felt immediate heat of longing. No, instead it was filled with something less defined. It was as though we were pulled together by a magnetic force, like we needed to come together, but at the same time we both knew we shouldn't or couldn't let it go further. Despite it all, his hand moved from my cheek to the back of my head, pulling me closer as the kiss went on forever.

And when forever ended, I slowly opened my eyes, gazing up into his heavenly blue ones. "Why did you do that?"

"I've wanted to for a while." His voice was deep, raspy and, like mine, barely more than a whisper.

My heart sang a happy little ditty. He'd wanted to.

"I'm glad. I've wanted you to, as well," I made the admission in a voice filled with confusion at the need I felt. He had to feel it, too, because his mouth came back to mine.

This time he nibbled my lip, letting his teeth graze the lower one, sending electric waves through my body. I shivered, despite the oppressive heat of the day. I stood in his arms, pressed against his chest as the day stood still for us. What was happening between us? His mouth explored, tasted, setting off sparks, ready to touch off a flame.

The portable radio squawked inside the car, startling me, ending the heavenly kiss. "Chief, Fred and Dave are at it again. When Greg intervened, he got a punch to the face."

Caleb sighed. "I need to go."

I nodded, already knowing this moment was over, but instead of pulling back, he lifted my chin to place yet another gentle kiss on my lips. "Grace."

I heard it in his tone, knew what he was going to say before he did. "This—"

I pulled away, physically and emotionally "No. I get it."

He took my hand to kiss my palm and my heart twisted. "I can't explain, but we can't be together."

"It's okay. I didn't come here looking for a relationship. I'm only here until August. It's good. Fine."

He looked away again, but before he did I saw the distant look in his eyes. He'd shut down again. More secrets. He pulled me into his arms, hugging me close, letting his lips skim over my forehead for the briefest of moments. It was as though we were both lost and with each other we'd found a connection. "Come. I'll drive you back into town."

While it sounded like an invitation, part of me still wondered which Caleb had asked: the man who'd kissed me and wanted a few more moments together, or the police chief, ensuring I didn't find a way to leave town.

Chapter Twenty

Monday.

I felt like I'd been in this town forever, but when I looked at the calendar in the school kitchen, I discovered it was only the beginning of my fourth week. Jackie prepared the inedible selection of food for hot lunch, slamming pots as she went. Sheila, from what I was told, was currently in labor.

I could handle the older woman on my own for this final week of school. Come next week, who knows what my job assignment will be. Knowing that my humming drove the stern boss mad, I pasted a big smile on my face, sang songs completely out of tune—I'm sure with the wrong words—and served the students by name.

After my long work day, I headed to the hospital to see Sheila. They didn't have a specific maternity ward, the hospital was too small. Instead, I was directed to her private room.

Her entire family was there. I said hi to her husband, Cole, and to her oldest three children, Louise, Erin, and David whom I knew from school. Sheila's parents held the younger two, Michael and Anthony.

Sheila introduced me to her newest addition, Christian. I tentatively accepted the newborn when he was put in my arms. While I liked kids, for the most part, babies were an enigma. I preferred when they were old enough to actually tell me what they wanted. When the little bald-headed bundle opened his eyes to stare up at me, I'll admit to being just a bit enamored.

I left as soon as I could, avoiding any chance encounter with Dr. Todd and escaping the oohs and ahhs of parenthood. Who has six kids these days anyway? As I headed back toward The Square I spotted Kevin, one of the kids from the bus. One of 'us'. I stopped at the end of the lawn and waited for him to pull up to me on the John Deere tractor and shut the engine off. He wore a huge grin on his nicely tanned face. "Hey, Grace, how ya doin?"

I smiled back at him. "Doing good. This is your job?"

He gave a quick nod. "Landscaping. I love it. Mowing, mulching, weeding, trimming bushes. It's a lot of fun."

I nodded. "It's a great summer job."

"In the winter, I'll be helping with plowing."

That caught my attention. "But in the winter, you'll be back at college."

He shrugged. "Maybe. I don't know. I like it here. I asked if I could stay and they said yes."

Of course they did. What was it about this freaking town that everyone wanted to stay, everyone except me?

"You should finish college. And what about your family? What would they say?"

He climbed back onto the tractor. "My mom died when I was ten and my dad has a new girlfriend. He won't care. As for college, I can either go locally, or complete courses on-line." He gave me a quick wave and started the engine again. "I've got to finish this chore. I'm behind because of the rain last week."

I walked past the police station and my heart skipped a beat. I wondered if the chief was inside. If I went in, would he kiss me again? I got warm just thinking about it.

No. He wouldn't. Caleb was too…Reserved? Strong-willed? Proper?

That made me laugh. As much as I wanted to see him again, I moved on toward the shuttle bus stop only to see Jake, Hope, Leland, Aaron, and Caroline heading my way.

My tiny blonde roommate was practically skipping; her happiness kept her usual exuberance at an all-time high. "We were hoping we'd find you. We decided to go to the diner for supper tonight."

The group pulled tables together in the small restaurant and sat talking and laughing as though we'd been friends for a long time, not three weeks. The waitress came over to take our orders but she stopped when she got to me. "Oh, you're Grace."

I wondered why she'd singled me out. "Ah, yeah."

"You're working over at the school right now. Do you know what you will be doing when school's out?"

I fidgeted in my chair. "No. Been wondering the very same thing, actually."

"Would you consider working here?"

Jake laughed. "I hope you don't mean serving customers. My friend here has a reputation."

I kicked him under the table but looked back at the waitress. "I don't know." I didn't want to sound rude so I followed up. "What I mean is I don't know if I have a choice. Last time they assigned us to the work places."

She nodded. "I can talk to my brother. He might be

able to put in a good word if you're interested."

The waitress didn't wear a name tag. Then again, why would they need to, everyone knew everyone else here. I shrugged. "I guess. Who's your brother?"

The woman gave a sheepish grin. "Sorry, I forgot you wouldn't know. I'm Mary, Caleb is my brother.

She stuck out her hand and I took it. I was being offered a job in the diner, across the street from the police station. Across from a certain man that distracted me in ways I shouldn't be distracted. Did I want to be that close to him on a daily basis? To see him and want him to kiss me again, knowing it would never happen. No. Definitely not a good idea to work this close.

"So, um, I guess if you want to talk to him that would be okay with me." I never claimed I made smart choices.

Our waitress nodded then got back to business of taking food orders. Jake nudged me under the table with his foot. "Do you think working here, with food, with a town of people who tend to piss you off is a good idea?"

"Why?"

He waved a hand. "I'm thinking when you dump a plate of spaghetti on, say, the head of one of the councilmen, the owners aren't just going to ban you to the back office to do paperwork."

"Probably not, but maybe I'll do something that will cause them to say they don't want me here at all and let me go home early."

He pouted at me. "You would leave me here? Alone?" then he mouthed: *With her?*

I tried not to laugh as his summer fling tugged on his arm, wanting his attention back on her. "You made your bed, my friend."

****

Mary must have spoken to her brother immediately, because he showed up at the school the next day. Without Sheila, I was extra busy. Jackie had already left for the day, leaving me to finish cleaning the popcorn machine.

The school bell had rung about an hour before, so when I heard footsteps in the cafeteria, I expected to see the janitor come lumbering through the swinging doors to the kitchen area.

I looked up and did a double take when I realized it was Caleb. I stopped my scrubbing and leaned against the counter. "Hi."

It was the first time I'd seen him, talked to him, since The Kiss. The one that wasn't supposed to happen. I wanted to act like it had been nothing, but suddenly I felt shy and awkward.

A feeling I don't believe this man has ever experienced. He remained near the door, half a room away. All business. "I heard you had a job offer down at the diner."

I nodded. "I met your sister."

"Mary. Yes. She came to see me last night. Said they could use help for first shift, seven to two. It would be Tuesdays through Saturday."

I twisted the sponge in my hand, fighting the urge to move in his direction. I wanted to touch him; to run my hand along his firm jawline. I wanted to press my lips against his. But I took my cue from him.

"Okay. So it's back to the restaurant business I go." I hadn't meant for it to come out the way it did.

"Grace, if you don't want—" He ran a hand

through his hair, the first sign of exasperation I'd ever seen from him. "I know you wanted to leave that business for the summer, and if you don't want to work in the kitchen, I can find something else for you. My sister came to me so I thought I would ask. You went to school for business management. Maybe I can find something along those lines."

I cocked my head to the side as I took in his stance. He wasn't looking at me directly. Could he be avoiding me? Had he been as affected?

Of course not. He probably wanted to forget it had ever happened. He'd made it clear Sunday we shouldn't have gone down that particular path.

"What else could I do? I'm not allowed to use the computers and, with everything tracked by these bracelets, I'd think it would all be fully automated."

"Most of it is. The outgoing at least. The incoming needs to be input manually."

Hmm. Could be interesting. "Where?"

He remained silent a moment. "All the records from the trucks coming in and out are processed at Town Hall."

Two things struck me at once: One: I wasn't aware trucks came in and out of the town. Of course, if they didn't, how did the town get produce and products for the stores and diner? Two: Roger worked at Town Hall.

"I don't think I could work in the same building as the councilmen."

The corner of Caleb's mouth tilted slightly. "Probably not the best of ideas."

With a slight dent in his stand-offish stance, I felt my heart jump and the need to move closer bubbled to the surface. So I did what I had to do: I turned back to my tasks.

I sprayed more chemical on the glass and stretched my arm inside to wipe away the oil. "The job at the diner will be fine."

There was a moment of silence and I half-expected he would leave. Instead I heard him walk farther into the room. "Here. Let me help.

He moved to the other side of the center counter where I was working. He tipped the popcorn machine back slightly, giving me better access to the inside glass without having to stretch as much.

I gulped. With a counter and a machine between us, there was still plenty of distance, but I couldn't stop the way my eyes kept drifting beyond the oil on the glass to the chest on the opposite side. Or the tingles running through my body at the mere sight of him.

"Thank you," I murmured. Is this what Caroline felt when she was around the almighty Aaron? Is this feeling of want and lust why she followed a near stranger to a secluded town for the summer?

When I finished scrubbing, I grabbed a towel and wiped the inside surfaces dry. Before I could do anything else, Caleb lifted the machine and carried it to the other side of the kitchen, placing it gently on its stand.

I hung the towel on a rack to dry and looked around the room, looking for something else to do, every surface was spotless.

"It's late, are you done for the night?"

Just his voice did something to my insides. I had to stop this. I had to stop thinking about a momentary lapse in judgment and remember this man was a critical reason I wasn't allowed to go home.

"Yes, I believe so." I moved to exit the kitchen. He had longer legs and was across the room, holding the door open for me before I'd taken two steps.

I brushed by him, careful not to look up. If I did, eagle eyes would see what I wanted; what I knew he couldn't give me. But I was oh-so aware of him as he walked beside me out of the building. Aware of how much longer his legs were compared to mine, and how he slowed his stride to match mine.

"Would you like a ride home?"

Yes, my brain screamed. Was he just being a gentleman? Did I want to be in a closed up car with him?

More than anything.

"No. I think I'll walk. I've been indoors all day. The fresh air is nice."

He gave me one of the slight nods he was so good at and I gave a half-wave. "Have a good night," I offered and turned away, determined to put distance between us before I said or did something I would regret.

I walked fast, hoping to outrun my fluttering heart. The next couple months were going to be difficult if I couldn't get my wayward thoughts under control. Caleb was off limits. End of story.

I only wished I could forget his kiss.

Chapter Twenty-One

The weekend came and we spent Friday night with our regular routine of listening to Straight and True play at The Hall. Leland was extra attentive and wanted to dance every song, while I spent the evening pushing his wandering hands back to a more respectable position.

I did get a chance to dance with Jake, though the entire time all he did as lament about his girlfriend.

"Damn, the girl runs hot and cold. I've never gone four weeks with someone and not had sex."

"You poor thing." I glanced over at the siren currently helping herself to a bottled water. "But, do you have to sleep with her?"

The usually graceful man nearly stumbled over my feet. "Why? Jealous?"

I rolled my eyes. "You've slept with more women than years I've been alive. It's this place, and the people here. I don't trust any of them. I think banging her would be bad."

He looked past my shoulder to the one in question and brushed off my concerns. "She knows I'm only here for the summer and yet she is all over me, sending me all the right signals. I'm not doing anything she doesn't want. It's just she encourages me to go so far then throws on the brakes last minute. I'm almost regretting leaving Layla behind. Almost."

"Think about it. The entire town is populated by her relatives. It's not like she's out there having casual affairs. Don't let her test the waters with you."

He spun me around the dance floor. "I see your point. I'll be a good boy."

If only I could get Leland to be as good.

****

Saturday was game day. The weather worked with us, meaning no rain. However, heat and humidity were not as kind. Then again…

I wore shorts and a tank top under my red mesh pinnie vest. I tucked my pony-tailed hair under my baseball cap as I started on a bottle of water before the game began. Today was going to be a scorcher and not just due to the weather.

I discovered most of the players, except for the women on the team, decided to play sans shirts, using only the color-coded vests for their team. My mouth went dry as I watched from the red side dugout as one certain male from the blue team stripped his gray t-shirt over his head before grabbing for his vest. But not before I'd been given one clear view of his broad chest and ripped abs.

It was official. I was not going to make it through this game without making a fool of myself. I turned away and gulped my water.

"Grace, there is both water and sports drinks in the cooler," Aaron called out. "Make sure to stay hydrated today."

I nodded, lifting my bottle in acknowledgment.

Perhaps it was the heat, but the game moved at a slow pace. There wasn't a lot of hits from either team and when someone's ball did connect, there was a quick and easy out.

At the bottom of the fifth, Blue team was leading, one-zip, when I went to bat and hit into the outfield. I ran past first and headed to second when A.J. cut across my path and we collided.

I jumped to my feet and went nose to nose with him. "What the hell do you think you're doing?"

Before I could get into any sort of altercation, Aaron was off the pitcher's mound and between us, pushing me back. Caleb moved into my spot in front of his teammate. With the two larger men's quick intervention, I'd been quickly and effectively removed from the situation.

"I made myself clear last week you were to leave Grace alone."

The younger player became defensive, his hands folding into fists. "Yeah, I heard you, but you're not my father. I don't have to listen to you."

In an aggressive move that seemed uncharacteristic of the usually calm chief of police, he grabbed the bully by the vest and hauled him up onto the toes of his shoes. "I know I'm not your father. Our father was banned from this town. Do you want to end up like him?"

"Holy—" My jaw dropped. "Are they brothers?"

Aaron looked down at me as he still held my arms, keeping me from interfering. "You didn't know?"

I shook my head as the two continued to argue, with the refs surrounding them.

"Half-brothers, actually. Caleb's father had an affair with a runaway. Caused the first divorce in almost thirty years here. Quite the scandal. But when he had another affair later, the town ousted him. He's not allowed to return, or to see any of his children."

"Oh." I continued to stare as the brothers argued and the referees worked to separate them.

"Looks like the refs are calling the game."

"But we're only in the fifth inning."

The team pitcher smiled down at me. "It's not the major leagues, kid. When the fighting and arguing start, the game ends."

I made my way back to the dugout. A.J. stormed off and Caleb headed back to his side's dugout. I watched as he slid his t-shirt back over his perfectly sculpted body. Damn, I had it bad.

I suddenly felt hot and grimy so I pulled my hat off and poured half my water over my head, reveling in the coolness as it slid down my neck.

"Are you okay?"

I jumped and squealed when I heard the unexpected voice from behind. I dropped my water bottle spilling its contents on the ground.

"Jesus, Mary, and—" I spun around and stopped mid-sentence as I got a raised eyebrow for my sins. "Sorry," I mumbled, "I didn't expect you to sneak up on me."

"I asked if you were okay. You were knocked down pretty hard."

I was eye level with his broad chest and bulging biceps. The man was a sculptured Adonis. I know he asked a question, and I think I am supposed to say something. Anything would be good, but all I could think about was how I'd poured water on my head and now I probably looked like a drowned rat.

"I'm fine." But leave it to me, when I did find my voice, not to leave well enough alone. "How did I not know before now that A.J. is your brother? Not once did it come up even when I made the crack about going to his dad."

He closed his eyes as he took in a deep breath. "Not intentional. We sometimes forget outsiders don't know all the family dynamics here."

I pushed water off my forehead. "Sure. Whatever. I've been harassed by him for the past few weeks. We've talked about him more than once, and you couldn't say word one, so now I look like a damn fool." The bleachers had emptied, as had the dugout, and I suddenly felt claustrophobic despite being outside.

"I have never once thought you a fool."

Once I started, I couldn't stop. "So much makes sense now. The first day, out in the woods, when they said to run because big brother was coming, I thought they meant that as an analogy, not, well, you get my point."

I drifted off because Caleb's eyes were wandering up to my forehead, where another droplet of water was about to fall from my hair. When it did, he reached out to catch it and his fingertip landed on my chest, on the bare skin above my shirt.

I suddenly felt electrified. The cool water, his warm finger, the unmistakable heat in his cobalt eyes. He slowly wiped the droplet from my skin, his gaze never leaving mine as he left a fiery trail from my chest up to my shoulder where he finally dropped his hand.

He didn't say a word, and once again, the silence begged me to fill in the gaps. But what do I say to a man who'd made it clear we shouldn't be together and whose eyes had a habit of shutting off emotion with a single blink.

I had a more difficult time shutting down, but I would do my best. My tirade was over now. Instead, I was left breathless as I attempted and failed at a casual escape. "Well, I should go. Shower. Cool down. Uh, you know, from the game."

"I thought you were joining us at Aaron's tonight," he reminded me. "I heard you made dessert."

Crikey's. It almost sounded like he wanted me to go. Or was that wishful thinking on my part? "Oh. Right." Aww, hell, I'd become a stammering mess. "Yes. I'll be there after my shower." I turned on my heel and walked briskly away.

I should never have let that man kiss me. Now every time I see him, I can't think straight. It was like he'd scrambled my brain. And all the kings horses... How many weeks until I was back on the bus home? Not soon enough.

My hand moved to my chest where his finger had skimmed and I briefly closed my eyes. My mind says no, but my heart says I can't wait to see him again tonight.

****

There were not as many of the players at Aaron's parents' house as I'd expected, but I still managed to keep my distance from Caleb. Or maybe he stayed away from me. Leland stayed glued to my side as we ate and later as we sat in the backyard, exchanging stories.

In all, there was about a dozen of us, which made staying quiet almost unnoticeable. I laughed at all the right places and I don't think anyone noticed my glances across the darkened yard to a certain off-limits officer of the law.

The crowd began to dwindle around nine-thirty; by ten I decided it was time to leave. Leland was currently in the house; Aaron and Caroline had disappeared a while before; and the man I'd been avoiding had left to put his children to bed.

Jake saw my high sign and pushed his girlfriend from her position on his lap. "Sorry, baby, but I'm going to call it a night. Why don't you take your brother home and I will make sure my friend makes it back to her door."

His girlfriend pouted. "Why don't we all walk Grace home, and then you can walk me home, too." Her voice lowered but not to the point where I couldn't hear her. "And maybe have a little good night kiss?"

He laughed. "I'm thinking you want that too much. I'm going to make you wait. Maybe tomorrow night."

The tall blonde threw an angry glare my way before storming away in a huff. Her power pout didn't faze my friend as he stood and put out a hand to me. "Your escort home awaits, me lady."

"Aww, you are so sweet. Foregoing a lip-lock with Goldilocks on my behalf."

"I was hoping you would stand in her place, for my chivalry."

That earned him an eye roll. "Dream on, lover boy. Come on, let's say our goodbyes and blow this place."

Before we could move, Caroline rushed at me from the corner of the house. With a loud squeal, she jumped into my arms. "Oh, Grace, you won't believe it." She gave me a huge hug and then stood back to do a little dance. "It's wonderful, wonderful, wonderful."

Jake and I exchanged a glance that asked, now what?

"If it's so wonderful, do you think you could fill us in?" I reached out to stop in her place and turned her to face me.

She grabbed my hands and bounced up and down. "Aaron asked me to marry him and I said yes."

Chapter Twenty-Two

Time managed to stand still despite my roommate spinning around like a top. "What?"

"Isn't it just fabulous?"

"No. No it's not." She barely heard me. "You've only known him a month. You can't get engaged this soon."

"Oh, Grace, you don't understand. He's the one. He makes me so amazingly happy. I feel complete when I am around him."

I sent Jake a glare, begging him to help me.

"I'm glad he makes you happy," he chimed in, "but you are planning on having a long engagement, right? Finish your last year of college?"

Thank you, thank you, thank, you. I was too much in shock to have come up with any sane reasoning. I spotted the man in question coming toward us and I wanted to get through to my friend before he arrived.

"Yes," I said. "Please tell us that is your plan."

But she had spotted her new fiancé and rushed to him, grabbed his hand, and pulled him to us. "They're not happy for us."

Ugh. Not fair. "I am happy for you. Truly. I want nothing but the best for you," I explained, "but you barely know each other. You need more time."

They wrapped their arms around each other. Two as one. "Please be happy for me. I want you to be my maid of honor. In two weeks."

"Two weeks?" I screeched. "*Two? Here?* What about your family? You can't possibly get married without them. And to a man they know nothing about."

"Grace, Aaron is everything I ever wanted in a man, in a husband. And this place is perfect for me. I fit in. I belong."

I looked to the two men standing beside us. "Can you excuse us for a moment?" I pulled my friend away, into the darkness by the house. "Caroline Parker, I love you. You are my best friend. I have been blessed to have you as a roommate for the past three years. However, you can be a bit naïve and unworldly at times." I held up my finger when she went to interrupt. "But please, please, please, tell me you are not rushing things because you are horny."

Even in the dark shadows I saw the blush creep up her face. "Aaron is such a gentleman and we have barely done more than kiss. I want to be with him and he said he won't touch me until we are married."

I groaned. I hate when I'm right. "Exactly my point. If he is the right one, waiting will only make it better. You have to wait. When the summer is over, bring him home to meet your parents. Come and visit him for Christmas break. Finish your degree and plan a true wedding for next June. Have the fairy tale, white-gown, choirs singing, walk down the aisle type of wedding you've dreamed of all your life."

"But I am," she assured me. "Aaron said if we plan this for two weeks out, we will have time for me to order a dress and get our rings."

Aaron this. Aaron that. He had her completely under his spell. There was no way I would make her see any sense. "Then you will be without a maid of honor. I can't watch you rush into this."

I turned on my heel and stomped away, despite the hitch of a sob from my friend. As I walked the streets alone heading back to my host home, I felt my irritation grow. When I saw lights on at Caleb's house, I redirected and pounded on the door.

I'm not sure what I would have done if his mom or stepdad had answered, but fortunately for me the man I wanted to see opened the door.

"Did you know about this?" I demanded. "Did you know Aaron was going to propose?"

"Ahh." He stepped outside and closed the door behind him.

"What does that mean?"

He motioned to the rocking chairs on the front porch but there was no way I was sitting down. "You haven't answered me."

Caleb took my lead and instead leaned against the porch railing. "No, I wasn't aware of any proposals."

I paced back and forth. "You're his friend. You have to talk him out of it."

"Why? He's happy."

I whipped around. "They are getting married in two weeks. *Two!* Tell him they need to wait. He needs to meet her family first. Caroline needs to finish her degree."

As usual, the man beside me remained calm as my own agitation grew. "What makes you think I have any say in this?"

"For Christ's sake, someone needs to talk sense into him."

I trailed off as the front door opened. Rita popped

her head out. "Everything okay out here?"

"All set, Mama. I'll close up if you want to head upstairs."

"The windows are open, so please watch your language."

"Sorry, ma'am," I muttered.

The moment the door closed I continued my tirade, this time keeping my voice low. "Do you have your phone on you?"

I noticed a slight straightening of Caleb's stance. "Why?"

"I need to call Caroline's parents and tell them their daughter has gone off her rocker."

He shook his head. "I can't. No phones. For any reason." He stood and moved toward me and I tilted my head back to look up at him in the dim light of the porch.

"No, you're wrong. She is my friend, and I can't stand by and watch her rush into something she will regret later." I held my hand out again. "You have to let me use your phone. It's an emergency situation. If there is any time to bend the damn rules it's now."

He stood his ground. "Caroline is old enough to make her own decisions. It's not up to us to interfere."

"Fine, I'll get it myself." I reached out and patted his right front pocket. Nothing. Then his left. I felt the outline but before I could slide my hand inside, my wrist was grabbed in a steel vice.

"Enough."

I felt tears of frustration welling to the surface. "I came to this stupid town to make sure my impulsive roommate didn't make a mistake exactly like this. If she won't listen to me, and you won't help, then I need to call her father."

"I can't help you. I took an oath to uphold the laws and rules of Wellington. Currently you are under contract that states no phones. I cannot be a part in allowing you access."

I pulled my hand away and turned to pace before I had another idea. "But you are allowed phone access. You can call her parents for me."

He looked above my head, the shuttered look in place. "I don't think so. I can talk to the Council on Monday, but I don't think they'll approve it."

"Agghh! You are useless. If you won't help, I'll find someone who will." I brushed past him to go down the front steps and turned back toward the town square.

"Grace?" Caleb called after me. "Where are you going?"

I didn't answer. He wouldn't like it anyway. I kept going but his legs were longer and he was beside me in a few strides. "Grace?"

"Don't worry. I'm not planning an escape."

"So where are you going?"

"To find a phone. I am calling her parents."

"And where do you plan to do that?"

I hadn't thought my plan through, yet, but there were places with phones readily available. Such as the hospital. Or the police station.

Chatty Connie, the switchboard operator, had mentioned outside calls went through police dispatch. That should be interesting.

"Go home," I bit out. "Pretend you are not the police chief for a moment and pretend I didn't come asking for your help."

"But I am and you did."

Damn him for being so cool and calm all the freaking time. I turned left, heading down Main Street toward The Square. Hospital or police station?

"What if I said I just need to walk for a while to blow off steam? Would you go home?"

"Nope."

"Fine. I'll head home. No passing go. No collecting two hundred dollars. Are you happy?"

The infuriating man continued to keep pace. I passed the police station and kept going. No use going anywhere with this man beside me. A few short hours ago, I wanted an opportunity to have a quiet moment with Caleb, now I wished he would disappear.

Then again, maybe this was a good thing. Strutting into a police station and demanding to use a phone probably is not the brightest idea I've ever had. I would have to use the phone at my host home and ask for the outside line and avoid a direct confrontation.

"He must have been one hell of a guy that broke your heart.

I turned abruptly to face him, walking backward. "What? Where did that come from?"

He shrugged. "You've been against Caroline and Aaron from the beginning. I figure someone broke your heart and now you have something against love."

I turned my back to him, picking up my pace. "One has nothing to do with the other."

"So someone did break your heart."

"I didn't say that." He was confusing me with this change in conversation. "Why won't you go away?"

"It's late. My momma taught me to walk a lady home."

"Agghh." I threw my hands up and turned another

corner. I kept my mouth shut while I stormed down the streets until I reached my temporary home.

"I'm here. You did your duty, now go."

Caleb stopped at the end of the walkway and gave a little salute. "Have a good night, Grace." And he waited until I was inside.

I leaned against the door. If I waited long enough, he would leave. So I stood for an eternity. Without a watch, I don't know how long it was, but eventually, I moved upstairs and peeked out the front window. I didn't see him.

I went to the phone on the table in the corner and picked it up.

"Operator, how can I help you?"

I didn't recognize the voice. It wasn't Connie. Instead it was the voice of an older woman. "Yes, could you put me through to an outside line, please?"

"One moment while I put you through to dispatch."

There was a series of clicks before a man answered. "How can I help you?"

"I'd like an outside line, please."

"This is Grace, right?"

I hesitated. Should I lie? If they knew it was me, they'd say no, but they probably already knew which house was calling and knew it wasn't Amy.

"Does it matter? I need to make a call."

"Sorry. Chief already called. You are under contractual orders to have no outside contact during the length of your stay."

"Well, you can tell your chief what he can do with the damn contract." I slammed the phone down on its cradle.

I had two weeks, fourteen days to find a way to

contact the Parker family and the chief had made sure it wasn't tonight. There was no way I'd be sleeping so I headed into the kitchen and the cooking commenced. By morning, I had cookies, brownies, and a half-baked plan ready to go.

****

I wrote a note for my hosts, telling them I'd had a late night and a bit of a headache. I said I would meet them at church and asked if they could take the treats to the fellowship hall with them, then I headed down to my bedroom to wait.

I yawned as I heard the couple moving around. Lack of sleep was catching up with me, but determination alone kept me awake. When they were gone, I took a quick shower and when I was done the numbers on the clock reassured me ninety percent of the town would be inside the church listening to the sermon.

I zig-zagged the streets to avoid The Square and the church in its center and came up on the hospital from behind. Being Sunday, I knew there was only a bare minimum of staff on sight as even the doctors were only on-call.

I didn't recognize the woman at the hospital front desk as I approached. Her name tag said: Nicole. I squinted my eyes and held my hand to my head. "Hi. I have a bit of a migraine today and was hoping to get something to help ease the pain."

The woman looked me over and I'm sure my lack of sleep helped my cause. She nodded and asked me to swipe my band for identification.

I gulped as I did, certain that damn police chief had a buzzer for whenever I did something out of the ordinary. I was told to sit in the waiting room while she paged the doctor. I did, but chose a chair facing the door, ready to bolt if the chief came in.

I waited two minutes then went back to the desk. "I'm sorry to be a bother." I wasn't, but she didn't know that. "I know everyone is at church right now and the doctor could be a while. Could I possibly go and lay down? These lights are hurting my eyes."

I think I had the poor nurse convinced. She gave a concerned look and told me to follow her. She led me down the hall to a private room where I lay down and the nurse kindly turned the lights off for me.

Once I heard the patter of her feet disappear, I crept to the door. The halls were empty. I tip-toed down the opposite end of the hall, turned a corner and discovered an unattended nurse's station. I moved around it and spotted a telephone on the corner of the desk. Jackpot.

I picked up the receiver and put it to my ear. No dial tone. What the hell? I looked around until I spotted the gadget to scan the wrist bands and my heart immediately sank. I had to register my ID in order to use the phones.

Screw it. I'd come here for a reason. I swiped my bracelet and lifted the phone again.

"Operator, how may I direct your call?"

Here we go again. "Please patch me over for an outside line."

I heard the clicks and then another voice. "Dispatch."

"Hi, this is Nicole. Dr. Todd has requested an outside line in order to get additional medical history on a current patient."

"Nicole? The ID is reading the name Grace."

I knew this wasn't going to work, but not one to give up, I continued anyway. "That's our patient. She's with me now. Her bracelet must have been closer than mine when I picked up the phone."

The man on the other end was silent for a moment and I thought for sure I was busted. Then he spoke again. "What is the number?"

Yes! "Eight-Oh-two, four-four—" I gulped as a figure stopped in front of the desk and motioned for me to hand over the phone.

Damn this tracker bracelet.

I stepped back from the counter, keeping a firm grip on the handset. "—Zero, one-three—" The phone went dead as Caleb leaned over the counter and pushed the button down, disconnecting the line.

"Shouldn't you be at church?" I taunted.

He motioned for me to put the receiver down. "I could ask you the same thing." His voice was low, dangerously low. The man was not happy.

"I'm not really the church-y type of gal." I let go of the receiver, letting it swing down before I took a step back away from the counters.

"That's too bad, because your contract says you are."

I cocked my head. "No, I don't believe I read that anywhere."

He moved, coming around the counter and sauntered toward me. I had nowhere to go. "I do believe the contract you signed specifically stated you would follow all town rules and policies which includes no drugs or alcohol or acts considered to be immoral. Here in Wellington, we keep the Sabbath as holy and attending church is mandatory, unless you are sick or on an assigned work duty. I'd be happy to show you the town rules and policies back at the station."

I had no interest in seeing the policies and he knew it. Without taking his glance off me, he placed the receiver back on the phone. "While you may not have been aware of that specific rule, you are quite informed that during the duration of your contract, you will not have access to phones or the internet. Am I correct?"

I was one hundred percent screwed. "You know I had to do this. You know my entire reason for being here this summer was to make sure Caroline didn't do something impulsive."

He stopped in front of me and I craned my head up to look at him. This was the Caleb from day one when I boarded the bus. The man whose very presence took the breath from my body and made my knees quake in fear. This was the Caleb I didn't want to mess with. I'd broken the rules, again, and he was the law-man who was going to make sure I suffered the consequences.

"What happens now?" My voice was barely above a whisper.

"I can't trust you to play by the rules. You have broken the bonds of your contract several times already and given the opportunity, I believe you will continue to do so."

Despite my growing fear, I tried to reason with him. "In my defense, all the other times were within the first couple days of being here. I have been exceptionally good for the past three weeks."

He raised an eyebrow.

"Okay, except for the time at the pharmacy." When he continued to give me a look of expectation I continued. "So I didn't tell you the whole truth about what happened at the school, but that time I was the victim."

He closed his eyes for a moment, as though he needed a moment to gather his thoughts and figure out what he was going to do with me. "As of this moment, you and I are the only ones who know about this incident. Let's go back to the Fellowship Hall and you can make your presence known without causing any further issues."

"Does that mean I am off the hook?" It didn't make sense, but I held out hope the nice, fun Caleb was returning.

He shook his head. "On the contrary. Cause and effect. Action and reaction. Let's make our presence known and I will deal with you later."

He stepped aside and I sulked as I passed him. I had a feeling I wouldn't like the consequences metered out. As we headed down the hallway, Dr. Todd came toward us and I stopped short.

Just the sight of the man had me nearly hyperventilating. Caleb stepped up beside me, placing one hand on the small of my back. Ironically, despite my current feelings toward the chief, I found the gesture comforting.

"Grace, where are you going? I was told you had a migraine."

I gave a frozen stare and it was the man beside me who intervened on my behalf. "Actually, Todd, I spoke with your patient, here, and after she told me she'd done a marathon night of baking, I convinced her what she needs is sleep and not medication to cure what ails her."

The doctor looked back to me and cocked his head.

"You do look a bit pale, though, are you sure you don't want me to do a quick exam?"

I may have gone sheet white, or perhaps it was my hand curling into a fist, but Caleb's hand moved from my back to instead clasp my hand in his. With him as a lifeline, I found enough of my voice to answer.

"No, thank you. The chief is right. All I need is sleep and perhaps a bit of tea and I'll be fine in a couple hours."

"I applaud you, dear. We pride ourselves on using medication as a last resort when there are healthier alternatives."

We moved to leave and the chief tactfully placed himself between me and the doctor as we passed in the hallway. Once we reached the outdoors I sucked in a deep breath, taking a few minutes to find my composure.

"Ready?"

Despite the fact he was not happy with me, and was about to dish out some unknown punishment for my alleged crime, he still managed to show compassion and understanding for my reaction to the town's medical personnel. For that I was thankful.

I pulled myself together and we walked in silence the couple blocks to The Hall. Church had let out and the place was crowded. Caleb remained by my side as we filled our plates, then he leaned down to speak quietly in my ear. "Enjoy your food. Meet me at the station at one and we will discuss consequences."

Chapter Twenty-Three

I found the table where my usual group ate and slid onto the bench beside Caroline who immediately put her arms around me and squeezed. "Gracie, I was afraid you were avoiding me."

I looked beyond her to her, *gulp*, fiancé. "I want to talk to both of you."

Aaron bit into a piece of extra crispy bacon but nodded and held his finger up for me to wait. Then he spoke. "I understand your wariness of how quick we've moved, but I want you to know I love Caroline very much. I've loved her from the first moment I saw her."

I pushed food around on my plate, not recognizing what I'd loaded it with. "I don't doubt it. She came back to our dorm, swooning. But do you realize that was only eight weeks ago? After four weeks of seeing you outside a coffee shop—which I find ironic now—she followed you home. But I came because of this very reason. You two need more time to get to know each other.'

My best friend held my hand. "I don't need more time. I know without a doubt we are meant to be together."

"Then wait." I pleaded. Even if it's until the end of the summer when our contract is over and you can go home. Right now, you're not even allowed to call your parents to tell them. You told me during our freshman year the reason you went to college was to explore and expand your life knowledge."

Her mouth twisted. "My family dynamics are different than yours. I'm the youngest and all my siblings are out of the house, married with children. While my parents may have said they wanted us to go out and get a great education, the lesson all of us learned the most was the importance of family. That's what I see here in Wellington. It's like one big, blended family, homeschooling their kids in one building.

"Coming here opened my eyes, Gracie, to how much I want to have a big family and give them what I had, only on a bigger scale."

My heart sank. Caroline was a lost cause. She'd made her mind up so I focused on her partner. "Do you hear what she is saying? Family is important."

"Of course. We both agree."

"Great, then how can you let her get married here, alone, without her family giving their blessing, when you are surrounded by your own?"

I saw a spark of doubt fleck in his eyes. Bingo.

"I am not telling you not to get married. All I am saying is you need to do it so you are making two families into one, not just adding a single member into your home."

When the meal was over, I believed I'd driven the point home for the newly engaged couple, or at least had them thinking. When I stood to clear the table, Leland appeared at my side. "Why did you sit way over there? I missed you down on our end of the table."

"I wanted to talk to Caroline this morning."

He walked beside me to the food table as I collected the platters my desserts had been on. "We all decided it would be fun to go on a hike this afternoon. Want to come?"

"Can't," I mumbled. "After I bring these home, I have a meeting."

He laughed. "What kind of meeting do you have on a Sunday?"

"Doesn't matter. I can't go with you."

He put a hand on my arm to stop me. "Are you avoiding me?"

I closed my eyes and prayed for patience. "No. I have things I need to do which don't include you, okay?"

I saw the pout before he changed his expression as he threw on the charm. "I'm sorry, sweetie, I didn't mean to make you upset. You're different today and I want to make whatever is bothering you better."

I spotted Jake waiting by the door for us, while Hope pulled on his arm, trying to get him to leave. He gave me a thumbs up sign and I nodded yes seconds before the jealous girlfriend pulled him from my sight.

"Go have fun, Lee. I'm sure we'll get together throughout the week."

He walked me outside then peeled off to join the group as I headed back to my host home to clean dishes before meeting with my judge and jury.

****

I arrived at the station and wiped my sweaty palms on my shorts before walking in. Being Sunday, the place was empty. There was only one row of lights on. I spotted the chief inside his office; someone was in there with him.

I moved slowly, hoping I'd have to wait. I wasn't in any hurry to have this follow-up, but he spotted me and motioned me to enter.

The man sitting in a chair across from the desk looked to be around Caleb's age, with dark hair and glasses. He had a laptop open and he stopped typing to give me a smile.

The chief had his quiet stern face in place as he motioned toward the other man. "Grace, have you met Randy?" The man held out a hand and I tentatively took it for a quick shake. "He is my computer guru. Anything I need with regard to our security in town, he's my guy."

I gulped, not sure where this was going.

"I have asked Randy to update your security restrictions to alert me when you are not at your usual locations. So, when you enter or leave your home, I will get an alert. Same as when you enter and leave your job."

I shifted on one leg and glared at him. "Are you saying that isn't already in place? How did you know where I was so soon this morning?"

I swear the man was a robot, devoid of any emotion as he spoke. "I ran into Kurt before church as we brought our food into The Hall. After last night, I asked where you were and he mentioned you'd overslept after baking all night."

I rolled my eyes. "Whatever. So now when I arrive at the diner in the morning, you'll know."

"Actually," he paused and I had a strong feeling I wasn't going to like what he had to say. "Your job assignment has also changed. You will now be working for me, here at the station."

That got the fire stoked. I'd maintained a civil tongue up until now, but the latest turn of events shot my adrenaline up to a thousand percent. "Doing what?"

"Whatever is needed. Typing reports. Cleaning the cells. Getting our lunches."

"That's a sucky job," I huffed. "The diner is expecting me in the morning. It's across the damn street. There's no reason why you can't monitor me from there."

"Sorry, Grace, actions have consequences. Randy, how are the security updates going?"

"Good to go."

I turned on the man in the chair. "How does someone get to be a computer genius in a town with limited computer access?"

The man in the chair closed the laptop. "I wasn't born here. I met Caleb at boot camp. We became friends. When he moved back here two years ago, I came with him, fell in love with his sister, and stayed."

I folded my arms across my chest. "Figures." I looked back at my security enforcer. "Am I free to go?"

He nodded. "I will see you here tomorrow, oh eight hundred, sharp."

"Bite me." I turned on my heel and exited. I heard a distant ping and I had an idea. I was going to bounce all over the place today and have that man's stupid phone pinging him constantly.

I walked, fumed, and walked more. I headed to the school and out to the woods behind. I left there and made my way to the baseball fields, taking a few minutes to let out every curse I could think of even though there was no one to hear them. Once I walked back to town, I spotted the shuttle station and decided to hop on board the one headed south. I got off at the end which was near Jackson's farm.

And prayed to every higher power in existence that Caleb's phone was pinging off the hook.

I didn't go down the dirt road to the homestead, instead I walked along the fence and eventually made my way to the line of trees on the far side of the property. I spotted a path and kept walking. The overhang of trees gave shade to an otherwise hot day, and after what must be nearly two hours of rambling, plus a night of not sleeping, I was almost regretting my impulsiveness of wandering the town.

I kept walking until I came to an opening and sighed in relief. I'd stumbled upon the lake where we'd swum a couple weeks ago. Perfect. I took off my sneakers and waded up to my ankles in the tepid water, letting the calm of nature wash over me.

Maybe I was being childish, running all over town like this, but everything about this place was like a noose on my neck, strangling my freedom. My tantrum last night and today had only tightened the rope, with no beacon of hope in sight.

Finding a phone still seemed the best course of action, but how was still the burning question. There wasn't anyone I could trust to help me make contact outside of town. Even Jake was blinded by this Stepford town, or at least by a blonde sex siren.

I found a place to sit down to rest and watched as the sun moved across the sky. I put my sneakers back on but let my fingers brush against the almost brown grass. I'd bet if this spring hadn't been so dry, the grass would be an amazing contrast to the crystal clear blue of the lake. Despite its lackluster color, it had been recently mowed. Was there any part of the town not perfectly manicured?

While I was back to hating Wellington and everyone in it, this tiny patch of land was medicinal. A butterfly briefly touched down on the ground before taking flight again. I heard the chatter of squirrels in the woods behind me. I lay back, put my hands behind my head and stared at the fluffy white clouds until my eyes closed.

****

I was floating. On a raft on the gentle water, drifting away while the sun wrapped its warm rays around me. I half wondered where the raft would take me. Would I float away from this crazy town?

Could this all be some crazy dream? Maybe Wellington didn't really exist. Maybe it was like the town in the play my grandmother took me to a few years ago, where the town only appeared once every one hundred years. What was it called?

I shifted, my face rubbed against something warm and unyielding. Not a raft. Bed? Nope. I was definitely moving. My mind struggled to keep up with my rambling thoughts.

"Brigadoon," I muttered.

"What did you say?"

I felt the brush of fabric under my cheek and I struggled to open my eyes. Last night had been a mistake. I'd never been good at all-nighters. When I did manage one, I usually ended up crashing for fourteen hours the next day to make up for it.

"It's a play. Brigadoon. Wellington. Maybe they are one and the same."

I felt the slight rumble in his chest as Caleb chuckled. "No magic here in Wellington."

"Oh. Too bad." I yawned before opening my eyes.

He'd carried me from the field, down the path. I must have stiffened because he tightened his hold on me.

"Relax, I've got you."

I was more awake and all the frustrations from the day immediately surfaced. "Why are you being so nice?

"I've told you before," he continued, walking with an easy stride. "I'm a nice guy."

"I'm still mad at you." I made the admission but instead of insisting I could walk, I lay my head on his shoulder.

His warmth felt good. He smelled good. And truthfully, I was too emotionally spent to argue again. What had today accomplished?

When would I learn not to be so competitive? To keep my mouth shut and think before I acted? It never ended well for me, especially in this place. Despite that, I wrapped my arms around his neck and gave up the fight, at least for today.

When we reached the end of the path, he set me down long enough to open the back seat of his cruiser and I slid in.

"Caleb?"

"Yes, Grace?"

"I hope your stupid phone pinged all day."

I saw a small spark of amusement in his blue eyes as he closed the door.

"Mission accomplished."

Chapter Twenty-Four

I woke rested but with trepidations about my upcoming new job. I wore my green work shirt from the cafeteria, not knowing what color I would need to wear for the new *position*. I packed a lunch and boarded the shuttle.

The only officer in the station was Greg, an older gentleman who'd semi-retired a few years ago but filled in once a week. No Caleb. I couldn't tell if I was happy or a bit disappointed that he was nowhere to be found. Happy. Definitely happy.

"What can I do for you, Grace?" the silver-haired officer called out from his desk.

"Um, I'm working here now. Didn't the chief say anything?"

"Not to me, but I haven't seen him today. I guess you can have a seat at the desk in the corner, though."

I put my lunch on the desk and sat, swiveling the chair back and forth as I waited.

Caleb arrived about fifteen minutes later with a young man in cuffs. I watched as he brought the man to the cells in the hall on the far corner of the room.

"Is this really necessary, Chief?" the prisoner whined. "I apologized."

"You threw a chair through a window, Chris," he stated. "There are better ways to get your point across instead of violence."

"I really like Isabelle and Nate keeps trying to steal her from me."

Hearing the other summer intern's name perked me up in my seat. The quiet girl from the bus now had not one, but two admirers fighting over her. Fabulous. I would place a bet she had no plans to head home in August, either.

"Destroying property isn't going to win her over, bud."

When the man in charge finished, he came around the corner and immediately set his sights on me. My reprieve was over.

"Morning, Grace." His tone said he was all business this morning.

I could do the same. "Chief."

"Come into my office. I have work ready for you."

I followed him determined to be professional, but my eyes betrayed my mind as they cruised across his wide, broad shoulders, where the mic to his portable radio sat. Downward to his waist, where his utility belt fit oh, so nice. And further down, noticing how well his jeans fit.

As much as I wanted to hate this man, I couldn't deny I found him attractive, but I was not going to let him know. No way. No how. And I most definitely would not mention yesterday at all.

I jutted my chin up and was ready to face him when he rounded his desk and lifted a pile of folders from the corner and turned to hand them to me.

"The computer has been programed for you. I will show you how to maneuver through the software so you can update these files."

I nodded. "In what way has it been programmed?"

I followed him back to the outer office and took a seat in the chair he indicated while he pulled a chair from another desk, rolling it across the floor to sit next to me.

"There is no internet access. Think of it as a word processor. Whatever you input will be saved to the general server."

He slid closer and turned the computer on. When the password prompt showed up, he had me swipe my wrist band against a little box like the one I'd used at the hospital yesterday and the desktop screen appeared. The next half hour was torture as he walked me through the software program. It took all my willpower to not react to being so close to this man.

It was hard to believe I'd kissed this man. Well, he'd kissed me, but I had enjoyed it. I'd forgotten what a control freak Caleb could be.

The paperwork was old files from before they'd had computers and needed to be put into the system. I learned quite a bit about the pious residents of this perfect town and how many of them had some sort of police record.

Another thing I learned, and most important, was that Wellington was in Pennsylvania. I'd been here a month, not truly knowing my location. At least I had one positive about this re-assignment.

At noon, I'd typed in half of the file content on my desk when my new boss came back out of his office. "Did you bring a lunch?"

I looked up from my task at his brusque tone. While he'd had been more than polite, he'd been a step up from cold around me all morning.

If he could be terse, so could I. "Yes."

"I would appreciate it if you would go and pick up lunch for Greg and me today."

I closed the file on my desk and stood. He'd warned me yesterday I would be nothing more than a glorified, 'go-to' gal. At least I wasn't cleaning the toilets in the cells. Yet. "What would you like?"

I stopped him before he could grab the pen from his desk. "I worked in a restaurant. I know how to memorize food orders."

Mary was working when I went in. Today she was behind the counter instead of working the tables. "Hey, sweetie, heard my brother switched things up at the last minute."

"Yep. I screwed up. I'm not always the best at following rules to the letter."

She handed off a milkshake to a waitress but continued talking with me. "He is a bit of a stickler for the rules. He's fair, but everything is black and white with him."

"Lori, order up," she called out. "So, sweetie, what can I get you?"

I put in the order and added a milkshake for me before taking a seat on a stool at the counter while I waited. Twelve to one was lunchtime pretty much everywhere throughout town, so the diner was busy. Mostly everyone who worked in the town square area came to the restaurant. But, because it was a small town, the chefs knew most of the standing orders and everything moved quick and efficiently.

Back at the station, I sipped on my shake and nibbled on my sandwich as I typed, being sure to stay out of the chief's way. With this kind of work environment, the rest of the summer was going to suck.

Around two, Rita came in with the kids and I witnessed a total transformation as the scowl disappeared and the crease in his eyebrow was a thing of the past. His mom had to go to Town Hall for an errand and the kids made themselves at home.

I stayed out of their way, but the half hour he had his children with him, he was the easy-going man I'd seen from time to time. The moment they left, he holed himself up in his office. Other than his one cell resident, it was a quiet day around the police station.

The older officer left at three and I sat in the quiet station, the only noise the taps of my fingers on the keyboard.

The next visitor to the station had me biting my lip. Leland strolled in as though he owned the place. "Hey, Chief," he called out as he let the door slam shut behind him.

"Lee." The name practically came out as a drawl and I swung my glance to Caleb, who stood at the doorway to his office, arms folded. Relaxed and in control, as usual.

My visitor wasn't affected by the older man's tone. Instead, he strolled over to me and put his hands on my shoulders and kissed the top of my head. "Hey, sweetie."

I froze. What the hell was he doing?

"What time are you springing my gal from work today, Chief?"

"Leland." I nearly bit his name out of my mouth, but instead his hands tightened and began a gentle massage.

Caleb looked across the room to the wall clock then back to me. "You can go at four, Grace."

I nodded. Ten minutes.

"Lee, you can wait outside for her so she can finish her work for the day."

He kissed the top of my head again and gave another squeeze to my shoulders. "See you soon, sweetie."

He turned on his heel and strolled out. I looked from the closing door back to the chief and caught the smirk on his face before he moved back behind his desk. He was amused at my suitor's show of testosterone preening while I was far from the same.

I cleared off my desk and shut off my 'word processor' at exactly four o'clock. I rubbed my palms on my thighs before walking past the chief's office. "Do you need anything else?" I stopped myself short of saying 'sir'.

"No. Have a good night."

I had made it through one entire day working with my parole officer and not doing anything to piss him off. Someone else, on the other hand, with his unexpected visit, had earned himself top priority on my hit list.

I strode outside and the humidity slapped me hard in the face. Summer had hit fast and I hadn't heard any reports on the radio of relief any time in the near future. The heat was a perfect echo of my ire as I spotted my new nemesis gracing the wall with his poster boy looks.

"What the hell were you doing in there?" I sputtered as I stormed to him.

His pretty boy smile and casual shrug showed he was unaffected with my wrath. "Can't a guy go visit a friend at work?"

I narrowed my eyes and gave him a stern glare.

"That was no display of friendship. That was you staking a claim."

He pushed away from the wall and ran a finger down my face. "Your cheeks are red. Heat getting to you?"

I pushed him away. "What is with you today? Friends, Lee. That is all."

He leaned down and captured my mouth with his for a quick possessive kiss. "Sure, Grace." He nearly whispered the words. "Just friends."

He took my hand in his and pulled me along the sidewalk, leading me across the street toward the diner. "I think we need to have a talk about what I mean by friends."

When he opened the door to the diner and motioned me inside, I looked back at the station and saw Caleb at the door watching everything. How long had he been there? Had he witnessed the kiss? Is that why Leland had kissed me?

****

By Friday, I was mentally exhausted. The job itself was easy, however my boss was job-oriented and barely had a smile or a casual word. Each day had been a near repeat of Monday with the exception of which officer was on duty.

However, I had discovered the hallway to the opposite side of the station. It led to Randy's office and his elaborate computer system, and also—joy of joys—to the police dispatch area. Finding it and having a chance to make friends with those with powers to contact the outside world were two different matters.

Both the security office and the dispatch area had glass windows the length of the hallway, which meant if I were to go into dispatch, the chief's right hand man would be on high alert. Besides, I had a feeling very few people crossed the head honcho of law enforcement.

When I joined the usual crew in The Hall for Straight and True's weekly Friday night gig, I needed to blow off steam.

The band couldn't play enough fast songs. I danced with Jake, much like we had done a few weeks ago, but it wasn't enough. I even danced with Leland, teaching him a few moves, but all it did was cause him to become more hands on, especially when things slowed down.

After the band's final song, the lead singer joined us and immediately pulled Caroline in for a heated kiss, I turned to move away but I still heard Aaron's words, meant for his fiancé's ears only, I am sure.

"One more week, baby, and we will be together. I can't wait to be your husband."

Despite my pleas to wait, the two still planned to go through with the wedding. I was running out of time.

Jake was no help in my crusade to have the couple wait longer before taking their vows. He was too busy off in the shadows having another grope fest with the all-too willing goddess of seduction.

And with the couples around us each copping a feel, Leland advanced on me. What harm could it be to allow him one little kiss? I'd avoid a lecture from him on loosening up, or even being a tease on the dance floor—we had gotten a bit out of control. So when he leaned in for a kiss, I let him.

The weeks of me holding him at bay, now became flood waters. He tugged me into the shadows on the opposite corner of the building and backed me into the wall. Once out of sight of the others, he deepened the kiss, his mouth pressing harder and his tongue pushed past my teeth.

I forced my head to the side so I could breathe. "Slow down."

Instead, he worked his lips down my neck. "Sure thing." But instead of slowing down, he captured my lips again as his hand grabbed my breast and squeezed.

I grabbed his hand and pried his fingers away.

"Relax," he mumbled against my lips. "Everyone else is doing the same." He body pushed into mine, forcing me farther against the brick wall of the building.

I twisted his fingers back until he yelped. "Stop, Leland."

He stepped away from me, surprise evident in his expression. "What the hell?"

I pushed at his chest. "I've told you before, I am not going to be a summer fling. Touch me like that again, and I'll have you singing soprano for a month."

"Jeez, Grace. I mean, you've been sending mixed signals all night. The way we danced, it was all 'I want to have sex with you' and now after a simple kiss, you're an ice queen."

Another comment like that and I might have to bloody his nose. He threw his hands up in surrender as he continued. "Besides, I wasn't going to do anything else. I swear."

"Swearing is frowned upon in this town," I grumbled. "I'm going home. Don't follow me."

Saturday, I did my chores around the house, but I was in no mood to play baseball. Or, more to the point, I couldn't go and not admire the very fine body of a man who'd been barely civil to me all week. I also figured Leland would expect me to be there and I didn't need him cheering for me in the stands. Besides, I was down to one week with no solution to stopping a wedding.

What I needed was access to my confiscated cell phone, but I had no idea where any of those items had been stored.

As I listened to the radio in my room, I made notes in my notebook about my time so far in Wellington and a stray thought hit me. Hope had mentioned, way back when we'd been drinking in the woods, how they had ways of getting around things that were against the law.

Could I trust her enough to find out where our confiscated items were stored? I couldn't have her call on an outside line on my behalf. One: that would put her in an unfair position if she got caught. Two: she would get caught because I had no doubts the lines were recorded. So I definitely needed my phone.

And if Hope was involved, I needed Jake to intervene. I headed across town hoping to find him at his host family home.

I was in luck. My pace slowed as I spotted him painting the front porch. The sight of my friend with a paintbrush put a smile on my face. I would have thought Doc Collings' kid more of the Tom Sawyer type, finding a way to have someone else complete the task for him.

I watched from a distance and saw the intense concentration and serious focus to his task. Damn. As much as I hated to admit it, this summer program may actually be good for him. Maybe he'd found a niche with working with his hands, both with painting, but also at the furniture factory.

We hadn't even reached the mid-point of the summer yet. "Please don't enjoy this too much," I muttered as I finally moved into his line of vision.

"Hiya, Gracie. See my masterpiece?" He waved his hand and drops of white paint dripped onto his sneakers.

"It looks good."

He dipped his brush and returned to his task of painting a railing. "It's fun, too."

"Jake Collings, enjoying manual labor. I'm in shock." I sat on the front step and looked up as he worked.

"What brings you here, gorgeous?"

I looked around, making sure his host family wasn't in hearing distance. "I came to enlist your help."

"Will it put us jail?"

I worried my lip. "Possibly. It will most definitely piss off the police chief."

He grinned. "Cool. I'm in."

I groaned. "You don't even know what I'm going to ask."

He raised his eyebrows at me saying it didn't matter.

I put my hand up to shade my eyes as I looked up at him. "I still think Caroline getting married next week without her family knowing is wrong."

"Agreed."

"I've been trying, without success, to use the phone system here to make an outside call. Then it dawned on me, why not use our cell phones?"

He continued to paint as he spoke. "The cell phones they banned on day one?"

"Yep." Then I continued in a half whisper, not wanting to be overheard. "I thought you could use your charm on your girlfriend to get access to them."

"As long as she knows where they are, I can convince her in a nano-second."

That's what I loved about Jake. He had no modesty about his sway on a woman. "Are you sure you don't mind helping? I'm in enough trouble with the town law enforcer. I hate to get you in his cross hairs, too."

"Caroline's my friend, as well. I agree this is too big of a decision to rush into. Leave it to me, kiddo. I'll have a plan by tonight.

Chapter Twenty-Five

By Sunday afternoon, Jake had assured me Hope was on board. According to my friend, he'd played up the computer aspect of his watch and claimed he wanted to show her a few naughty websites. What he'd neglected to tell her, and what I already knew, was his watch was also a phone. Clever boy.

Tuesday was the weekly Town Council meeting and they determined it would be the best time for her to raid the police station locker for the booty. When the day arrived and the chief left as expected, I could barely sit in my chair, never mind accomplish any work, as I waited for my unsuspecting accomplice to arrive.

When she strolled into the building, I had to force myself to pretend I didn't know her intentions. She gave me her perfect smile and brushed her long blonde hair behind her shoulder. "Good afternoon, Grace."

"Hope. Not working today?" Casual conversation. I should take up drama class.

She looked over at Brent, officer *du jour*. "Jimmy is at it again. He's been listening to everyone talk about the drought and the need for water for the crops this year, so he decided to turn on hoses in everyone's yard to prove we have plenty."

Hmmm, had she come up with that ruse to empty the station? Not bad.

He yawned. "Yeah, I'll go check on him. Anything

else I can do for you?"

"I'm here to see Randy." She motioned toward the door leading to his computer room. "My scanner isn't working right."

"Oh, okay." The officer watched her disappear and when he shook his head, I had a sneaking suspicion he didn't care for the diva. He headed out the door to check on the teen's misdeeds and I forced myself to stay put in my seat. Curiosity was killing me, though.

A few minutes later, the leggy blonde re-appeared without a bracelet and I wished I'd sneaked down the hall to see the interaction which allowed her to roam without the device.

Before I could ask, she motioned for me to be quiet. She pulled out a set of keys and headed down the hallway housing the cells. There is a door on the other end I had not been through yet, that must be where she'd gone.

I so wanted to join her to locate my own cell phone, but in order for this plan to work, she couldn't know I was the catalyst for her boyfriend wanting his watch and phone.

She'd been gone only a minute when the security guru came into the room. "Have you seen Hope?"

I concentrated on my paperwork. "Ah, she mentioned restroom."

"Doors wide open. Try again."

Well, hell. Randy could be as intimidating as another former marine with his cold tone.

I looked around and shrugged. "How should I know? Use your tracking thingy if you need to find her."

He narrowed his eyes at me and strode across the

room. I coughed, hoping to alert the other woman but I had a feeling she was as good as busted.

A few seconds later she was practically dragged into the main precinct room and forced to sit. "Don't move." Randy picked up the phone. "Have the chief come to the station," he barked.

If I had been on the receiving end of that man's fury, I'd be a jumble of nerves, but not her. She picked at a piece of non-existent lint and waited patiently until the top cop arrived.

I turned back to the computer, keeping my back to them. I did a hunt and peck on the keyboard, pretending to be busy, but I was on high alert listening in on the conversation as the computer specialist filled in the chief on the visitor's reconnaissance. I couldn't help myself, I stole a peek.

Caleb casually leaned against the desk, his arms crossed over his marvelous chest. "What were you doing in the closet?"

"Just getting something for a friend."

I grinned. Vague answer. Something I would do. Something I know from experience would exasperate the man with the badge.

"Care to elaborate?"

"Not particularly."

Oh, how I wanted to swing my chair around and watch the tennis match of wits.

"Let's start over. Tell me what you were looking for, and for whom." Ahh, the no-more-Nice-Guy tone.

There was silence, and I tried hard not to squirm on the poor girl's behalf. If I'd learned anything in the past five weeks, she was more than likely getting the look which said he would sit there all day until he got an answer.

She broke. "It's just a stupid watch, that's all."

"Hand it over."

I glanced over my shoulder and saw her slip the watch out of her pocket.

Randy spoke next. "Did you also take the phone it needs to be synced to, as well?"

Her eyes widened and while I saw the hesitation as though she debated giving over the second item, she was completely busted. She handed over the confiscated item and I turned away to bite my lip to hide my own frustration.

The chief continued in his demand. "And your father's set of keys which I assume you used to get into the locked closet."

I heard those being slammed onto the desk. "I don't see what the big deal is."

"The big deal is you have no authorization to be in the evidence room, hence the keys were not issued to you. The big deal is your friend, Jake, signed a contract to not use internet during his stay here, so he can't have this back."

Caleb stood. "Get your bracelet back on, Hope. Go back to work."

I whipped around in my chair, my mouth open in shock, as she scrambled out of the office. "That's it?"

The chief raised an eyebrow as he turned his attention to me. "Do you have something to say?"

I couldn't help myself. "That's it? She just gets to walk out? She stole something from a freaking police station and you let her walk? If that were me, I'd be thrown in a cell and then be under house arrest for a month."

"Do you have a problem with how I run things?"

Oh, the things I wanted to say, but I put my hands up and swung my chair back around to face my desk. "None of my business." I muttered under my breath. "So unfair."

He came up behind me and leaned down, one hand on the desk, the other on the back of my chair as he spoke in my ear. My body went into high alert at his silky tone. "Tell me what I should do. Would you like me to investigate further? And if I do, will I find out the owner of those stolen objects put her up to it, because *you* put Jake up to it?"

I gulped as my hands stayed frozen over the keyboard. I slowly shook my head. Without another word Caleb pushed away and walked out of the station. How the hell does he do it? How does he know? I glanced at the black band on my wrist, wondering if it also contained a listening device.

I wouldn't put it past him.

When Leland arrived at four to pick me up, I was the one to take his hand when exiting the office. I couldn't get out of there fast enough.

The weekend arrived and despite my intentions, I'd failed at reaching Caroline's family. The wedding was happening. Like everything else around here, everyone participated. There were committees for every aspect. Decorations. Flowers. Even preparing an apartment for the new couple.

On Saturday morning, I was in the kitchen at the school, helping with the wedding cake. Despite my reservations about her marriage, I couldn't say no when she asked me to make it.

I had never baked dessert for four hundred before

and felt immediately overwhelmed until Karen and Rita, my helpers for the day, informed me all the kids get cupcakes. The three of us worked all day and in the end, I was happy with the finished product. I'd made her favorite: carrot. Instead of one towering dessert, we prepared several cakes of different sizes and placed them on multiple tiers. Tomorrow, they would be adorned with flowers for the finishing touch. We'd also made over a hundred cupcakes in vanilla and chocolate.

Despite my trepidation over the quick marriage, Caroline was still my best friend, and I was glad I'd made something beautiful for her to remember her day.

****

Someone transformed The Hall into a wedding wonderland. I gazed in amazement on Sunday morning after helping to transport the desserts. From the white tablecloths adorning each table both inside the hall and out in the covered courtyard, to filmy streamers wafting from the rafters. Candles and lanterns, placed strategically throughout the room, waited to be lit.

Carla, an elderly woman with gray hair flowing to her thighs, placed flowers on and around each of the tiered wedding cakes, giving them the finishing touch they needed.

In the span of two weeks, from the day Aaron proposed, the entire town stepped up and created a fairy-tale wedding. It was awe-inspiring and sweet.

With my job done, I rushed home to get ready and was back at the church to see the bride a full half hour before the church service. While I'd thought the decorations had been beautiful, it was nothing compared to my friend.

"Oh, Caroline, you look stunning."

She beamed, her blue eyes wide and glistening with tears. Her joy was evident. I pushed back all my doubts about her rushing things.

"Let me look at your dress."

I circled her, taking in the beauty of the gown's simplicity. The cap sleeves were perfect for the heat of summer; the neckline plunged, but maintained its modesty with the high sash line, accented in silver lace. The dress fell in small pleats to the floor; a short veil was attached by a floral headband.

With her bare feet adorned in flat white sandals, she looked like a throwback from the sixties; and it suited her. She fit in here. The farming. The one-big-happy-family. My sweet, charming, impulsive roommate had found an extension of her childhood in this secluded town.

"You've never looked more perfect. I wish nothing but the best for you both. I know you will be very happy together."

"Gracie, that means the world to me." The tiny girl engulfed me in a quick hug before grabbing her fresh-cut flowers. "This day is going to be amazing."

The bride and groom were seated in chairs on the altar as the regular mass commenced, and only at the end did they stand for the nuptials.

"Aaron and Caroline, please face each other and hold hands," Pastor Rick instructed. "Our heavenly father created humans to unite, both with him and with each other. We gather here today as a congregation, as a family, to praise our God, but we are also blessed with celebrating the love and sanctity of marriage of two of God's children. With the joining of your hands, you are also joined in the light of Christ's blessings. I now pronounce you husband and wife."

My best friend had never been happier and I was coming to terms with the whirlwind wedding. The church was as decked out for the festivities as much as the courtyard and fellowship hall and the Wellington community was thrilled to welcome Caroline as their newest 'daughter.'

I failed in my mission to ensure my roommate returned to Vermont with me in August. Maybe a part of me knew it was a lost cause before we even boarded the bus. Now I still had half of the summer to go until I headed back to college. If I tried hard, maybe I could keep my mouth shut and get through the second half trouble-free.

Chapter Twenty-Six

"I can't believe Caroline got to go home," I whined as Jake and I fed the horses on Jefferson's farm the following Saturday.

"I thought you wanted her family to know about her new husband."

I looked over at the twins, who'd insisted we come help while Aaron was away, as they led two more horses in from the paddock outside.

"Sure, I did," I sputtered. "*Before* they were married. Besides, they were holed up all this past week being all lovey-dovey in their new apartment."

Jake snickered. "It's called a honeymoon."

"Whatever." I waved the snarky comment aside. "My point is I didn't see her all week and then, *Blam!* she's on a bus to Vermont. Will she even think to contact our parents and have them spring us early from this prison camp? No. She'll be too busy with her own life to think of us."

That earned me a sputtering laugh from Jake who in turn received a piece of feed in the face.

"Lighten up, Grace. As of today, we are seven weeks down, seven to go. Finish your prison sentence and you'll be home free."

"Informants for the prison guards en route," I grunted under my breath as the siblings re-entered the barn. "Time for a subject change."

Jake shook his head at me but kept his mouth shut.

Hope brought a horse into its stall. "Storm clouds are moving in. We have maybe two hours before it hits."

Her brother came up behind her. "I spoke with Jefferson, and he said we can hang out or take a walk, but we should be on the next shuttle back to town at four-o'clock if we want to miss the worst of it."

Automatically I looked at my wrist for my watch—and found the black bracelet. "How do you manage to be on time if you don't have a friggin watch?"

Lee put an arm around my shoulder. "There are clocks everywhere." He pointed to a small one in the far corner of the building. "You're in a mood. What's wrong, today?"

"She's missing her best friend," my confidante tattled. I could have throttled him for that.

"I know just what you need. Come with me." Wonder Twin's arms tightened on my shoulder and he led me away from the barn, leaving the other couple behind.

"One of the best things about growing up here, is even as a child, we could come and go anywhere throughout town on a whim." His hand slid down to clasp mine as we walked across the field. "I always loved coming out to this side of town. At first it was because of the lake hidden within the trees, then I discovered I liked going south, past the horse pastures and into the open fields."

I didn't say much as I followed. I spotted one of the ranch hands in the distance but we headed out in the opposite direction. I was curious what would capture this man's attention more than the beauty of the lake. I climbed over one of the fences, struggling a bit in the oversized boots Shelby had lent me to work with the horses, and continued to follow from one field to another until my guide stopped short.

"Here we are."

I looked around. "We're in a field."

He nodded. "I know. No one around. It's quiet. Open." He pulled me to the ground and then lay down with his arms crossed under his head. "Look at the sky."

I followed his example and looked up. Gray clouds raced across, like soldiers moving into battle formation. Wind brushed the hairs on my arm causing them to stand. "Maybe we should go."

But he was in no hurry. "I've been telling you since you arrived how you need to stop and appreciate what Wellington has to offer. You're in farm country. Here, we welcome the rain. It's critical for our crops. If you pay attention to the weather, you can tell what is going to happen."

"Yep," I conceded. "I can tell we're going to get wet. Soon."

He leaned up on an elbow and looked down at me. "You're funny. Seriously, though, if you close your eyes and take a whiff, you can smell the weather coming. It's actually the plants and grass releasing a scent."

I did as he told and didn't smell anything more than horse manure. I opened my eyes to pay more attention. "You're really interested in this, aren't you?"

He had a sheepish grin. "Yeah."

While I wasn't always crazy about Leland, this was the first real thing I'd learned about him. "Then show me more."

He jumped up and pulled me beside him. His voice became animated as he walked. "There are lots of signs of a storm. One example is the low air pressure. Look close and you will see the birds flying lower than usual; or in the winter, when woods stoves are going, the smoke will hang low."

I tried to take it all in. "So you come out to these fields when you know it's going to rain so you can watch all of this?"

He gave a bit of a shy nod as we meandered back toward the barn. "I come here, or into the woods, or even sit on a bench in The Square and observe what is happening with nature to predict when the storm will actually hit, or how severe it might be."

I looked up at the darkening sky. "What do you think about this one?

We had reached the back of the barn and he leaned against the wall. "This one is going to be fierce and those are the most fun to watch."

We slid down to the ground, the building blocking a bit of the wind. As Lee talked to me about weather patterns I didn't pay much attention when his arm went over my shoulder, pulling me close to him as he explained how cows lie down in the field and huddle close together.

"You really know your stuff. Why don't you go to college and study meteorology?"

"Nah. That would mean working outside Wellington. I like it here."

I enjoyed this side of him. Usually I think of him as a grown-up teenager, not knowing what he wants to be when he grows up. This was the first time I saw what he was interested in. Passionate about.

I was intrigued enough in what he was saying to not notice how close he'd shifted to me. Or how he'd subtly slipped my hat off my head in order for me to have a better view. Or when his hand began to slowly move up and down my back.

But when I turned my gaze back from the horizon to look at him and found him staring at me with *that look*, I knew he was seconds from kissing me.

"Lee, I—"

"Shh. It's nice to see you relaxed, Grace." He put a finger on my lips. "I've enjoyed today with you."

I gulped. I had to stop things before he went further. "Sure, it's been a good day, but—"

"I want to kiss you."

"Whoa. I've told you before that I—"

"We've been doing this dance all summer, when are you going to give in to the inevitable?"

"There's nothing inevitable about this." I pushed at his chest as he made his move. "I'm going home soon."

He didn't budge. "Haven't you figured it out, yet?" His face was mere inches from mine as he gave an exasperated sigh. "You're not going home. You were brought here to get married and I picked you. Look at Caroline. She understood."

The words were like ice, freezing me in my spot. I'd thought it. I'd joked about this town needing fresh blood for marriage, but I hadn't really believed it. Not until now.

My hesitation was enough for Leland to take his advantage and before I realized what was happening he had me trapped between his body and the ground.

"No. This is not going to happen." I pushed at his

shoulders, but for a skinny guy, for a guy more about his looks than even Jake, I couldn't get him to move.

"You should be flattered, Grace. My father is an influential man. He is grooming me to take a place on the council someday and you will be there by my side."

He tried to kiss me but I turned my head away and pushed at his face. "Stop fighting it. Hope and I have it all figured out. We'll have a double wedding."

My stomach clenched. When I was a freshman, the college had a seminar for woman about being aware of predators and what signs to look for. On campus, I was always careful. I rarely walked anywhere alone and always went to parties with a group. I'd had one situation my freshman year that had put me on high alert. I'd promised myself I'd never let myself get into something similar.

I tried to remember the tips they'd given at the course. Kick him in the groin? Nope, not in the right position.

Jab him in the eyes? Maybe. I went for his face, but he was quicker. He grabbed my wrists and forced my arms over my head. This couldn't be happening. I screamed but it went nowhere.

I thought I heard the wind howl, but I wasn't sure as it competed with the screams in my head. I needed to get away. The best I could do was bite his lip and he lurched his head back enough to yelp. "Stop fighting."

"No. Get off me."

Then he was gone.

For a nano-second I thought maybe a hurricane or tornado had ripped Leland off me but then I saw Caleb holding him like a rag doll.

"What the hell are you doing?"

The older man's voice was like the thunder approaching. My attacker didn't back down. "Damn it, Caleb. You're supposed to be at the bus station with Aaron and Caroline."

"I'm back." With a flick of his wrist, the police chief dropped Leland who stumbled as he tried to get his footing.

"You're ruining everything." He practically stomped his feet and in that instant was back to being the spoiled man-child I'd seen all summer. "We had a plan and you interrupted."

"If your plan included rape, than you sure as hell better be glad I interrupted."

I nearly quaked at the cold, harsh tone of the chief's voice, but the younger man didn't seem to notice. "You need to stay out of it, Caleb. I chose Grace. She's going to be my wife."

"Not this way."

My head spun with emotion. I scrambled to sit up, staring at the two men standing in front of me. One who reminded me of the raging wind ripping through the trees across the field, and the other who, given the chance, would crack like lightening.

Another male voice interrupted. My head snapped to the side where Roger appeared, Jake in tow. "Caleb! This man just defiled my daughter."

Leland threw his hands up in the air. "Damn it, everything is ruined. All I needed was a few more minutes." He spun and kicked out, connecting his boot with my ribs. I went down with a groan.

One second my attacker was standing over me, the next he was on his knees. In a swift move, the usually unflappable chief had the boy's arm twisted behind him and, even in the howling wind, I heard it snap like a twig.

And all hell broke loose.

The kid screamed in pain; his father barreled toward Caleb; Jake was released long enough to zip his pants; while Hope stood in silence watching the melee.

Not knowing what else to do, I scrambled to my feet and ran.

Chapter Twenty-Seven

The cloud cover was heavy, cleaving a path through the woods filled with shadows. The rumble of thunder continued in the distance, but large splats of water plopped on my head as I ran. I stumbled in the oversized boots, so I slipped out of them and continued in stockinged feet.

I couldn't escape what I'd heard or seen. Leland telling me I'd been brought there to marry him. Roger dragging Jake from the barn screaming for Caleb. Jake zipping his jeans one-handed, what he'd been caught doing obvious. Hope, with her blonde hair mussed and a sly smile on her face. The pain in my side where I'd been kicked. The distinctive snap of bone when the police chief lost his usual cool and took matters into his own hands.

I stepped out into a clearing, my heart pounding in my chest, my breathing labored. I stopped and bent over, putting my hands on my knees, taking deep breaths and looking around. I'd come out at the lake, on the opposite side of where everyone went to swim.

I wasn't going home. That's what Leland said. We'd all been brought to Wellington, not for a summer work program, but to be married off. What the hell had been in the contract I'd signed in May? I should have read it. I shouldn't have just signed it, assuming it was exactly as Hope had summarized. What had she said?

What had Caleb said when repeating it to me?

I walked out into the field by the water and sat, watching the dark water ripple in the wind, as the rain pelted it, and me, with more force.

For the duration of your stay. Those were the words they'd both used. Had there been an end date on the contract? I never looked. Had I truly signed my freedom away?

I'm not sure how long I sat in the rain, but I wasn't surprised when I felt movement behind me.

"The storm is moving in fast, Grace. We need to head back now."

"I don't really care."

I heard his sigh a second before he knelt beside me. "Did he hurt you? How are your ribs?"

I bent both knees, wrapping my arms to pull them close to my chest. "It doesn't matter. I want to be left alone." Flashes of lightening lit the sky; I knew the clap of thunder was only minutes behind.

"We're sitting ducks out here in the open," Caleb stated. "We need to find shelter immediately."

Cool. Maybe I'd be struck by lightning. If I died, I wouldn't be forced into marriage. If I survived, maybe I'd be disfigured and they'd send me home.

"Oh, hell no." I heard the exasperation. "I've seen that look before and this is no time to be stubborn. We are leaving this field now. You can come of your own free will, or I will carry you."

I tensed at the ultimatum and responded with a glare. His raised eyebrow, daring me to defy him. He was twice my size and strong as a horse. Fighting him would be a losing battle. He knew it. I knew it.

"Fine." I pushed to my feet and waved an arm as

the sky lit up again. "Lead on."

"Where are your shoes?"

I looked down at my feet, my white ankle socks covered in mud. Caleb shook his head. "We're not going to make it back to Jefferson's house in this and the winds could bring down trees." He contemplated for a moment then with a nod, motioned me toward the tree line. "I know a place. Does it hurt to breathe?"

"What?" I followed his gaze and realized I was rubbing my side. "I'm fine."

"Want me to check to see if you have any broken ribs?"

"Lay a finger on me and, Lee won't be the only one with something broken."

No amused smirk. No retorts about how he was bigger and could overpower me. Instead he turned and led me back into the woods. As the wind howled, I was thankful not to be alone. Branches snapped and fell in the distance. We continued to hike the path upward.

We'd taken the horses on these same paths earlier in the summer. While I wouldn't call it mountainous, the incline was more suited to the animals than to someone already mentally and physically exhausted. I regretted taking off the boots as my feet slipped on the muddy path.

Thunder and lightning marched toward us and I shivered. Despite the earlier heat of the day, the temperature dropped drastically with the change in weather; I was now completely soaked to the skin.

Caleb stopped at a giant rock that seemed to grow out of a hill above our heads. The overhang left room to barely fit one person, never mind two. "Crawl in there. I'll be right back." He turned on his heel and disappeared.

As depressed as I'd been and as much as I wanted to be left alone before, now I felt abandoned and the last thing I wanted to do was crawl under a rock, literally. When the next boom hit, I yelped and dove under the overhang and clasped my upward knees as I waited and prayed for his return.

He wasn't long. He brought several branches and placed them upward against the overhang, creating a protective barrier against the rain. He left again and again until he'd covered most of the opening then crawled in beside me. With the storm and now the branches, it could have been midnight with the amount of light we had. At least we were no longer barraged with pelting water.

I yelped again with the next clap and hid my face in my knees. "One, two, three, four, five." *Boom*.

"Are you scared?" The space was tiny. Caleb was a big man; I felt the heat emanating off his body.

I could lie. I hated showing weakness around this man who was an unwavering pillar of strength, but maybe because it was dark and he couldn't see me, or maybe it was that I jumped at every noise anyway, but I told the truth.

"Yes." It came out nearly a whisper. "I usually enjoy watching storms. Sarah and I like to go up to the attic and watch them from the window to get a great view, but I've never been trapped outside with one. Especially with it right on top of me."

"Come here, then."

I hesitated but as the storm raged around us, I couldn't help myself. It took barely a shift in position to be pressed against the strong, hard body. His arms wrapped around my waist sliding me closer.

"This doesn't change the fact I am super pissed off with everyone, including you, about why we were all brought to Wellington."

"I understand."

I rested my head at the crook of his arm and shoulder, his wet tee-shirt only a thin barrier between us. We sat in silence for a while but my thoughts wouldn't turn off.

"Can I ask a question?"

"Umm hmm."

"In the past, when you've brought students here for this summer program thing, have they all stayed without question?"

He hesitated a moment. "The summer program is something new this year."

I shifted to look up at him, his firm chin only a shadow inches from mine. "It is?"

"In the past, and even during the time I was away, if the younger adults did not head out to the colleges in the nearby communities, we had a few 'recruiters' who would venture out and befriend young homeless or runaways and bring them to Wellington.

"In all instances I am familiar with, they all found our town to be welcoming and somewhere they could feel included and needed. It's always been their choice to stay."

"What changed? Why travel outside of the state?"

He shifted a bit. I couldn't tell if he was uncomfortable in the small, cramped space, or if it was from the topic of conversation.

"This was Roger's brain-child. He's overprotective of his children and doesn't like them outside the gates so going to a conventional college was out of the question for them. And as far as he was concerned, the homeless and runaways were not good enough for his kids."

"But he let them go with you to recruit us."

Caleb let out a bit of a snort. "Under strict supervision. Everyone was separated into groups at the different colleges in different states, but the twins were to stay together and I was to be their chaperone at all times."

"Lucky you. This town takes protecting their own seriously."

"Yes."

I thought about the interactions I'd had with the boys and men during my stay and spoke without censoring my words. "Don't you think by sheltering everyone in this town to the degree they do, that they've interfered with the natural dating rituals? I mean, look at what happened today. I don't think Lee really knows how to gradually move forward with a girl. It's either hold hands or have sex."

"Are you defending his behavior?"

It was my turn to snort. "Hell no. But I was thinking about something Phillip said to Jimmy about what makes a man and that's having babies. If they truly believe it, and all they have around them is relatives, it's no wonder when someone new arrives in town, they all want to prove themselves."

I cringed when another boom of thunder sounded. Caleb's fingers slowly drifted up and down my arm in a soothing motion. While I'm sure he meant it to calm me, his touch started a different, more intimate emotion. Instead of pushing away, like I knew I should,

I stayed still, allowing his fingers to skim up and down my arm. My body reacted by melting further against his chest.

"It's not how I was brought up." he spoke softly, his tone gentle and even, despite the storm raging around us. "Even with a father who screwed around, I was taught to respect women and I learned those ideals living here in Wellington. Families are cherished, protected. It's part of why alcohol and drugs are forbidden. Drugs alter your state of mind and people tend to forget how to behave properly when under the influence."

"People are people, Caleb. Drugs and alcohol might enhance who they really are, but it doesn't change them."

"How did you get so smart at a young age?"

He tightened his arm around me after another clap of thunder sounded, protecting me from my own fears. The wind whistled, but the branches he'd positioned around us stayed in place.

The conversation was a needed distraction. "Growing up working in a restaurant, you get to see a lot of different behavior in people. I've seen how men treat their dates, how parents treat their children, how children behave out in public based on their parents care of them. Alcohol sometimes contributes to the behavior but not always.

"My biggest issue was not keeping my mouth shut when I didn't like what I saw and why my parents banished me to the office most of the time."

"So you've always had spunk?"

I snorted. "My mom calls it an exasperating personality."

"I think it's charming."

I don't know why his comment meant so much to me. "Thank you." I whispered. Leaning against him, I felt his body tense only slightly and the air changed between us. His fingers no longer moved up and down my arm but stayed firm in place, still protecting, but almost afraid to touch anywhere.

He'd shifted in the dark, his face looking down at me. "You miss them."

"Yes, I do. That's the point. I have a family. One I plan to go home to."

We were nose to nose in the close confines. His breath was warm against my face. "I know."

With one arm still around my waist, he lifted his other hand to my face, lifting my chin, positioning my lips so he could take my breath away with a brief, tender unexpected kiss that ended much too soon.

I didn't know what to make of it. He'd made it clear the last time that he had to stay away from me. Before I could even contemplate his reasoning, he changed the subject.

"You've never mentioned a boyfriend, Grace."

It was a statement, not a question, yet I knew he waited. "I, ah, am not seeing anyone."

"That surprises me, someone as beautiful as you on a college campus."

I gulped. I didn't want to talk about my past. No, I wanted his firm mouth on mine again, making me forget everything and everyone. This time, I reached up, rubbing my hand along his firm jaw, noting the soft stubble of facial hair. Instead of taking my hint, Caleb stopped my hand with his own. He was waiting for an answer.

"I had a boyfriend. Things didn't end well and I decided to spend my time concentrating on my studies. I'll get my degree and go back to work at the restaurant."

"Were you in love with him?"

I grimaced in the dark. "It's complicated." I jumped as another clap of thunder crashed overhead. I didn't think we could get any closer but I practically crawled into his lap, seeking comfort in his hold.

"We've got all night." At first, I thought he meant something else, but maybe those were my own wayward thoughts wishing to meld our lips together. He only wanted conversation.

It was dark under the rock overhang. The rain pounded around us but his voice was calming and his touch soothing. So I talked. "I had a boyfriend all through high school. He was a year older and I thought it was serious, but when he went off to college he broke up with me so he could enjoy the college experience."

I hadn't spoken about this in a long time and realized I no longer felt the bitterness that had followed me for a long time. "When I went off to Burlington, I decided I'd take things slow and easy with my next relationship. I met a guy and we dated a few months and I could tell he was getting frustrated."

I started to pull back as the memories of a certain night came back, but there was nowhere to go. Caleb continued with his fingers stroking my arm. "There was a party the night before we were all to leave for winter break and I had decided I would finally sleep with him. What I didn't know was his friends had been giving him a hard time that I wasn't putting out. He decided to take matters into his own hands."

Caleb's hands stopped and his body tensed. He guessed where this was going.

"He roofied my drink."

"Shit, Grace."

I shuddered at the memories. "The thing is, he'd bragged to his pals about what he was going to do and it got out. A few of my friends heard about it and showed up at the party before anything bad happened. I don't remember much about that night. They had to carry me home because my legs wouldn't work."

He pulled me closer, his arms protective but I felt the tension in his hold.

"About the only thing I do remember is being violently sick, but my friends had my back."

"I suppose you never reported it?"

"No. I was humiliated." I heard his resigned sigh. "I went home for break and came back determined to never be in a situation where I wasn't in complete control again."

This time he groaned. "And then you came here and were drugged on day one. I'm sorry, Grace. I can't say that enough."

Then he tipped my chin up, and we were so close again. "Whoever he was, he was a fool. You're worth waiting for."

More words were spoken when his lips met mine. Apologies and regret mixed with a heavy dose of attraction and want. The day had been an emotional ride but in this moment I welcomed what Caleb had to offer.

His kiss deepened and I felt from him the same attraction I'd been trying to deny for weeks. The lightning from the storm was not the only electricity happening. I tingled from my head to my toes. Where our bodies pressed together, my right side to his left, we become one entity and I turned my body more, to press further into his chest and I heard my own moan as our bodies melted together.

We'd been fighting this for weeks. With the storm raging around us, I needed this moment. I opened my mouth and allowed his tongue to explore. His hand traveled downward until his fingers could slip under my damp shirt. They were warm and rough from callouses and made my skin come alive. I gripped his shirt front as his mouth released mine and moved to my neck and his hand continued to move against my hyper-sensitive skin, moving to my ribcage.

"Oww," I murmured into his neck, not able to help the groan.

He immediately pulled back. "Damn it. You are hurt." I heard frustration in his tone. "Let me check."

"No, I'm fine. Kiss me again."

He rolled in the cramped space until my back was on the ground and he leaned over me. He kept my head cradled in one large palm as his tongue plundered my mouth and I forgot all about the outside world. About the storm. About Wellington. All I felt was his heat, his strength. His hand on my bare midriff as he pushed my shirt upward.

My hands moved up his chest, across his shoulders, and up to his head, pulling him closer. I was lost in all sensation as I felt his fingers make a swirl pattern on my tummy. My bones melted beneath his touch. By my own admission, he knew it had been a while since I had felt a man's touch in this way. Maybe too long. My body reacted quickly. I expected at any moment Caleb's callused fingers would find their way to my tightening nipples.

Instead of moving upward, though, his hands moved to my side, trailing softly, mesmerizing me, until I almost didn't feel how his palm flattened, or how his fingers became a bit more clinical.

I broke the kiss. "You bastard." But there was no heat to the words. I wasn't mad. At the moment, I couldn't be upset with him, I wanted him too much. "I told you I was fine."

His thumb and forefinger pressed further against what I was sure would be a bruise by morning. "I don't feel anything broken, but your twinge tells me he got you good."

"You saved me." I shook my head in wonder. "You broke his arm."

Caleb's palm stilled on my skin, and I heard the pain in his voice when he spoke. "I wanted to rip his limbs from his body for hurting you. I am truly sorry he did what he did."

He placed a kiss on the top of my nose and I knew the heat of the moment had passed, but not the attraction. He twisted again, this time onto his side, his back to the branches as he positioned me in order to spoon under the rock overhang.

"When I brought you here, all of you, I never expected any of this to go so far." He sounded sad. I'd never heard that from him before.

"I believe you."

"I'm sorry, Grace. I am sorry you have been unhappy. I am sorry Leland hurt you."

"Thank you for saving me." I rubbed my finger across the back of his hand at my waist. While the moment of passion was over, I was thankful to still have his body pressed against mine. I wasn't ready to let go.

"No, don't thank me. You shouldn't even be here." I felt him sigh, felt him distancing himself. "I'll get you out of here, Grace. I'll get you, and Jake, too, if you want, both home to Vermont."

I felt a slight zing of anticipation. "You will?"

He kissed the top of my head. "Yes. It might take a couple days, but I'll figure it out."

The wind howled as the worst of the storm raged over us. If I'd been alone, each whistle of wind through the trees, each snap of a branch, every crack of thunder would have had me quivering. But Caleb was with me. His strong, warm body was wrapped around me, protecting me from any and all harm.

I shifted back against him, scooting into a position to lay my head on his outstretched arm. As I did, my behind pressed to him and I felt the unmistakable fullness behind the zipper of his jeans at the same time he sucked in an audible breath.

"Are you comfortable?" his voice was tight. I didn't know if I should apologize, but the thrill that went through me caught me off guard.

He was aroused. And it was because of me. I'd been fighting my attraction—well, trying to fight it—for weeks, and now, when getting home meant more than anything else, I was faced with the hard and fast fact that he was also attracted to me.

So I did what I shouldn't. I shifted again.

"Damn it." It was like a painful whisper in my ear.

I grinned in the dark. "Ah, sorry?"

His hand pressed against my belly. "Are you?' I shook my head, knowing he couldn't see me, but he knew.

"Oh, Grace." He kissed the top of my head. "I'm a man of my word. I told you early on I am in charge of your safety and I just promised to get you home. Please, I am begging you, don't make this harder than it has to be."

Just my luck. I'd found someone in this God-forsaken, Podunk town who I could actually like and who obviously liked me and he was going to get me home.

Home. Yes, definitely more important than the few kisses, no matter how hot and amazing they'd been. Despite my first impression of Caleb, he'd turned out to be a good man. Too bad he lived in Camp Davidian.

"Grace, you realize I can't promise to get you home tomorrow. I need to make a plan."

Made sense. The place was locked down tighter than Fort Knox. "I know."

"While I do, would you consider—" He hesitated. I turned my head to look over my shoulder at him as he finally rushed out the words. "Would you have dinner with me?"

My heart did a rapid pitter-patter in my chest and I silently squealed a high-pitched Yes! "Okay. Yes. I'd like that."

I thought, for a moment, that he'd kiss me again. He didn't. Instead he flashed a smile at me in the dark. "Good. I'd like that, too. Try to sleep. We'll head back to town in the morning."

I placed my hand over the one he had at my waist and snuggled into his warmth. Despite the storm raging around us, I fell asleep with the first breath of hope I'd had in seven weeks.

Gina Leuci